The Reluctant Flirt

Also from Jennifer Probst

Outer Banks Series:
Book of the Month

The Twist of Fate Series:
Meant to Be
So It Goes
Save the Best for Last

The Meet Me in Italy Series:
Our Italian Summer
The Secret Love Letters of Olivia Moretti
A Wedding in Lake Como
To Sicily with Love

The Sunshine Sisters Series:
Love on Beach Avenue
Temptation on Ocean Drive
Forever in Cape May
Christmas in Cape May

The Stay Series:
The Start of Something Good
A Brand New Ending
All Roads Lead to You
Something Just Like This
Begin Again

The Billionaire Builders:
Everywhere and Every Way
Any Time, Any Place
All or Nothing At All
Somehow, Some Way

Searching for Series:
Searching for Someday
Searching for Perfect

Searching for Beautiful
Searching for Always
Searching for You
Searching For Mine

The Marriage to a Billionaire Series:
The Marriage Bargain
The Marriage Trap
The Marriage Mistake
The Marriage Merger
The Marriage Arrangement

Standalone:
The Charm of You
Summer Sins
Executive Seduction
Dante's Fire
The Grinch of Starlight Bend
Love Me Anyway
All For You
Unbreak my Heart

The Sex on the Beach Series:
Beyond Me
Chasing Me

The Steele Brother Series:
Catch Me
Play Me
Dare Me
Beg Me
Reveal Me

The Reluctant Flirt

Jennifer Probst

BLUE BOX PRESS

The Reluctant Flirt
By Jennifer Probst

Copyright 2025 Triple J Publishing Inc
ISBN: 978-1-963135-40-4

Published by Blue Box Press, an imprint of Evil Eye Concepts,
Incorporated

Author's Acknowledgments

This book is dedicated to MJ Rose.

MJ, you were a champion for this series from the start. Every word in this book had you in mind—your love of fashion; your exuberant laugh; your addiction to romcoms that made you feel good; and the way you told amazing stories. You are so missed. You have changed so many lives. Thank you for allowing me to write with 1001 Dark Nights and Blue Box Press. Thank you for letting me experience the beauty of your soul.

I love you.

Liz, Jillian, thank you for letting me part of this special family and your endless support during such difficult times. There's no other place I'd want the Outer Banks series to be!

Prologue

"Shoes speak louder than words."
– Jimmy Choo

Eight years earlier…

Sierra Lourde reached up with trembling fingers and touched the delicate chain around her neck. The breath stuttered in her lungs, making it difficult to grab a deep inhale. With half closed eyes, she fought for control. This was the most important day of her life. She could not lose her shit.

The white wedding dress itched her skin. The veil tickled her nose. Her pearl-encrusted Jimmy Choo shoes—which she'd scored for fifty percent off—pinched her feet. And she felt moments away from doing the runaway bride thing.

Mom, am I making the right decision?

The desperate question pinged from her thoughts into the universe. Sierra waited for an answer. A sign. Anything to help her calm down, open the door, and walk down the aisle to the man she was supposed to desperately love.

After a few precious moments, her eyes flew wide open as her answer echoed in the small waiting room of the chapel.

Nothing.

What had she expected? Neither of her parents had given any type of sign they were still with her over the past year. All of those people who gushed about feeling energy and receiving signs were liars. Or even worse?

Mom and Dad didn't care enough to stick around to watch over their daughters.

The pain flared, raw and messy, but as usual, she had stuff to deal with and little time for self-reflection. In a few minutes, she was set to marry Patrick. Her first serious boyfriend. Her first love.

He was a good man. They'd met in college, and he was easy to be with, easy to care for. Besides being kind, he was ambitious and would provide a good financial foundation. God knows, since there wasn't much life insurance after her parents' death, she needed a solid plan to keep taking care of her sister, Aspen. The bitterness mixed with her grief, offering a cocktail that didn't taste like champagne.

Once, she'd been like Aspen, and believed her parents were living the ultimate love story. All of her friends dealt with divorce or conflict. They were jealous of her parents' constant honeymoon phase, even if the physical affection was sometimes embarrassing. It was only later Sierra began to lose the rosy blinders and realize the cost of such an intense love was ranking second. Or third.

Mom and Dad always chose each other first.

Sierra and Aspen were often left alone. Her parents were on a lifelong adventure that didn't seem to include their children. How many times had she woken up to find Mom and Dad packing to leave for a big outing, confident Sierra and Aspen could take care of themselves? How many times had they forgotten to leave groceries, or pay bills—too focused on their next big experience?

Sierra was in fifth grade the first time they decided she could handle a long weekend by herself. She'd tried so hard not to be a baby and cry; to be adult enough to take care of Aspen while her parents took a vacay. At night, she'd been terrified of the dark and the creepy noises coming from the basement, dreaming of monsters snatching them forever. When her parents called Sunday night to let her know they were delayed, Sierra dealt with breakfast, packing lunches, and making sure they made the bus for school.

Mom and Dad declared she'd done so well, they felt comfortable doing it again.

And now, those exact pursuits had caused their deaths. A last-minute island trip on a small single engine plane ended in disaster. The crash killed the pilot and her parents instantly. Once again, leaving Sierra alone and in charge.

She paced back and forth, her long train trailing behind her. This past year had been a blur and nonstop roller coaster ride. Endless nights crying with her sister and puzzling out their next steps. Struggling to make sure Aspen had what she needed to continue college. Packing up her parents' belongings and quickly becoming the adult she needed to be.

When Patrick proposed everything had suddenly made sense. She'd have both stability and a way to keep Aspen in college. It was time to grow up and make some tough decisions for her life.

Who cared if she was suddenly having doubts about how much she loved him?

Sierra grew up knowing love was the most important thing to live for. Mom always advised to choose a partner who completed your heart and changed your life. She'd show them endless movies and cite books where love saved everyone in the end. Aspen had fallen into the dreamy goal, and was now embroiled in a relationship with her English professor. Sierra disapproved of the whole toxic affair, but Aspen insisted Mom would've understood.

Sierra may not feel the magical butterflies with Patrick, but it was a decision best made with her head rather than heart. After all, look what had happened to her parents. To Aspen. To anyone who sacrificed everything to go after a reckless longing of the heart.

Disaster.

Pain.

Death.

She'd be different.

Marrying Patrick would be the start.

The breath suddenly rushed into her lungs as she confirmed her decision. Sierra listened to the mocking silence. Her hand rose to her neck again, running her index finger across the smooth white gold surface, the slight bump of rubies spelling out the word LOVE.

Her mother's favorite necklace burned her skin in a sense of betrayal. Slowly, she unclasped the chain and tucked it into her beaded clutch. It didn't feel right to wear Mom's bold motto. She was choosing a different type of relationship, with a man who was steady, trustworthy, and safe. A better type of love. Sierra would commit all she had to make him happy and build a life of stability for both of them.

Calmness settled over her. The final door within slammed closed, shutting out the remnants of hope that her mother would appear and give her all the answers. The tears of grief stuck in her throat as she swallowed them back. From now on, she'd focus on the things she could control and move forward.

Sierra adjusted her veil. Smoothed her palms down her dress. Stepped through the door where her sister waited.

And got married.

One year ago…

Kane Masterson sat in the holding room and waited for the lawyer to spring him from jail.

He clenched his fists to stop the shaking. It was just a mistake. He'd done nothing wrong, and eventually he'd be back in his office while John laughed his ass off about the whole experience, telling him it'd be a great story to tell one day.

His sluggish mind kept repeating the words thrown at him.

You have the right to remain silent…

You have the right to an attorney…

Fraud…

Embezzlement…

A shudder wracked him. He hated the way he felt at this moment; just like he did when he was a kid dealing with filth and violence.

Shamed. Dirty.

A failure.

Kane drew in a breath and calmed his mind. He was a grown-up, dammit. He closed million-dollar deals, wore Armani suits, and was a power player in the most competitive city in the world. He'd worked for Global Investments as the top property developer for a few years now. One mistaken night in jail couldn't take away his accomplishments.

God, he hoped his brother didn't find out. Derek needed to focus on himself during rehab, and this would set him off.

The door flung open and a guy in a sharp charcoal suit walked in. His whole presence stunk of lawyer—from the slicked back hair, conservative clothes, and sharp-eyed, predatory gaze. He placed his leather briefcase on the crappy table and reached out his hand.

"Gary Parkers. John sent me."

Relief coursed through him. "Kane Masterson. Thank God, you're here. Did you talk to them about the charges? None of them are true—I'm not sure what the hell is going on but I spent the night in here."

Gary didn't seem bothered by him locked in a cell with a toilet and dirty cot. He took a seat on the folding chair across, opened his case, and began shuffling papers. Kane would have felt better if the guy had a laptop and immediately apologized about the misunderstanding, but at this point, he didn't know what was going on in this *Black Mirror* hell.

"I've gone over the charges and spoken with the partners at Global. I'll be honest here. There aren't many great options."

Kane blinked. "What? I'm innocent. I never touched any funds—they're all John's accounts."

Gary looked up. Ice trickled down his spine as Kane realized there was something else going on. Something bigger that he never even considered. And in this moment, his whole life was going to change.

"You had full access," Gary said sharply. "You were able to move money around and the trail clearly shows large amounts of money being withdrawn and disappearing. Global wants to press full charges. With the evidence they have and their legal team, you're looking at serving ten to fifteen years."

Kane shut down the threatening panic and forced his brain to work. It took him a few moments to begin looking at the whole situation with cold rationale. "Gary, are you my lawyer? Or Global's?"

"Neither. I'm John's lawyer. I've come to offer you a way out."

He stared at the man's neutral features; his perfect hair; his thin lips. But it was his eyes that finally gave it away. Shrewd. Manipulative.

The truth hit him like a tsunami.

He'd been framed.

Kane clenched his fists tighter as the room spun. John, his mentor, his boss, had set him up. The man he trusted with his life had stolen those funds and had sent his shark to make sure the truth never came out.

He'd been so stupid. Hadn't he learned not to trust anyone in this fucked-up world? And now he'd pay.

Kane let the numbness wash over his body, even as his mind fired up.

"I see. You're here to cut a deal."

Gary continued without answering. "John thinks highly of you. Doesn't want something like this to ruin the rest of your life, or take away your freedom. He'll talk to the partners and make this whole thing go away. The charges will be dropped. You'll leave Global. And everything will stay quiet. You'll just need to agree not to talk about the situation with anyone, or work at another competitor here in New York."

Yes. It made sense now. John could cover his crime by framing him, but it would only work if Kane disappeared.

"Is there a payout?" he asked coldly.

"No. You walk away with nothing. Everything gets wiped away."

Holy fuck. All of his money was tied up in the company, and he'd just used all of his cash to invest in a high-risk deal John had encouraged him to do.

Still, in that moment, he didn't care. He'd fight. He'd expose the truth. He was innocent and damned if he'd let another monster ruin him.

"Fuck you," he said calmly. "You tell John I'll be his worst nightmare."

Gary didn't even flinch. A small smile played upon those thin lips. "Too bad. I'm sure your brother will be disappointed to be thrown out of rehab."

Shock hit him. Derek. He'd forgotten about Derek. He was finally at a top-notch place that cost thousands after almost losing him brother to drugs and suicide. How could he pull him out of the first rehab that was actually working?

It was over then. Kane knew it. So did Gary.

John had played his trump card. There was only one vow Kane would never break; a vow that had kept him surviving through it all.

Protect his brother at all costs.

His life wasn't a movie of the week. It was reality, and the ones with the most money and power always won.

Slowly, Kane nodded. "If I agree, Derek's rehab needs to be paid in full. I'll want it in writing."

"Understood. So, you agree?"

A part of him died in that moment; the last ounce of innocence and hope he'd been holding onto, but there was only one answer.

"I agree."

Chapter One

"I still have my feet on the ground, I just wear better shoes."
– Oprah Winfrey

"I swear, the man is such a snack, all I could do was drool," Plumeria said, shaking her head as she folded the pile of t-shirts and arranged them neatly. "If I hadn't been on a date, I would've totally tried to approach him last night at Sunfish. How have you not met him yet, Sierra?"

Sierra Lourde grinned at her new part-timer, a college student who adored fashion and wanted to study retail. Her youthful energy brought a welcome spark to Flirt, even though she had no experience and needed training. "My sister has been trying to set us up, but we keep missing each other. He may be a little old for you though, right?"

Plumeria sighed, her dark eyes dreamy. "Who cares? I don't want to marry him."

One of the customers overheard their conversation and cut in. "I agree with Plumeria. I told my cousin to take one of those wild horse tours so she could meet him. Besides being attractive, he's the sweetest man. Do you know he's been the most active volunteer for Judy with the sea turtles?"

Brooklyn, her manager and close friend, called out from behind the register. "I heard that, too. Plus, he's been helping Marco install a whole new financial software program since the store is doing so well. I can't believe he's from New York. He fit in so quickly here."

"Maybe he'll stay," Sierra said, amused at the enthusiastic gossip. The Outer Banks may be a stretch of gorgeous beach that beckoned endless tourists, but Corolla was a small town. The locals loved an interesting newcomer, especially a mysterious, gorgeous man like Kane Masterson.

In a short amount of time, Kane had captured the town's attention. Seems he'd appeared one day at Brick's door and began working for Ziggy's Tours, showing tourists the wild horses. Her sister, Aspen, had come for a summer visit from New York and began dating Brick, so she'd been quickly charmed by his best friend. Women were crazed to date Kane, but every time Aspen pushed her to meet him, Sierra backed off.

She wasn't interested in chasing after the town's hottest bachelor.

She wasn't interested in any man right now.

"Maybe you'll actually give this one a shot," Brooklyn said cheerfully. "Lord knows, you've turned down every other single guy around here."

Sierra gave her friend a warning look. "Don't start, or I'll declare a clearance sale and

make you work late. Our customers don't need to know about my love life."

"What love life?"

Plumeria and the lone customer laughed. Sierra drew in a breath, though she was used to her friend's ribbing. "Let's focus on the lunch rush and making some sales, shall we? I'm sure Kane Masterson will still be around at closing."

On cue, the cheery sound of the bell alerted the influx of a new group of customers. Sierra happily fell into her daily routine of running Flirt, her beloved shop she'd created from scratch. The buzz of happy conversation mingled with the scent of lavender. Soothed from the feminine energy bursting around her, Sierra's gaze swept over the space with pride.

The boutique was located in Duck, set beside a café and toy store close to the busy center of town. When she first decided to open her own business, she knew she'd never be able to afford the spaces by the water, but she'd gotten lucky snagging this last commercial spot near the action. Sierra signed her lease at a time when the landlord just wanted his last empty store filled.

Flirt was filled with unique clothing, jewelry, and accessories with a beach vibe. There were no cheap T-shirts or mugs here. Instead, shelves displayed delicate perfume bottles, jewelry boxes, and candles. Artwork by local artists was strategically placed on the walls. Sierra knew décor was one of the most important draws for a store, so it was roomy enough to move and everywhere a customer looked, something grabbed the eye. Bold color, a glittery stone, the mix of jade or wood, an elegant curve to a candlestick; it was not only a clothing shop, but an experience. Sierra wanted each item to serve a shopper's impulsive ways and wandering gaze.

God, so much had changed these past few years. When her ex-husband had first dragged her out here from New York, she'd struggled. She'd wanted to be near Aspen, but he'd gotten a big job at a well-respected wealth firm, and Sierra knew she had no choice. He'd been the moneymaker. Sierra had barely graduated after her parents' death, managing to squeak by with a sociology degree.

Yeah. That'd been a real smart move.

She ended up in Corolla with no friends, no family, and no job. How many years did she struggle to make a beautiful home and become what her husband needed? How long did she struggle to figure out what she really wanted in life?

Now, she had carved out her own path, with a tight group of friends, her sister, and a thriving business. It was a long way from the unsure, lost woman who'd just discovered her husband cheating, blowing every part of her life to smithereens.

Sierra had never believed fashion could be her career. In her head, people who ran shops went to the Fashion Institute or knew secret things about the industry, but once she began working at a boutique after the divorce, Sierra quickly figured out most of the staff had no clue.

It took her under a year to know more about running the place than the owner, and when she spoke up too many times, she'd gotten fired.

It was one of the best things to happen.

Sierra loaded up on business and online master classes, then applied for a bank loan to open her own place. It was as if the universe had finally opened up the path clearly before her, removing all obstacles. And now Flirt was a success. She'd built a steady client base, even during the off-season, and woke up energized to start her day.

If only she had someone to share it.

Pushing the thought out of her mind, she refocused on the responsibilities of the day. Groups were already flowing through the aisles and clustered around the jewelry cases. Brooklyn chatted up some teens who were trying on charm necklaces, complimenting them all with her usual warm energy. Plumeria worked the register, and the hours passed by in a blur.

Finally, there was a lull, and Brooklyn walked over. "Plumeria, go take your break. I appreciate you staying with me during the rush."

The girl lit up at the praise. "No problem. Hey, do you think you can put the new silver hoop earrings aside for me? I get a discount, right?"

Brooklyn grinned. "Thirty percent. The Jasmine Concept collection, right?"

"Yes, they're so dope."

Sierra laughed. "I just persuaded her to give me more of her stuff. We'll definitely keep them for you but don't make me put a limit on your purchases. You need college tuition."

Plumeria gave a cheeky grin. "But I need to look good first. See ya later." She strode out, her distressed denim jeans, cute crop top, and dark braids the perfect walking advertisement for Flirt.

Brooklyn sighed. "Remember us at that age?"

"Nope."

Her friend shook her head, walking to the back to pull her salad from the refrigerator. "Well, I do. I was partying nonstop, and in love with someone new every month. I was also worried about the future, and thinking I wasn't skinny or fabulous enough. What a waste."

Sierra began refolding graphic t-shirts with signature quotes. "Youth is wasted on the young, remember? Can't tell them anything because they need to experience it, just like we did. At least you settled down and married a nice Jewish man like your Mama wanted."

Brooklyn sat down and popped opened her Tupperware. "Trust me, she was worried for a while. She loves Greg more than me by the way she acts around him. Like he did me this huge favor by marrying him."

"Did he?" Sierra teased.

Brooklyn gave her a mock glare. "Funny. Speaking of marriage, I wanted to see if you'd be open to meeting someone."

"Oh, hell, no. Not after the last so-called meeting you tried to trick me with."

"Come on, Sierra! How was I supposed to know the guy still lived in the basement at his mom's house? Greg said he had just gotten a promotion and was moving up the corporate ladder."

"I'm not starring in *Failure to Launch*. I'm tired of blind dates and trying to force connections. I'm happier staying home. The universe will send me my person when I'm ready."

Brooklyn stared. "Did you get a brain transplant? Because trusting anything other than your own power is *not* what you do. You make things happen, remember? You believe in yourself."

Sierra straightened the candles on the shelf. "Please tell me I don't say that crap. Sounds like a self-help influencer. If a man is meant to be mine, he'll show up at my doorstep or deliver my pizza or—I don't know—just appear! Until then, I'm thinking of making a big move and want your advice."

"I'm here. And yes, you should definitely get on a dating app."

"Brooklyn, this is serious. I'm talking real commitment serious."

Blue eyes widened and she nodded. "Okay. I'm ready. Tell me."

"I may get a...cat."

Brooklyn blinked. "Are you kidding?"

"No. God, just the thought of it makes me nervous, but somehow, it feels right to take this next step? Bring a living creature into my home that I have to take care of. It'd be a rescue, of course. I haven't even mentioned this crazy plan to Aspen. What do you think?"

Brooklyn slumped in her seat and focused on her salad, looking disappointed. "I think your announcement sucks. I'm afraid if you get a cat, you'll never leave the house again."

Sierra laughed. "Childless cat ladies can rule the world in their own way."

"Okay, you got me there."

"Getting a cat will go with my new philosophy. Maybe I'll meet a childless cat guy and we can live happily ever after."

"You're so weird."

That got them both laughing, and then new customers came in. The rest of the afternoon was busy until late evening, and by the time they closed, Sierra was ready to collapse. Unfortunately, she had a ton of spreadsheets waiting for her so it'd be a long night. Maybe it was time to hire a bookkeeper. Her profit margins were healthy, but taking on another employee was a huge step. She looked at anyone who worked at Flirt as her responsibility, and she'd hate to hire too quickly if the budget got squeezed. Offseason was always the tightest time on the island, and her landlord had been acting strange lately. She had a feeling rent was going up, but every time she tried to pin him down on re-signing her lease, he made an excuse and disappeared.

Her Spidey senses were tingling. And not in a good way.

She reminded herself things were going perfectly. She loved her life, though watching her sister and Brick fall hard for each other set off a deep longing she didn't know how to soothe. She was happy for Aspen, but wondered if she'd ever be able to truly let another person in again.

Her thoughts flashed to *him*.

A shiver raced down her spine. The one night she'd let herself go and experience the type of passion her parents embodied. The type of surrender written about in books and movies that promised happily ever after but mostly led to disaster. The memory of that night was a constant companion, but belonged in Pandora's box, never to be flung wide open. She'd walked away, sensing if she stayed, her life would have been led off course.

Losing her parents and experiencing a divorce taught her two valuable lessons she wasn't about to repeat.

She was never chosen.

And everyone left.

The thought was a pang in her gut, but she was used to smothering the feeling. Better to stop the endless dating cycle and be happy on her own. But it was definitely time to push herself to make a new commitment to something that could offer growth.

After all, her marriage may not have worked out, but her shoe collection?

Worth the care, investment, and patience. It was legendary.

A cat may be the perfect next step.

Sierra was almost ready to take the leap.

Chapter Two

Kane Masterson pulled into the parking lot of Ziggy's Tours and cut the engine. "That concludes our tour for the day, folks. I hope you enjoyed it."

As he personally escorted them from the Jeep, flashing his customer grin, he noticed the three girls in the back row were nudging each other and giggling. They were obviously students on vacay and had him in their sights for a fun fling. His usual tour dialogue had received suggestive statements and jokes containing the words *wild*, *riding*, and *stud*.

Though they'd be a fun distraction to party with, no way was he getting involved with anyone below drinking age.

The leader, a leggy redhead with a cute sprinkling of freckles, grabbed his hand in an intimate shake. "I can't thank you enough, Kane. You're a wonderful tour guide."

"Thanks, Marcee. It was truly a pleasure."

He noticed she held a twenty and hoped he'd still get it after the rejection he'd need to bestow.

A flirty smile curved her lips. "We'd love to hear more. Want to join us for a drink later?"

He schooled his face in disappointment. "Normally, I'd jump at the chance, but my sister's in town with my niece. I'm on babysitting duty all week."

The girls shared a look. Marcee's smile turned into a small pout. "Oh. Bummer. Well, we'll be around tonight and tomorrow if you get any time off. Here's my number."

She pressed the bill into his hand with a slip of paper. He pocketed both smoothly. "Sounds good, ladies. Fingers crossed!"

"Definitely!" They disappeared, shooting lingering looks over their shoulders while he waved.

He unloaded the Jeep and walked into Ziggy's Tours where Brick waited behind the counter.

Smirking.

"Did you use the niece thing again or are you meeting them for drinks?"

Kane shot his friend a suffering look. "Niece. They're practically jailbait."

Brick laughed. "You're really raking in the dough for me, man. Who would've thought that pretty face could be such a gold mine?"

"Fuck you."

His friend laughed harder, but Kane really didn't care. He'd accepted his good looks as a gift years ago, and didn't take himself too seriously. Though it wasn't fair, society still rewarded such things by bestowing more opportunities, and Kane grabbed every single one. Sometimes, it had been the only factor allowing him to survive.

"Want to join me and Aspen for dinner tonight?" Brick asked.

He lifted a brow. "Aren't you afraid I'll steal her from you with my apparent pretty face and charm?"

"Nah, she said you're ugly."

Now, it was Kane's turn to laugh. "You wish."

Brick's face turned serious. "No, for real. Join us. I really appreciate you stepping in and helping me get this business profitable again. In a matter of a few weeks, you carved out a place here. Helping Marco and Judy. Hell, I even heard Mr. Pitts took a liking to you, and he hates everyone."

Mr. Pitts was an elderly man who lived next door to Brick. He terrorized children, animals, and his surrounding neighbors. Whenever people spotted him, they took care to duck or hide to avoid the man's sour face and blistering tongue. Somehow, Kane didn't take offense. Mr. Pitts was lonely and obviously miserable. At least he never tried to hide behind a fake veneer. Kane respected the truthful way he was awful to all equally.

"I think liking is too strong of a word. I took his garbage out since it was raining last week. He bitched me out for taking away his choice."

"Yeah, but he left it out there. When I tried, he dragged those cans right back to prove his point."

"What can I say? People like me more than you."

Brick grinned. "But not Aspen."

Kane grinned back. "You got it bad, huh? Listen, I appreciate the offer but I actually have a date tonight. An overnight one, so I won't be coming back to your place."

Brick's eyes lit up. Yeah, he'd done the right thing by lying. Aspen didn't like to sleep over at Brick's place when Kane was there, so it was best for him to make an excuse and give them the space. It was time Kane figured out a new plan.

When his life in New York blew up and he was released from jail, he'd found himself with nothing but a suitcase of clothes and some credit cards that wouldn't last long. All of those years in the property development industry, working his ass off night and day, only rewarded him with betrayal and the threat of a fraud conviction. An image of his old mentor, John, flashed in his mind, and he fought back the bitterness. How many times had he been taught his trust always led to pain? Between his asshole father and the boss who'd ruined him, Kane learned quickly not to depend on anyone but himself.

The memory was still a raw ache he doubted would ever heal. With his brother, Derek, in rehab, and no other family, Kane found himself seeking out his best friend as a last resort. He'd headed to OBX and hoped Brick would take in his sorry ass.

And his friend had. No questions asked. It was supposed to be a quick stop to get his shit together, but as time slowly passed, Kane realized the beach town was a place he could make a new start.

For years, his world had been controlled with the pursuit of more. More money; more power; more opportunities. It was a gnawing hunger he never seemed to satisfy, but when it was all ripped away, he realized maybe Corolla was the perfect town to re-create himself.

The people here seemed different. Instead of with suspicion and distance, he found most welcomed him with enthusiasm and openness. He liked knowing his neighbors and greeting the same people at the coffee shop and bars. Brick had introduced him to his friends, offered a guest room as long as he needed, and hired him on the spot to be a tour guide.

Kane was surprised how much he'd taken to the job switch. Learning the history and facts about the wild horses was satisfying. Much different from hard sales, manipulative moves, and high-value, cutthroat contracts. Teaching others about the land and animals that lived here gave him some peace, and he'd taken to driving out there sometimes to think about his next step and watch them race across the sand.

Brick interrupted his thoughts. "Listen, can you be careful about who you date, please? I told you—this town is different than New York. One night means something. You don't want these women to be discussing you at the support group."

Kane waved a hand in the air. "Not worried. You and Aspen have a great time. I'll see you in the morning."

He walked out and wondered where he'd crash tonight. Probably a hotel room outside of Corolla so no one spotted him. Soon he'd be able to get his own rental place, but he'd need a steady job to pay the bills. There were some possibilities he'd look into. Kane doubted he could find a high-powered property development firm out here, but it was time to start looking.

Thoughts of everything he'd left behind competed with the pull of a bright, clean future where no one knew. Once again, he'd fought his way out of ugliness, but he was able to cherish the two most important things he'd managed to protect.

His freedom.

And his brother.

Kane focused on the other emotion flickering inside him, refusing to be dimmed.

Hope.

Sierra looked longingly at the television and wondered if she could cancel.

The week had slowly turned awful, and she craved pj's, a glass of wine, and the new erotic thriller on Netflix. Instead, she'd promised Aspen they'd all go out so she could finally meet the mysterious Kane. Normally, her sister would understand she was tired, but lately, Aspen was all giddy over Brick and wouldn't stop bugging her to resume dating.

No. Thanks.

The knock on the door made her grumble as she went and opened it.

"Why are you not ready?" Inez asked, dark eyes squinted in suspicion. "Don't even think you're ghosting tonight."

She gave her friend a long-suffering groan. As usual, Inez looked gorgeous in her skinny jeans and black crop top. The outfit was simple but emphasized her curvy butt and flat abs. Her braids fell down to her waist in a fall of sexiness that made every man she passed take a second look. Her nose piercing flashed as she shook her head and marched in. Inez was a numbers genius and ran her own finance firm, though most couldn't match her tats and rebel style with the staid, boring reputation of math.

Sierra had fallen for her immediately, loving her unapologetic ways and strong personality. Once Brooklyn joined in, their trio was a perfectly balanced circle of trust and fun.

"I had a hell of a day. Pru's on vacay and the store was mobbed. I have a buyer's trip this week and need to research. And my new shoes needed breaking in so my feet hurt."

Inez gave a snort and threw her purse down on the table. "Don't care. It's Friday night and you're not staying home alone again. Aspen will kick your ass if you don't show." With a snap of her fingers, she headed toward the bedroom. "Your house is amazing but it's becoming a prison, girlfriend."

Sierra trudged after her friend, looking around. She may have bought the house with her ex, but she'd turned it into her true home. Each detail was carefully chosen to work with the décor of an elegant beach retreat. Home was her haven and the place she felt most comfortable, other than Flirt.

Shades of cream, butter, and bright white created a neutral background to emphasize the pops of color splashed in accents and thoughtful details amidst the rooms. Sierra kept her beach theme threaded through with aquamarine seashell pillows, sea glass portraits of seagulls, and gorgeous handmade vases holding colorful wildflowers. The throw rugs were aquamarine. Wicker baskets and driftwood décor added to the chic vibe, but the furniture was oversized and comfy. The kitchen with its massive island, multiple granite countertops, and generous padded barstools was a chef's dream.

As they reached her bedroom, Inez yanked open the closet and studied the options. Her king-size bed was set on a massive platform with a silver velvet headboard. Shades of lavender and light gray created a soft, feminine retreat. A shimmery crystal chandelier sparkled in the light. A generous cosmetic center with a padded stool and beveled mirror sat in the corner. The chaos of dozens of brushes and bottles were carefully organized in various containers. Frilly lace curtains covered the windows. Each detail had been lovingly crafted to make her feel indulged.

"Here. You should look slutty tonight."

Sierra caught the silky red number and shook her head. "Hell, no. I want comfy. It's only Sunfish!"

"You're such a pain in the ass. Fine. We'll go big on the bottom and slutty on top. Try this."

The faded flare jeans gave her plenty of room to move, accentuating the white halter top that tied around her neck and plunged in a deep V. Sierra sighed. "You're such a bully. Isn't that too skimpy?"

"No, you have fab breasts and more men need to see them."

Sierra smothered a laugh and gave up the fight. Inez always won anyway. "Fine."

"Now the shoes." The second closet opened and Inez gave a shudder of pleasure. "I swear, every time I look at this, I have an orgasm. You have the best shoes in the world, girl."

Sierra had to agree.

The walk-in closet had been converted to showcase shoes. From Louboutin to Prada, Gucci to Dior, every style and mood was accounted for and lovingly worn to evoke a feeling. Open shelves and compartments were color coded with a dazzling variety of colors, from sandals and flats, to boots and loafers. Fuck-me, sky-high heels happily sat beside platform pumps and every heel height in between. When Sierra gazed at her closet, her insides stilled, and she was dragged into the moment and that one important choice of the day.

Over the years, Sierra found herself drawn to shoes. Every woman had a thing, whether it was handbags, makeup, or the new hottest trends. For her, a day spent with the right shoes could be the difference between a good and bad day; of success or failure; of happiness or feeling lost.

Her ex-husband mocked and made fun of her obsession. He used to grab the credit card bill and scold her like a toddler when she spent too much on a pair. Afterward, she leaned in hard to a hobby that made her feel powerful and in charge, saving money by expert shopping with re-sale sites, flea markets, and even garage sales. Most women didn't realize the treasures they had with a pair of designer shoes.

She sold a few pairs at Flirt, cultivated for the impulse beachwear accessory. They never stayed long on the shelves. She had a talent for knowing what women craved in their footwear. Aspen had a bigger size foot and had been horrifically jealous of her when they were younger. Now, she admitted Sierra could have been the next big shoe designer of the century. But she liked wearing them, not creating them. It was a pleasure she now refused to apologize for.

Inez took a few moments in worshipful silence, then plucked a pair of platform white sandals with embroidered daisies on the wide crossover strap. Betsey Johnson knew how to create a whimsical, yet sexy shoe that was legendary. "Good choice?"

Sierra smiled with pleasure. "Perfect. Give me fifteen."

She was efficient with her make-up, and Inez helped curl her hair so it fell soft and loose around her shoulders. Grabbing a small denim bag from Ed Hardy, and spritzing some Dior perfume, she faced Inez.

"Ready."

"You look hot, bitch."

Sierra laughed. "So do you."

They headed to Sunfish but as they were getting out Inez got a text. "Oops, Brooklyn needs a ride. Grab us a table and I'll be right back."

Sierra grinned. "Means she's drinking tonight."

"The kids must be on their worst behavior today."

Inez took off. Sierra spotted Aspen, who'd managed to snag a large table. She squished in and gave her sister a hug. "Long time, no see. Inez is bringing Brooklyn. Where's Brick?"

"Should be here soon. You look amazing. I cannot wait for you to meet Kane!"

Sierra sighed. "Babe, I don't want you to get disappointed if we're not interested in each other, okay? Every woman I know in town is panting after him. I'm not really into competing."

"He's not like that." Her brown eyes held a plea. "I just want you to find a guy who's worthy. You have so much to give, and I'm afraid you're beginning to close off and no one will see what I do. That you're so special, Sierra."

Her heart softened to mush. "That's really sweet. But right now, I'm doing okay. Let's talk about Brick instead and how happy he makes you."

"Did I hear my name?"

Brick kissed Aspen and slid in next to her. Sierra watched her sister melt and make googly eyes at him. Oh yeah, they both had it bad. She wondered briefly what it would feel like to experience such highs again— that giddy roll of lust and possibility when you looked at a man. The comfort of touch and the safety of snuggling next to someone at night. The beautiful routines she sometimes missed and craved.

Sierra blinked hard, shoving those disturbing thoughts aside.

She meant what she said to Aspen. She was doing okay. She was happy.

It was enough.

They chatted. Inez and Brooklyn came in, and soon, a crowd of friends clustered around the table. Sierra stood up to stretch and make her way around the bar. One drink turned to two as she relaxed. It was good she'd come out. Another reminder she enjoyed her life.

After a quick stop to the restroom, Aspen intercepted. "Kane's here."

Sierra chuckled. "If I finally meet him, will you promise to stop talking about how great he is? You're being a meddling matchmaker."

Aspen threw up her hands. "Just looking out for you, sis. Inez may fight you for him, though."

"Hos over bros, babe."

Aspen cracked up. Hurrying over to Brick, she pulled at his arm and whispered something. Amused at the drama, Sierra waited patiently while Aspen pushed her forward.

"Kane, this is Sierra. Sierra, this is Brick's friend, Kane. He's visiting from New York and helps Brick out with some of the tours."

Her gaze lifted and collided with familiar emerald green eyes.

Everything stilled. Her entire body froze in shock, trying to keep up with her spinning mind that kept repeating the same word over and over and over.

No, no, no, no...

Her hand jerked and the glass she was holding dropped, shattering on the floor.

Still, she couldn't move, couldn't breathe, as her sister's voice repeated her name, and applause broke out in approval of breaking something in a bar.

It was him.

The man who'd haunted her dreams for the past four years. The man who'd stolen a piece of her heart and soul that one perfect rainy night. The man without a name.

That man was Kane Masterson.

Dear God, he was just as sexy and devastating as she remembered. Thick auburn hair that fell in a wave over his forehead. A lush mouth and chiseled jaw that was a work of art. His lean muscled body was clad in pressed khakis, a starched white shirt, and beautiful leather shoes. Broad shoulders and powerful thighs forced the fabric to yield and surrender, just like she'd done under his talented hands and fingers. His scent of spice and clove drifted to her nostrils and sparked erotic memories that she wasn't ready to confront.

But God, his eyes. She was already drowning in the green-gold depths, framed by thick lashes. That gaze drilled deep and pinned her in place while she swayed on her feet, helpless underneath the intense male stare, as shocked as hers.

"Sierra?"

She shuddered. The low, gravelly voice raked across her ears. He'd never spoken her name. The raw intimacy of hearing it for the first time from his lips shot her into a total panic.

She wasn't ready to confront her past in the middle of a crowded bar. Sierra jumped, realizing Aspen and Brick were both staring at her with concern.

"Umm, hi. Nice to meet you, Kane."

The words flew from her mouth automatically. Something flashed in those beautiful eyes. Pain? Regret? Anger? She had no time to process. The voice inside screamed for her to flee.

Sierra forced her gaze away, turning toward her sister. She pressed a fisted hand to her trembling mouth. "Aspen, so sorry, I gotta go. I've got an…awful headache. Tell the girls I'll see them later this week."

"Wait, I'll go home with you."

"No!" She blinked, forcing a smile. "No, stay. I want you to stay. I just really need some sleep and alone time. Bye, Brick. Talk to you guys later."

She shot out of the bar like Satan was trying to snatch her soul. Her drive was a blur, as the past and present crashed into each other and left a broken trail of memories behind.

By the time she arrived home, there was no more fight left.

Sierra pressed her back against the door. Slid down to the floor. Closed her eyes.

And remembered.

Chapter Three

Four Years Ago

"You gotta hear this one. A man walks into a bar and…"

Sierra Lourde stared at the guy who was rattling off bad jokes and held back a groan. Really? She expected such behavior in her small beach town—tourists were notoriously chatty and tipsy on vacation—but this was New York City. At the Carlisle hotel. Wasn't that fancy enough to guarantee loud, sloppy men wouldn't try to pick her up when she just wanted to sit by herself and drink a glass of overpriced wine?

The overweight, almost bald man guffawed at the punchline, not caring she didn't break a smile. "Hysterical right? Let me buy you another drink." He made a motion to the bartender but she reacted quickly.

"No, thanks. I'd prefer to be alone right now, but appreciate the offer."

He blinked red eyes in disbelief. Then grinned like he'd misheard her. "A pretty woman like you? Nah, I'm a great listener. Try me."

Sierra glanced around the mostly empty bar and tamped down a sigh. Once again, she'd have to take care of things herself. Why hadn't she learned there was never someone coming to save her? The lesson kept slapping her upside the head enough times to get a concussion. Yet, here she was. Still hoping for a white knight to step in, get rid of the guy, and not expect a thing in return.

The men that Mom always spoke about, she thought with a touch of bitterness. The ones from those awful movies she played over and over, telling Sierra love was the only reason for living, and to go big or go home.

Oh, she'd gone big alright.

And then she'd gone home. For good.

"Look, I just want to—"

A deep, gravelly voice interrupted her from behind. "Sorry, honey, I ran late. The kids are in bed but I think Sylvester came home with lice, which I may have caught—oh, hi. Keeping my wife company? Thanks so much."

Her jaw unhinged but she snapped it shut, refusing to ruin the save. Sierra caught his scent before she actually saw the stranger; a mix of clove and whiskey that was so sensually male, she almost gave another sniff just to confirm. The joke guy almost stumbled back when he was offered to shake hands, and she bit her lip to keep from laughing.

Must be afraid of catching lice.

Sierra smoothly picked up her role. "Dammit. I was hoping to clear my thoughts but I guess that's not happening." She gave a deep sigh. "I think lice is even worse than bed bugs, don't you, darling?"

"I agree. We should've never sent Sara to camp."

Joke guy took another step back. "Uh, I'll leave you to, ugh, figure things out."

In seconds, they were left blissfully alone. Sierra swiveled her head around to thank her savior, then turned mute.

He was…breathtaking.

Thick, russet hair with touches of gold tumbled over his brow. His features were classic Irish but held a carved symmetry that kept him from looking too pretty. A short, clipped beard hugged his lush lips, giving him an edge. But it was his eyes that held her motionless.

A deep-set emerald, gleaming with both mischief and ruthless intelligence. A swirl of gold and green that demanded a woman's full attention, because she'd be helpless under his stare. Sierra didn't have to study him to note the cut of his designer suit, or the lean muscled body beneath. She knew immediately he was way out of her league, but damned if she'd give him the satisfaction of stumbling over her words. God knows, he was probably used to it.

Thankfully, she found her voice. "Sylvester and Sara, huh? Creative. Was there going to be a third?"

Those gorgeous lips quirked in a half-smile. "Salvatore. He has chicken pox."

She nodded. "As parents, we're screwed."

He gave a husky laugh. His hair was damp from the rain. He brushed off the lingering raindrops and tugged at his Burberry raincoat. "Hope that was okay. I made an executive decision you didn't want company."

"Your decision would have gained you a promotion. Appreciate it."

Her heart beat madly in her chest but she remained calm as that piercing gaze studied her. She knew what came next. He'd offer a drink, sit down, and give her a bunch of charming pick-up lines. It was a rainy Monday night and other than the vanished joke guy and the bartender across the way, no one was here. Her one-time savior would try to close the deal and the good feeling he gave her would be gone under the eventual smarm of wanting to sleep with her.

God, she was so cynical.

God, she was so tired.

What had she expected? It wasn't his fault. She'd come alone to a hotel bar, which pretty much screamed her intention to get drunk and have sex with a stranger.

Holy crap, what if he thought she was a hooker?

Sure, she wasn't wearing provocative clothes—her loose black pants, cold-shouldered matching top, and high heeled red boots screamed city chic, but escorts were classy now. Except with this man, if she was an escort, she'd offer him a freebie.

Sierra waited, and wondered if she'd just give in. He was male perfection, and though she wasn't comfortable with one-night stands, she'd come here to escape her tangled thoughts and insecurities.

This man would remove both.

He treated her to a full grin, bringing a roguish Irish charm her sister, Aspen, would have written about in her novels. "You're very welcome. Enjoy your drink."

Then with a graceful tip of his chin, he headed to the opposite end of the bar and settled on the chair.

He ordered a drink and Sierra spun back around toward her own cocktail.

Well, dayum. That was embarrassing.

Caught between shame from the rejection and laughter at her ego, she chose humor. Aspen would never let her forget this moment. Her sister was always whining that Sierra could get any guy she wanted, so she'd crack up at this bold turn-down.

Lifting her glass, she sipped her Cabernet and allowed herself to grin.

"That seemed too amusing not to share."

Her nerve endings shimmered with awareness. His voice stroked all the places inside her that hadn't been stroked in way too long. She ignored her body and cocked her head. "Just remembering all those witty jokes from my previous companion."

A sexy snort echoed across the bar. He lifted his glass—looked like whiskey—and took a sip. "If the first ones were as bad as the one I caught, I'm concerned about your sense of humor."

"Be more concerned about Sylvester and Sara. You're on duty tonight."

A grin curved his lips. "You're funny."

A sigh escaped her. "Not really. My sister terms it "dry wit." A nice way to say I'm sarcastic."

"Nothing wrong with sarcasm."

Sierra shrugged, then went back to her wine. The hushed sounds of the bartender moving glasses and a low conversation from out in the hall added to the feeling of intimacy. Rich wood, glass bottles, soft music, and dim lights made it a good place to escape a cold, rainy night. Her phone lay on the gleaming mahogany, on silent, untouched. She didn't want the outside world to invade her bubble.

The silence stretched to fill the room. Curiosity spiked. Was he grabbing a drink before going home to his wife? Was he meeting someone? Was he drowning his sorrows in liquor? Was he hoping for an easy pick up?

His phone was perched on the bar but he wasn't scrolling, either. His fingers tapped the polished counter absently, seemingly deep in thought.

She jolted when he spoke up. "I'm celebrating. Closed a deal and had a good day."

"Congrats."

Another graceful nod. More tapping of fingers. "Thanks."

Sierra paused. "I'm celebrating, too."

"Yeah? For what?"

"Getting through a shit day. A few glasses of wine are my reward."

He turned in his chair to study her. That lush lower lip quirked. Her fingers itched to touch his mouth so she made a fist instead. "I'm sorry you had a bad day."

She blinked. "Thanks."

"Feels kinda weird talking to you from way over here. Can I get you another wine? Or I can stop talking if you just want to chill by yourself."

He sounded sincere, which threw her off. "I'm not a hooker."

A burst of laughter escaped him. The sound pleased her, and she mourned when he stopped. "Good to know because I'm not looking for one."

"You wouldn't need one anyway."

A delighted grin lit up his face. "You're flirting. I like it."

Her eyes widened. "Trust me, I never flirt. Just stating facts."

He shook his head and those emerald eyes gleamed with amusement. "A reluctant flirt, then."

Sierra had no idea why his statement pleased her. Her looks were solid enough to attract men, but she'd been told she was way too direct and serious. When she moved to Corolla, she'd been hopeful to absorb some southern charm, but it had never happened. She was too impatient to get to the punch lines. One of her biggest weaknesses.

Flirting was for women who played. Lingered. Women who enjoyed waiting for the payoff. Women who had...fun.

Hell, when was the last time she had actual fun?

Sierra pushed the gloomy thought aside. "Nope, not part of my makeup. But I'm sure you're used to every person in your path flirting with you," she said with a tiny snort.

His brow climbed. "Was that an insult cloaked as a compliment?"

"Maybe? Not that it's your fault you were born beautiful. I'm sure in some ways it's a terrible burden."

Another rich laugh. "For someone who doesn't flirt, you have the potential to be an expert."

"Now who's the flirt?"

Their gazes met and locked across the room and damned if that tingle blazed into a heat that warmed and melted her blood. A few seconds ticked by as they regarded each other. Sierra wasn't ignorant enough to think it was special. She was sure this man had a willing companion every night, but God, it felt good for her body to finally come alive. She'd been dead for too long.

He spoke with care and precision she immediately respected. "I'd love to sit closer and chat, but if you want your space, I promise to leave you alone."

Sierra studied his face. He was a stranger, but she believed him. And on this rainy, quiet night, she ached for some real conversation without any expectations.

"Why not?"

As she took a seat next to him, her nostrils filled with the scents of whiskey, clove, and fresh rain. He smiled and motioned for the bartender to bring her another glass of wine. "Hi. I'm—"

She lifted her hand and cut him off. "No names. If that's okay?"

It was so much easier to let go when there were no attachments. Her pain was something she'd been carefully hiding from practice—not wanting to drag her family or friends or co-workers into the mess. Here, with him, she'd be free not to care.

He glanced down at her hand. The empty patch where her wedding ring had been was a lighter skin color. "Married?"

His tone was neutral but his body stiffened. "Not any longer."

The tension eased. Sierra wondered if he had morals about sleeping with married women, or just wanted to know. His reaction said it was a line not to be crossed, but she knew nothing about him. "Okay."

The word seethed with meaning. Her shoulders relaxed. The bartender brought her another glass and she switched out. "Tell me about your good news," she said, taking a sip. The dry, oaky liquid slid down her throat with ease.

A tiny frown creased his brow. "Won't that make you feel bad? We can talk about your day."

She shook her head. "I'm tired of me. I want to hear about your big deal."

"Okay." With one graceful motion, he shed his jacket and hung it on the back of the chair. Her mouth watered at all those lean muscles moving underneath the crisp white shirt. "I'm in property development. I've been trying to buy this building for a while, but it was a long shot. Finally managed to snag it at a basement level price."

"How much?"

"Ten million."

She whistled. "Nice. What are you going to do with it now that you own it?"

"Tear it apart and turn the place into a storage unit."

She blinked. "Storage? What is it now?"

"There were a few tenants, but mainly it's used as an artist's studio and retreat."

Sierra considered his answer. "That sounds much better than storage. The world needs more creativity."

"Actually, it needs more space for New Yorker's storage. Have you seen the tight space in the apartments here?"

She fought back a smile. "So, you gobble up struggling properties that can be used for something better?"

"Mostly."

"You're the villain in the story."

His gaze narrowed with interest. "More like the Robin Hood of property. I buy them before they can fall into bankruptcy and give them a chance to make some money."

Sierra gave a snort. "You don't give your riches to the poor. Besides, I've seen *Pretty Woman*. You manipulate for a great deal, then dismantle someone's beloved business for money."

He gave a bark of laughter. Those green-gold eyes sparkled with mischief. "If you're not a hooker, I'm not the bad guy. No artists have been harmed during this deal. No nice old ladies have been thrown out of their houses by the big bad wolf."

"You don't strike me as a wolf."

"I'm glad."

"You're more like a hyena."

Shock flickered across his face. "Did you just call me a....hyena?"

"Yeah, wolves have no sense of humor. Take themselves way too seriously with all that alpha junk. You give off an aura of both cunning and humor. Bet you love a good joke."

"A man walks into a bar--"

She laughed and he joined in. It was nice to talk with a man who was good at banter. When was the last time she got to be silly? She had no motivation to impress or seduce him. The simple act of being in his company was a high, and Sierra could say anything she wanted. Her dry sense of humor was an oddity only her sister truly appreciated. And her ex, of course.

Until he didn't.

He ordered another whiskey. Then glanced over and their gazes met. Heat flared between them. She'd heard of physical connections that came out of nowhere but had never experienced it. Aspen had told her she experienced it with her professor immediately, citing with dreamy eyes how powerless she felt around him.

Odd. This felt different. More like a surge of feminine power washing through her. As if they were meeting halfway toward something bigger.

Sierra pushed the ridiculous thought away and seriously considered her options. Did she want to sleep with this gorgeous man who'd just closed a multi-million-dollar deal? He was probably dripping in money and power. Probably dated perfect women who did anything he wanted. She'd simply be another number to add to his list.

But tonight wasn't about him.

It was about her.

"Can I ask you a question?"

His voice lowered to a rumbly, sexy growl. "You can ask me any-thing."

"Is it easy for you? Getting anything you want?

Shadows gathered in his eyes, along with a flash of pain before it was quickly covered up. "No."

He didn't expand and she didn't need him to. Understanding pulsed within her. "I'm sorry."

He jerked back. "For what?"

A small, sad smile curved her lips. "For what happened before you became fabulous."

Surprise skittered across those masculine features. Powerful energy emanated in waves around him, drawing her in, but underneath she recognized the primal pain of a life with bumps and bruises. He hadn't gotten here easy. Sierra respected that type of journey. It was probably what made him so lethal to females.

God knows, they all loved a fixer-upper. Especially the sexy, rich kind.

"Why aren't you married anymore?" he asked.

Sierra was used to the trademarked responses she'd cultivated after her safe life blew up. A small southern town wasn't the best place to go through drama, and everyone loved a juicy break-up. She'd immediately gone into survivor mode, shoving down the pain and anger so she was able to present a calm, capable front. Sierra refused to play the role of the victim, and ruthlessly handled the fallout. Funny thing happened, though. After playing the role for a while, she'd begun to believe it. The breaks and broken parts only surfaced occasionally.

Tonight had been one of them, leading her here.

Sierra wondered what it would feel like to just tell the stark truth. All the sad, messy details she smoothed over, like one of Aspen's polished final manuscripts. After another fortified sip of wine, she spoke.

"My husband was cheating on me."

He winced, but didn't offer condolences or platitudes. So, she kept going.

"I caught him in our bedroom having sex with someone else. Afterward, he told me he was sorry but he didn't love me like he was supposed to."

"How long were you married?"

"Four years. We met in college."

He shook his head in disgust. "It's too cliché for someone like you. Please don't tell me it was his secretary who's ten years younger."

A smile ghosted her lips. "It was his boss. Same age. His name is John."

His brows snapped together. "Not cliché after all."

The smile widened. She didn't mind humor with her pain. "At least he spared me a boring story. "

"Yes." He seemed to be in deep thought as he studied her. She refused to squirm in the chair, suddenly sensing he spotted things beneath the surface she easily hid. "But being rejected by someone you loved, someone you trusted, isn't very funny."

Her lungs collapsed. The heaviness in her chest tightened. What if she told him the truth? The horrible, unvarnished truth of her marriage? She'd never see him again. It was like one of those movies her mother used to love: two strangers meeting one stormy night to share secrets, then part forever. Maybe she was meant to find him in order to unburden.

She opened her mouth. The words tangled in her throat.

He slid his hand over the polished wood, fingers barely brushing hers. Her body jolted at the contact, the heat and slow slide of his skin.

"Tell me."

The demand wrapped her in a sensual cocoon. Sierra fought a shudder.

"I think it was my fault. I think he was right. I never loved him the way I should and it forced him to find someone else." The relief from her confession allowed the rush of air to finally enter her fully. "I don't care that it was a man. I think love can come with anyone and shouldn't be restricted to gender. But there was this moment before I married him that I had terrible doubts if he was the one meant for me."

"Isn't that being human?" he asked gently, not breaking physical contact.

"Yes, but I lied because it was easier. I needed stability after my parents died. I needed to feel safe so I could take care of my sister. I knew I didn't love him the way I was supposed to but I married him anyway. It was my fault."

The relief of admitting her dark secret rushed through her. She'd kept the truth even from Aspen, who was wrapped up in her own angsty relationship and didn't need any extra stress. Sierra waited for the judgment, ready to accept the hit because she deserved it.

Instead, ferocity lit his gaze, which locked on hers. Waves of masculine energy beat from his aura, reminding her of a storm gathering on the ocean. "Fuck that."

She blinked. "What?"

"You heard me. Fuck. That. Did you try hard in your marriage? Did you cheat? Did you disrespect or ridicule or make him feel less than he was?"

"No, of course not."

"Then it wasn't your fault. He made the choice. He could have spoken with you. Asked for counseling. Fought to figure out if the marriage could be saved. Instead, he took the easy way and betrayed you. There's no instruction manual on the right way to love. You did the best you could at the time." He shook his head. "I can't imagine dealing with losing your parents and being there for your sister. Isn't love supposed to be trust and security? Why does it have to be only one thing?"

Astonishment held her still. She stared at him as his words sparked something deep underneath; a buried vault of guilt, shame, and rage that had been shoved into the dark. Instead of going away, it had been slowly blistering, making Sierra unable to see a path forward for herself.

At that moment, she wanted to lean into his strength and have him hold her. She fought hard against the neediness, not wanting to make a bigger fool of herself. As if he knew her secret thoughts, his gaze held her steady, a balm to the rawness of her confession. Heat flushed her skin.

Who was this man who seemed to sense exactly what she needed?

And why did he make her feel safe amidst such vulnerability?

"Don't pull back now," he murmured.

A ragged laugh escaped her lips. "What are we doing?"

"Getting real. Refreshing, isn't it?"

She tilted her chin up. "I'm not here to play games. I didn't come here for a hookup."

Mischief danced over his carved features. "Neither did I. But I didn't expect you."

Still unsteady from her admission, she sipped her wine and regarded him under half lowered lids. "What about you? You seem to know a lot about love. Are you in love now?"

Sierra cursed herself for dreading the answer. It wasn't as if they'd see each other again. He'd be a story to tell when she returned from New York. Someone to whisper and giggle about and play the what-if game. But it didn't matter. The primitive feminine portion of her soul craved there to be no one else for him.

Just for tonight.

"I've never been in love," he said. "Lust, yes. Friendship, yes. People say you'll know when you find it." His shoulders moved in a half shrug. "Do I want to find it? Maybe. Maybe not. Right now, I'm too focused on my work. I don't think I'd be good for a relationship."

"Even after a ten-million-dollar deal?"

"Yes."

She sifted through his words. "What if it's never enough?"

Ghosts shadowed his eyes. "That's exactly what I'm afraid of. For now, though, each deal I make is one step closer to getting to the goal."

"Which is?"

A smile flashed across his face. His front tooth was slightly crooked. She caught a faint scar by his upper lip. She wondered how he got it.

"Owning a property empire," he said. Resolution ground within his tone. Sierra sensed this man would do anything to get there, making him a bit dangerous. But it was the motivation underneath that intrigued her.

"What will that give you that love won't?" she asked.

Sierra watched as he jerked back, in the hot seat like she'd been. His gaze narrowed as if he was trying to figure out if he should try to answer, or laugh it off. She deliberately leaned in to crowd his space, forcing him not to break the suddenly seething connection. "Don't pull back now," she said softly.

He shifted in his seat. Seconds ticked by but she waited him out, allowing him to find the words or courage or both.

He lifted his glass and drained it dry. Studied the bottom of the expensive crystal as if it held answers. Then swung his gaze back to hers.

"Safety."

Emotion poured through her at his answer. Yes, he had demons. Sierra couldn't blame him. Money and power certainly kept one safe. They were on opposite sides of their goals. She was hiding behind her marriage for safety. She'd used love to get there.

He was hiding behind his career. Sierra would bet he used ruthlessness, focus, and workaholic tendencies to get there.

Together, they completed the most perfect circle.

The bartender glided over, refilled their drinks, and disappeared.

Sierra lifted her full glass. He did the same. They clinked them together.

"To safety," she said, pressing her lips to the rim.

It was then she caught the hunger in his eyes. Desire glittered darkly primitive, teasing out a delicious shiver as her body softened, ready to play. Somehow, this game had turned on them both, and Sierra wasn't sure where it would lead.

Or end.

He reached over and ran a finger over the back of her hand. She clutched at her glass, afraid to move as ripples of awareness rushed over her, through her, prickling beneath her skin. The breath got trapped in her lungs. One casual, simple touch and her entire body primed for his taking.

The air charged like an exposed live electrical wire. "If you were mine, I don't think I could have let you go."

Sierra ignored the jump of her heart and kept her voice steady. "Yes, you could. Because you're not done building your empire."

Regret flashed. Slowly, he nodded. "You're right."

"And I need to figure out who I am separate from being a wife."

"I didn't expect you tonight. I didn't expect...this."

Her usual caution and reserve had no place here, in this moment. "Me either. But I'm glad."

His lopsided grin was sexy as hell. "Good."

Chapter Four

They talked. Switched cocktails to sparkling water. Ordered a plate of finger food from the kitchen. No one else ever came in. It was as if the bar at the Carlisle was caught in a time warp, keeping them separate from the world.

The bartender stopped in front of them. His smile was polite, and his brown eyes warm. "I'm sorry, but the bar is closing. Is there anything else I can get you?"

They both reached for their wallets but he stopped her with a shake of his head. "No. I'm putting it on my room tab."

"You're staying here?" she asked, surprised. She'd assumed he was just stopping by for a cocktail.

"Yeah, I live downtown and have an early meeting next door. Figured I'd just stay and buy time."

He scribbled something on the check and they stood up.

"I kept you up too late," she said, grabbing her purse.

"No. You didn't." He treated her to another one of his devastating smiles and lightly touched under her elbow, guiding her through the bar. They stood before the doors leading out, stopping behind a large marble pillar. The lobby was shadowed and hushed, even as the rain pelted the windows with a fierce pressure.

They stared at one another. "Do you have a car?" he asked.

"No. I walked, but I'll call an Uber."

"I can get a cab for you—let me go to the desk."

She shook her head. "Uber's faster." She tapped the app. "One minute away once I order it."

He seemed to struggle with his next words. Her finger lay on the button to book her ride. The silence stretched as they waited for the other to do or say something, the connection between them humming with intensity. Hunger clawed at her belly for more of him. She wanted the opportunity to kiss those full lips; smell his skin; feel the bite of his fingers as she clung to his muscled length and surrender to her body. God, it had been so long since she felt like this.

"Will you at least tell me your name?" he finally asked.

Sierra hesitated. Once she gave it, this entire evening would become real. They wouldn't be seeing each other after tonight. Much better to keep their encounter anonymous, like a beautiful dream she could replay safely. "I'd rather not."

"Why?"

She smiled. "Because this is too special to name."

A soft curse broke from his lips. "You're right."

Sierra clicked on her phone and ordered the Uber.

"Can I ask you a question?"

"Yes."

"Why did you decide to come sit with me?"

The answer sprung to her lips without hesitation. "Instinct."

Satisfaction flickered over his face. Slowly, he nodded. "Yes."

It was time to go. Every second spent this close to him wore down the last of her barriers. Sierra couldn't get greedy. Being with him for these hours was special. He reminded her there was something else for her other than the marriage that had slowly eroded her own identity.

"Goodbye," she said.

His eyes sparked with regret. "Goodbye."

He bent down to brush a kiss to her cheek, but she tilted her head upwards at the same time.

Their lips slid together in a whisper light touch.

Her entire being jolted at the contact. Her muscles clenched in a desperate effort to take a step back, but her senses were already demanding more, automatically leaning in. A growl vibrated in her ear. Hard hands gripped her hips as he did it again, pressing another barely-there kiss against her trembling mouth.

He pulled back an inch. Sierra held her breath. Heat burned between them. His glittering green-gold gaze crashed into hers.

And then they were kissing, a wild, hungry tangling of tongues as they pressed together in an effort for more. Sierra's head spun at the taste of him—stinging whiskey and spice that made her spin. She opened her mouth to the silky, demanding thrusts of his tongue and let herself go under.

He broke away. Jaw tight, he grit out the words she barely registered. "Cancel the Uber."

Sierra managed a jerky nod.

Then followed him to his room.

He ushered her inside without a word. The room was dark and neither of them reached for the light.

Other than her first year at college, Sierra didn't have much experience with one-night stands. To her, they were drunken, fumbling events that were more for release than connection. Events that were barely remembered in the morning after separation. But with this man?

Sierra wouldn't forget a moment.

The fact scared her enough to speak up. "This can only be for tonight."

He looked at her, then slowly nodded. "Okay. One night."

"No names."

A smile touched his lips. He closed the distance between them. "No names." He reached out his hand. "Shake on it?"

She smiled back and took his hand and then he was holding her and it was all over.

Over and over, through the hours of the night, they faded into one another; bodies slick with sweat, sheets tangled, the smell of sex lingering in the air. As dawn threatened, they finally collapsed into sleep.

The last words that drifted in her hazy memory were his ragged whisper against her ear.

"I don't think I can ever let you go. And I don't even know your name."

Then there was nothing.

Sierra woke up.

Body sore, throat parched, she tried to move and found she couldn't. Fighting down panic, she scanned her surroundings until her memory caught and held.

Last night, she'd slept with a stranger.

Last night, she'd fallen a little bit in love with a man who was nameless.

Turning her head, she gazed at him in sleep. Russet hair mussed from her fingers running through the strands. One muscled arm was slung over her, chaining her to the mattress. Full lips were slightly pursed. The sheets were tangled around his waist, giving her full access to the map of matted hair on his broad chest and hard abs that led in a perfect line to a secret garden of delights that she'd taken advantage of over…and over…and over.

Every memory slammed through her, ravaging the shreds of her control.

Oh, the things they'd done together. Things that made her scream and beg and shatter into multiple orgasms.

But it wasn't just the sex. That would have been fine. It was the emotions already tearing her heart apart as she gazed down at him. Tenderness and hunger spiraled, making her want to reach out and touch him. Her entire body throbbed for more in any way she could get it.

Sierra closed her eyes and bit back a whimper. This was too much. How could she know someone so intimately without knowing anything about his current life? How could one night form such a bond, as if they were already deeply connected?

Panic struck.

She had to get out of here.

Glancing at her watch, she knew there was a small window of time before he woke. His breathing was deep and even, gorgeous face smoothed out in sleep. With careful motions, she removed his arm, and slid out of the bed.

He grunted. Frowned. Moved. Then settled.

Relief flooded her. She moved quick, gathering up her clothes and phone, quietly dressing like it was the apocalypse and she couldn't wake the zombies. Heart pounding, she paused at the door, hand on the knob.

She could leave a note. Leave a number. Leave a clue. Something that would lead them back to each other. Because Sierra sensed she'd never meet a man like him ever again.

Her life flashed in slow images.

She worked at a clothes store in a small southern beach town. He was a millionaire and lived in New York.

She was newly divorced. He wasn't interested in relationships or love.

She had no idea who she was anymore and she was tired of pretending she did. He knew exactly what he wanted and who he was without apology.

They were on different paths; different lives.

She wasn't ready for someone like him.

It was time to figure shit out. On her own. Being with this amazing man in the real world may be another blockage or detour she couldn't afford right now.

Emotion choked her throat. She gazed at him one last time, memorizing his face. She'd never forget last night. He'd changed her. Sierra was no longer afraid to begin tearing things apart to find her happiness. It was overdue. Staying in a loveless marriage and settling for satisfaction wasn't the path any longer.

Better to leave now before she got more attached. There was no way she'd be able to walk out of here if he woke up and reached for her.

Sierra walked out the door and didn't look back.

Chapter Five

Present Day

She'd run from him.

Just like she had that morning.

Kane sat on the edge of his bed in the guest room with Dug. The small, very ugly dog had wormed his way into his heart, even though he tried not to show it. Brick had inherited the canine, who looked like a rat monster with a long snout, overbite, and stuck-out tongue. He shuffled when he walked, drooled, and had no idea what a command meant.

Yet, right now, as if sensing his distress, Dug plopped his butt on Kane's bare feet and stood guard. The company helped ease some of the ache in his chest.

Her name was Sierra.

It sang in his mind like an aria—haunting and lyrical. He'd never forgotten that night. He'd never forgotten her. For weeks afterward, Kane searched for her face on crowded streets, swearing he caught her scent and blindly following it to dead ends. He dreamed of those long legs wrapped tight around his hips while he buried himself deep inside. He woke up hard and aching, remembering how her lips opened under his like a bloom flowering in the sun.

Everything had changed that night for him. Their lovemaking transcended names. Sharing their deepest thoughts in the shadows bonded them.

He'd been so wrong.

She'd run and made him feel like a fool.

Kane's mind flashed briefly to that morning after.

When he decided to step in and save her from joke guy, he knew she was attractive. Caramel colored hair hit her shoulders in straight shiny strands. Her face was a beautiful symmetry of features that made him want to linger; heart shaped face, plump, bow-shaped lips; arched brows; thick lashes. Her body was banging—all luscious curves that would make a man pant. But it was his reaction that stunned him when he looked into those hazel eyes.

Recognition.

Like an electrical current, his body almost jerked, sensing a familiar connection he'd never experienced before. He wanted to stay and look deeper. Soak up the feminine energy curling and wrapping around him like a whisper of smoke.

Sure, he'd had some one-night stands, but this was different. It was as if this woman knew his very soul; was able to stare into his eyes and not only accept the demons but understand him. Too many saw what he presented to the world: a rich, powerful businessman who intended to rule Manhattan. A smooth, charming man who knew how to close a deal and get anyone to give him what he wanted. He rarely allowed anyone into his inner circle.

But with her, all of his defenses crumbled the moment she touched him.

She'd changed him. He craved her on a basic level he'd never experienced. Kane felt alive for the first time in too long.

He rang for coffee. Searched his room. And found she'd fled.

There was no trace she'd even spent the night other than the scent of her on his skin and the indentation on the pillow.

The despair ripping through him made no sense. His head whirled while he tried to figure out what had just happened.

She'd left without a word. Left him while he slept and dreamed of a future with a woman he'd just met. But she'd never intended for them to be anything but one night of sex.

How had he been so far off? How could he have believed what they had in those precious hours was all real?

A cocktail of shame, anger, and pain surged through him. He tried to convince himself she was a ghost. A dream. A fantasy conjured from what he'd always imagined would be his soul-mate. No one could be that perfect. He'd shared his truth and believed she'd done the same. But it all must've been a lie.

Dug whined, jolting him out of the reverie. He leaned down to pat his bony body, and his stubby tail wiggled.

Now, she was back. The sister of the woman Brick was in love with. A resident in the town Kane was thinking of settling in.

Sierra.

She hadn't faked her obvious shock when they met. There had been no games there, so at least, it wasn't like she knew who he was and had ignored him. But once he'd said her name, Kane hoped for an honest encounter. Stepping away from the group to talk. Some type of acknowledgement they shared a past intimacy. Anything that made that night real again.

But she'd denied him.

Pretended not to know him. Put on that damn fake smile and made an excuse to flee.

Again.

Kane stared at Dug and tried to make sense of the whole thing. Why was she so afraid to admit they knew each other? It wasn't as if he was about to spill their secret, but he figured they could have pretended to meet in New York and left their story open. Instead, she'd shut the door hard a second time and left without another word. Like he was nothing.

The pain was surprising. Even after all this time, Kane had never stopped thinking about her, and what he'd do if she came back into his life. He just hadn't anticipated this ending.

He sat with the uncomfortable feelings in silent misery. Dug kept a faithful watch. Slowly, he came to one final conclusion.

He'd been an idiot, but it didn't give her the right to treat him like nothing. Damned if he'd allow her to dismiss him and their encounter when he hoped to make a place for himself here. She owed him a conversation. There was no way the woman he'd fucked for hours, who'd cried and begged for an orgasm, who laughed and shared and listened could be this cruel.

Sierra may have run four years ago, but now there was nowhere left to hide.

And he was coming for her.

For the past forty-eight hours, Sierra had been a nervous wreck. Barely able to keep up a façade at work, she spent the torturous hours prepped for a confrontation. Each time she got into her car, she expected to see him. She kept picking up her phone to check her notifications, positive he'd text or call. She walked by the window of Flirt a hundred times, peeking at the busy streets for a flash of his russet hair and broad shoulders.

But there was nothing.

Aspen asked a few times about her impression of Kane, but Sierra quickly shut her down. She agreed he was hot, but simply not her type. Aspen seemed to accept the answer with a bit of disappointment.

Lying to her sister hurt. Sierra thought about confessing the truth, but after her performance and further thought, it was best to keep up the ruse. Maybe she was overreacting. After all, it had been four years since their night together. Maybe he didn't care that she disappeared the next morning. Maybe he'd been relieved, and Sierra was making this a huge deal in her head. Maybe Kane had laughed and shrugged the whole episode off.

Maybe he wouldn't even pursue a further conversation. Her imagination was overtaking her.

She'd been hanging around a writer too long.

Sierra closed up Flirt and drove home. Her nerves slowly settled. There'd be no need for him to privately seek her out. Maybe next time Kane and her ran into each other, they'd have a moment to quietly acknowledge their past. He'd be going back to New York soon. Sierra dove headfirst into a Google search, greedy for information, and confirmed Kane had made all his dreams come true. Unfortunately, ambition came at a price. Sure, he made his millions and carved out a reputation, but her focus had lasered in on the small article pretty much buried on the Internet unless someone was really looking.

He'd been in jail.

The fact both shocked and concerned her. The man she remembered hadn't struck her as a criminal, but with money and greed, anything was possible. There wasn't much detail—just the facts the charges had eventually been dropped, and he'd quietly left Global Property Inc. The dates coincided with his appearance in OBX so Sierra figured he'd come to visit Brick and let the heat die down. Since Ziggy Tours had been struggling, he must've decided to stay and help his friend out before heading back.

No way would he be happy in a small beach town. Kane Masterson craved the fast-paced life. He was probably setting up his next moves to rebuild his career. He'd never be interested in picking up with her after all these years.

Finally calm, she pulled down her block and into her driveway.

Where he was waiting.

The breath exploded from her lungs in a rush. Sierra fought the impulse to close her eyes and stay safe in the locked car. Instead, she sensed going on offense was best. Cowering or hiding from this confrontation would prove she had feelings that went way beyond one night of sex.

Stiffening her spine, Sierra got out of the car and slowly walked to her front porch.

He lounged on her white rocker, one ankle crossed over his knee. Linen pants, a pink shirt, and Armani loafers screamed billionaire playboy vibes. Thick auburn strands blew in the wind, giving his hair that freshly out of bed look. The perfect amount of scruff hugged his jaw and mouth to keep him from looking too pretty. Her gaze went immediately to the small scar on his lip her fingers had once glossed over and traced. When she'd asked, he told her it was the result from a scuffle with his father. There were no words to offer, so she'd pressed her lips to the mark and then he'd tumbled her back to the mattress, spread her legs, and—

"Nice place you got here."

The familiar, gravelly voice hit her body with an explosion of heat. She'd forgotten his ability to overwhelm anyone within a close distance. His aura practically crackled with sensuality, from those lazy green eyes, muscled body, and intense scrutiny. The spicy scent of him drifted to her nostrils in the summer breeze. Even though they were outside in daylight, she felt squeezed in; attuned to every slight movement or glance; her body already softening in welcome, remembering.

"Thanks. Nice of you to drop by without an invite."

That lower lip quirked. "Figured you wouldn't want to have this conversation in public, surrounded by friends. But if you'd rather wait, I can leave now."

She ached to wrap her arms around herself in protection but the gesture screamed defense. "No, you're right. Better to get it over with."

One ginger brow arched. "You sound like my company is a dentist appointment. I think I prefer when you scream and beg for your orgasm."

The scene slammed against her vision.

"You taste like a ripe peach," he growled against her naked thigh. Green eyes glittered with lust as he stared up her body. "I can't get enough."

Vibrating with need, her voice came out ragged. "Oh, please."

"Come against my mouth. Let go, beautiful."

Heat flushed her face, and other more intimate places. The sharp words rushed out in a tumble. "Sorry, I didn't realize one nameless night years ago gave you the right to show up on my porch."

His eyes flashed with something that looked like pain, but it must've been a trick of the sun. His face reflected nothing but cool amusement. "Guess it doesn't. But with Aspen and Brick spending all this time together, I figured a chat was needed."

Sierra tried to hide her wariness. He made a good point. She'd keep things polite. "You're right. Sorry, I was taken off guard. What do you want to talk about?"

"You pretended not to know me."

His casual tone contradicted the hard gaze that pierced and shredded her defenses. She jerked back, then raised her chin. "I panicked."

"Understood. But you ran away. Again. Why?"

She practically squirmed with discomfort but tried to answer honestly. "I thought it was best for both of us to forget. Neither of us believed we'd ever see each other again. I didn't want any awkwardness, especially since Aspen and Brick are together. I had no idea what your reaction was going to be, so I ran."

He tilted his head, considering. She tried not to study his beautiful face and remember how many times throughout the night she'd kissed that full mouth, ran her fingers through his hair, caressed his rough cheeks. "You get points for honesty."

Temper stirred. "This isn't a game, and I'm not being judged by you. You agreed to the rules. No names. Just one night. Don't try to pretend there was any more than that between us."

Her words must've hit a hot spot. Kane rose from the chair in one graceful movement, and stood inches before her. Face tight, he stared back with challenge. "Is that what you believe? That our night was just about great sex and no more? Is that why you fled like a bat out of a hell, afraid to face me in the morning?"

In that moment, Sierra realized the shattering truth.

He cared.

The passion weaved within his words proved he hadn't forgotten her either. Kane was trying to push her to admit the real reason she'd run—because she was scared of what they'd found together.

Off balance, Sierra knew there were two roads to choose.

She could confess the truth, and open herself to a mess of vulnerabilities. If Kane knew how hard she fell that night, he'd want more. More time in his company would encourage her to fall harder, faster, leading to a relationship with the same type of challenges.

He lived and worked in New York. He was dedicated to his career. He was already the local playboy in town, so obviously he enjoyed being with a wide variety of women.

Sierra finally had her life together. She wasn't about to blow it up and take a chance at a broken heart with a man who was dangerous. She deserved someone safe and true and easy. Someone who didn't scare the living hell out of her.

Which led to path number two. She could convince Kane right now that night wasn't important. Just a fun time to blow off steam while she visited her sister in New York. That she hadn't given him a second thought until he showed up.

It would create the proper distance between them to get her through until he went back home.

Sierra didn't need long to make her choice, even as an inner voice branded her a coward.

She forced a tinkling laugh and shook her head. "Don't take it the wrong way, Kane. The sex was amazing. I got off so many times I should've left a thank you note, but I didn't think it was necessary." Sierra met his eyes and used all her willpower to tamp down on any shred of raw emotion threatening to reveal the truth. "Honestly? Seeing you drop into my real life freaked me out a bit." She shrugged. "No big deal. Kind of glad we're getting this straightened out now. Sorry I was rude."

Sierra allowed him to hold her gaze for a long moment, probing, assessing. Sweat broke out on her brow but she didn't move, didn't blink.

He took a step back. "I see."

Sierra pushed harder for the close. "You understand, right? I have a reputation in this town, and I don't want it ruined by gossip. Especially since you've stirred up some chatter around here." Another forced laugh. "Every woman I talk to is dying to get in your pants. Much better for me to claim ignorance and not ruin your vacay."

She hated every ugly word uttered but it worked. Distaste flickered over his features along with a hardening that made her heart ache. He turned with a derisive snort. "Got it. I won't say anything. We'll pretend it never happened."

Each step as he walked away was like a slap.

"I'm sorry, Kane."

The words spilled out softly, her own private apology for soiling a memory that had been precious to both of them. She hadn't expected him to hear but his retort was the final blow.

"I'm not. It's exactly what I needed to hear. See you around."

She jumped as the car door slammed.

Then he left.

Sierra let herself inside with shaky hands. Her gut lurched but her brain reminded her it was the right choice. It was much simpler this way.

The familiar silence closed around her. She ignored the emptiness and reveled in the safety.

It was done.

Chapter Six

Kane heard the bell and walked from the back room to greet the customer. "Hey, welcome to Ziggy's Tours…"

His voice trailed off when he spotted Sierra. She shifted from foot to foot, obviously uncomfortable at the surprise meeting. Since their confrontation a week ago, he'd tried to shut off any type of thought or emotion regarding the woman who'd crushed his heart.

Ridiculous, since she owed him shit. But her scathing words had cut, distorting that night into something else. It was as if a treasured memory was a gift, once perfectly wrapped, now torn to pieces and impossible to put back together. How asinine to think she'd been haunted by him all these years. He'd romanticized the whole damn thing.

"Hi."

"Hi." She cleared her throat. "I'm supposed to meet Aspen here. Her car is at the shop and she needed a ride to the bookstore."

"She went out with Brick to see the horses. I'm sure they'll be here soon."

"Okay. I'll wait outside."

"No need. It's hot as hell, take a seat." He almost winced at the obvious discomfort on her face. They'd already agreed to put the past behind them. Was it that damn painful to be in the same room? Annoyed, he pushed. "Want some coffee or tea?"

"No, thank you." She sat in one of the cushioned chairs and whipped out her phone,
  dismissing him.

Irritation hit. He took his own coffee over and deliberately sat across from her. "How've you been?"

She looked up, a tiny crease between her brow. He was already questioning the move to be near her. The scent of wildflowers drifted around him. Her outfit consisted of tiny white shorts that showed off endless expanse of bare leg, a red blouse that tied in the front, and red sandals with polka dot stacked heels. She'd pinned her hair up but some caramel strands loosened, framing her heart-shaped face. Tortoise shell sunglasses were perched on top of her head. Gold hoops hung from her lobes. Her lips were painted a deep blush pink, currently matching her cheeks.

"Good."

"You own a store, right?"

Her entire body stilled. Kane watched her with interest as she seemed to sense danger. "Yep. When are you heading back to New York?"

He stretched out his legs. "Don't know."

Those hazel eyes glinted with a touch of worry. "I'm sure you're bored to tears here."

"Not really. I like working for Brick."

The snort escaped her plump lips. "Doubt it's half the thrill as Global Enterprises and million-dollar deals."

Kane tilted his head, surprised. She'd done a search on him. Enough to know where he previously worked. Was she simply curious or was there something he kept missing? He didn't question her in case she closed up. "True. But maybe I've been missing out on other things."

The flare of panic threw him off, but then Brick and Aspen walked in.

Sierra flew out of her chair. "Hey, I've been waiting for you."

Her sister sighed. "I'm so sorry—I forgot to text you that Brick said he'd give me a ride. I suck."

Sierra shook her head but was smiling. "That writer's brain of yours is a killer."

Brick laughed. "I'm starting to understand now I need to fight for her attention with imaginary people."

"Stop! Listen, I just have to sign some stock and then we're grabbing lunch. Come with us."

"Okay, sounds like fun."

Brick moved to the counter. "We have no tours till three so let's just close, Kane. You both can hop in our car."

The reaction was instantaneous.

Kane watched as Sierra bit her lip, color flooding her cheeks. "Oh, I forgot! I need to get back to work for a meeting. Sorry—I'll take a raincheck on lunch."

Aspen frowned. "But you were going to drive me anyway?"

"Yeah, but now I can take the meeting and it's really important." She flashed a fake smile, refusing to meet Kane's gaze. "I'll see you tonight. Bye!"

She disappeared quicker than a flash of smoke.

"What's up with her?" Aspen murmured.

"Probably just busy, baby."

"I guess. She works too much."

"Says the writing workaholic," Brick teased.

Kane cut in. "She owns a clothes store in Duck, right? How long has she had it?"

Aspen wrinkled her nose. "About three years now. After her divorce, she worked in retail, then realized it was a perfect niche for her. She took some classes, opened Flirt, and is killing it. She's always been a badass."

The obvious pride in Aspen's voice showed another piece of the woman he'd thought he'd known. Until the word uttered made him still and spin around.

"Flirt?"

"Yeah, the name of her shop is called Flirt. Thought you knew."

A roaring filled his ears. He stared at Aspen as his thoughts began to whirl. "No, I didn't. That's an interesting name."

Aspen laughed. "I know! Cute, right? I asked her where she came up with the idea and she said it was from a conversation she always remembered. We better get going, I'm starving."

Kane tuned out their casual chatter as he got in the car, going over and over this new information.

She'd named her store Flirt.

Coincidence?

Odd that a thought kept circling his mind like a vulture, pointing to the weak spot. If their night together was all about sex and she didn't care, why was she so frantic to avoid him? He'd already agreed not to say a word. Why look panicked at the idea of sharing a simple car ride or exchanging pleasantries in the waiting room?

At first, he figured it was the awkwardness. Nothing like being stuck with an ex who you'd rather not see. But her reaction didn't add up.

He brought up the memory of their unexpected meeting at Sunfish and raked through for clues. She'd dropped a glass and hadn't even jumped when it shattered at her feet. Stared at him with not just shock, but an unusual mix of emotion he still couldn't figure out. There was more lurking beneath the surface. He'd been so caught up in her blatant rejection, Kane never stopped to think if there was another reason for her reaction. Was it possible Sierra pushed him away for a completely different purpose?

Out of all the names in all the world, she picked that one. *Flirt*. From a conversation she always remembered.

Their private joke.

Yes, maybe the answers were simple. Maybe it was his ego hoping to ease the sting of rejection.

Or maybe Sierra Lourde was hiding something she didn't want him to figure out.

Kane considered his options. Either way, it wouldn't hurt to dive deeper. If he stayed, they needed to be comfortable, and not consistently trying to avoid the other. And if there were other reasons Sierra was desperate to keep her distance?

He intended to find out.

Sierra stared in rising horror at the man rapidly closing the distance between them.

Was this a nightmare? A punishment? Or just Fate laughing her ass off at the unfortunate destinies of single women?

Her fingers clutched her wine glass in a death grip as Kane reached the table. "Sierra," he said, his voice a combination of velvet and gravel. "How are you?"

Not well. In fact, I'm about to lose my shit if I have to spend more than a few minutes with you. Wanna know why, Kane? Because when you're around all I think about is sex. Glorious, orgasmic, wild sex with you in my bed. Again. For more than one night.

Sierra forced a brilliant smile that stunk of desperation. "Great. Umm, sorry, why are you here?"

He sat down across from her. "Aspen mentioned she was meeting you for a drink but got delayed. Since I was passing by, I told her I'd let you know and keep you company until she arrived." His look was pure innocence. "You don't care, right?"

Sierra wanted to scream with frustration. Instead, she waved her hand in the air with dismissal. "That's nice but no need. My phone is my office so I can easily work till she gets here."

"A fellow workaholic, huh? I know how that goes." He peeled off his jacket and her mouth went dry. He reached down, freed each button on his cuffs and slowly rolled up each shirt sleeve. The expanse of corded muscles and tanned skin made her want to whimper. "Still, we both deserve a short break."

He lifted a finger. A waitress came running. "Cabernet?"

Sierra tried to speak past the lump in her throat. "Yes." If she was going to survive, she needed a bottle.

"Whiskey. Neat."

The exact cocktails they'd drunk all those years ago.

He leaned back in the chair with a casual confidence and gave a rueful smile. "I wanted to apologize for our last conversation. I came across much too strong, and understand your position."

She blinked. "You do?"

"Of course. Again, I have no intention of saying a word—we'll forget the whole past thing. But with Brick and Aspen together, I thought we'd at least try to be cordial."

He seemed to be over his frustration and hurt. Which was a very good thing. The pang of hurt was simply her ego. Sierra nodded. "Yes, I agree."

Their drinks arrived. She swallowed the last of the liquid from her first glass and gratefully grabbed the second. He lifted his whiskey and held it up. "Great. Then let's toast to new beginnings."

Sierra grit her teeth and clinked glasses. She'd give her soul to the devil right now to be released from this cocktail hour. She was going to kill Aspen.

"So, you like retail?"

"Uh, huh."

"I should come by sometime. See your place."

She choked on her wine and slammed the glass back on the table. "No need. As I said, probably best to keep our distance. Don't want anyone to get the wrong impression."

"Oh, sorry, I forgot. Are you seeing anyone special?"

"Not right now."

His brow lifted. "Looking for anything serious?"

"No," she said forcefully. "I'm very happy the way things are."

Kane drummed his fingers on the table. "Hmm, that's good. Relationships are hard. Work is so much easier, right?"

Even though his questions were casually framed, Sierra felt like something was off. Best to keep up her defenses until Aspen got here. "Probably."

"Funny how you can see things more clearly in a different environment. New York had me on the hamster wheel, which I loved, but I didn't realize there were other ways to live."

Her nerves screamed danger. "You'd get bored without the chase," she said, trying to look unconcerned. "No million dollar deals or fancy boardrooms. Just horses and beach and local gossip."

"There's Duck Donuts."

"You'll have to give up bagels."

A slight wince. "Point taken. Still, Brick seems happy. So does Aspen. It may be time for a change."

"Maybe you can move to Brooklyn."

His lip quirked. "Let's not get hasty."

She refused to smile. "I'm sure there's a ton of skyscrapers that need overtaking." Curiosity urged her to prod. "Unless there's another reason keeping you away?"

She kept an impassive façade, not ready to challenge him on his brief jail stint. Better for him not to know she was poking around in his past. It would blow her ruse of not giving him a second thought.

His gaze sharpened, but after a moment, those broad shoulders lifted in a shrug. "My chosen profession is full of pressure. Sometimes, it pushes people to do things. Another good reason to step away from the game."

She'd sift through the mysterious words later. Right now, Sierra got ready to double down on all the reasons he shouldn't consider staying longer, when a female voice interrupted them.

"Kane—your ears must've been ringing. I was just saying how I keep playing phone tag with you!"

Sierra took in the woman standing next to Kane, her hand laid on his shoulder as if staking claim. Callie worked in the local bank and had been quite vocal about her interest in dating Kane, though Inez confirmed date was a pretty loose word for what she wanted. The woman was known to like to break in the hottest tourists or locals before anyone else could sample the goods. Usually, Sierra wouldn't care—hell, she hadn't before she'd known who Kane really was—but the way Callie licked her lips like he was a buffet in Vegas was pissing her off.

Kane tilted his head up with a warm smile. "I'm honored you'd want to even play tag with me, Callie," he said, earning a ridiculous giggle. Sierra almost rolled her eyes at the awful line. "You know Sierra, right?

I'm just keeping her company until her sister arrives."

"Of course! Good to see you." Callie gave her a polite nod, then refocused on the prize. Sierra wondered why he'd been so specific about why they were together. Was he simply honoring her request not to start any gossip? Or was he trying to tell Callie not to worry?

She stayed quiet as they chatted, obviously flirting. Callie's hand squeezed his shoulder. Kane chuckled at something she said and touched her hip.

Sierra tried not to fume.

Finally, they broke apart with a promise to see each other. Kane resettled and gave her a satisfied grin. "Well, that was fortunate. Any idea where to take her this weekend? Someplace she'd really like?"

Sierra drank more wine. "Callie and I aren't close friends so I'm not sure what she'd like," she muttered.

"Hmm, then I'll go classic. Dinner and drinks at home afterward."

"You're living with Brick," she said, molars grinding painfully.

"Her place, then. You were right when you said there were plenty of women to enjoy around here. They're all so welcoming."

Temper flooded her bloodstream. The image of him kissing Callie, those overblown Botox lips opening under his, made Sierra cranky and a tiny bit reckless. "Be careful. She likes to gossip, plus you don't want to begin leading women on around here."

He cocked his head. Those bright green eyes delved deep, stirring up all the emotions she'd been fighting since he sat down. "Thanks for the warning. But as you mentioned before, sometimes sex is just sex."

The softly spoken words punched her in the gut. Her vision blurred with white-hot jealousy at the thought of him taking Callie to bed, giving her endless pleasure as she screamed his name.

Sierra struggled for calm. A glint of satisfaction flashed in his gaze, but it took all her concentration to stay in control and a stupid, fake, half-smile on her face. "Right. Doesn't matter to me what you do."

She finished her wine, realizing at this pace she'd need Aspen to drive her drunk ass home. If she survived.

"So you've said. At least me being with Callie will take any heat off you." His tone dripped with concern. "It's funny how things change, right? Think about it. Four years ago, I only cared about work, and you were getting out of a marriage. Now? You're a proud workaholic with no intention to settle down, and I'm starting to think that's exactly what I need." His finger traced the rim of his glass. "Get a nice place, a job that's more flexible, and a steady relationship. Chill out. Smell the flowers and walk on the beach. I think I'd like a serious girlfriend."

Her eyes felt as if they were about to bulge from the sockets. Was he serious? She leaned over. "I doubt you're ready to compromise for love," she practically hissed. "Especially with Callie! Corolla is not a place for you to settle in and get comfortable."

He propped his elbows on the table and moved his body forward, so their faces were inches away. "Is it wrong to realize you suddenly want…more?" Kane paused, dropping his voice to a sexy growl. "What about you, Sierra? You've rebuilt yourself, launched a successful business, and have a great home. Is that all there is? Or sometimes, do you also crave—more?"

Everything fell away except the scorching memory.

"What do you want, beautiful?" he asked, tightly gripping her hips, poised at her entrance. She gripped his hair and twisted wildly, the ache between her thighs driving everything from her mind except how bad she wanted him inside her.

The demand ripped from her trembling, damp lips. "More."

He thrust inside and she cried out. Slammed her head against the wall as she arched.

"Like this?"

She was out of control, squeezing her thighs around his hips, desperate to be torn to pieces with this agonizing pleasure. "Yes."

His mouth ravaged, tongue thrusting like his cock, and still he paused to ask her again. "What do you really want?"

She met his gaze head-on and surrendered. "More. Fuck me so I never forget."

Sierra jerked as the raw images slammed through her vision.

The wine glass toppled and spilled.

God, her wine was never safe around him. She jumped up. "I—need to go to the restroom." Barely able to breathe, she rushed down the hallway and locked herself in the stall. Her hands were clammy and a terrible heat burned between her thighs.

The hell with this. She refused to spend one more moment being slowly tortured. She should be thrilled he was no longer in pursuit, but her heart and soul still screamed in protest. She'd make some excuse, leave, and text Aspen they'd grab drinks at home.

Washing her hands, she composed herself and rejoined the table.

Aspen was in her seat, laughing at something Kane said. The waitress finished mopping up the spilled wine and eased past. Relief flooded her. "Hey, you made it."

"Yes—sorry I'm late. As usual. Did you guys have a good chat?"

Sierra tried to ignore Aspen's hopeful gaze. "Yes. I mentioned how nice it was for him to help Brick out. But with summer almost over, it's probably a good time to get back to New York. Crowds slow way down during off-season and things get boring."

"So, I've heard," Kane said. Amusement flickered over his face. "But chatting with Sierra was exactly what I needed. I've finally realized what's best for me."

Thank God. Sierra only hoped he'd be gone by the end of the week.

"What is it?" Aspen asked.

"OBX. Corolla." A satisfied grin curved his lips. "I've decided to stay."

Her sister clapped. "That's awesome! Brick will be so happy!"

A frown snapped her brow. No. She must've heard wrong. "Wait—you aren't going back to New York?"

His gaze swiveled to her and locked in. Resolve glittered within those emerald depths along with another emotion she was too unsteady to analyze. Her entire body froze; a predator to his prey; helpless under the sudden jolt of arrogant masculinity that promised the rules had changed, and she was way out of her depth.

But of course, that had to be her imagination.

"That's right," he drawled, not breaking his probing stare. "I'm staying, Sierra. Thanks for the pep talk. It really helped."

Her jaw unhinged but he'd already won.

She watched him talk with her sister, both excited about the future, while one thought spun over and over in her head.

She was so fucked.

Chapter Seven

"You can do anything you put your mind to, and you can do it in stilettos."
— Kimora Lee Simmons

Two Months Later

Sierra walked along the water and immersed herself in the crowds lingering on the boardwalk. She dragged in a lungful of air, scented with salt and sunshine, and allowed her mind to float with each smart click of her Stuart Weitzman camel-colored ankle boots with a shiny gold heel. It had been a busy day at Flirt. Switching over to new color palettes and fabrics for the change of season took endless hours and focus. With the cooler weather, customers craved earthy colors with pops of burnt orange, crimson red, and hunter green. Shoppers sought gifts for Valentine's Day, so jewelry sales boomed. Knits and boots replaced gauzy lace and sandals. All of her buying was done two seasons before, so it was fun to re-discover all the goodies ready to sell.

This whole weekend had been spent replacing the racks and bringing in new products from various designers. She'd been going nonstop, especially since Aspen had returned from New York and moved in with Brick. Seeing them flourish after such a roller coaster ride stirred up a longing in her gut. Her sister finally got the happily ever after ending she deserved. Sierra wondered if she'd ever be able to trust another person that much to commit one hundred percent.

Life had proved there were never guarantees. She was glad Aspen had beaten the odds, but there was one major fallout Sierra now had to contend with.

Kane Masterson.

His decision to stay in Corolla coincided with Aspen and Brick's break-up. Sierra hadn't seen him since the night Kane announced he was staying, that piercing gaze blowing away all her defenses, practically daring Sierra to protest.

It was easy to avoid him. If Sierra caught him out with Brick, she kept her distance. Sierra started to meet Brooklyn and Inez at places other than Sunfish, and had become a new weekly member of the local support group, now re-named The Bad Ass Bitches Club.

Sure, Kane remained a hot topic. She heard from the buzzing grapevine that he was dating, but Sierra tried to keep her head down and her ears blocked.

But now that Aspen and Brick were back together?

She'd be forced to see Kane more often. Even though she reassured herself his interest had passed, and he was carving out his own life here, the prickle of danger remained. There was nothing left to do but keep her cool if they ran into each other, pretend not to care, and refuse to give him a second thought.

The whisper broke free from the locked place inside and taunted her.

Liar. What about today in the shower? When you closed your eyes and imagined—

Sierra sucked in a breath and slammed the lid closed. "Not today, Satan," she muttered under her breath.

They'd both moved on. He was working at some property development firm now, gotten his own place, and forgot she ever existed.

Exactly like she wanted.

Deciding on a quick detour, Sierra headed to Duck Donuts. One little treat wouldn't hurt. It was either sugar or a margarita, and since she still had a ton of work ahead, the nonalcoholic option won.

Sierra stepped up to the counter. "Chocolate Coconut Dream, please."

"Bad day?" Greta asked with a knowing smile.

"Challenging."

"I hear ya. Things can get hairy in here, too." The pert brunette was the owner's daughter and learning the ropes. "I'll swing by to pick up my layaway tomorrow night. Gonna wear it to a party this weekend."

"No worries. It's safely tucked aside for you. I got some gorgeous earrings that match perfectly, so I put those away to check out."

"You're the best. Thanks, Sierra."

"Anytime." She swiped her card, picked up her donut, and headed out.

Then stopped short as she almost collided with a man on his way in, taking up all the space in the doorway and the air around him.

Kane.

Sierra froze. A fragment of her hoped if she stood very still and stayed quiet, he'd walk past her and pretend he didn't see her. After all, they'd been playing the game well for the past few months, and it was working.

Kind of.

Instead, he paused and let the door swing shut behind him. In the silence, their gazes locked, and within seconds, the slam of sexual energy gripped her in a vise.

Dear God, he was perfect.

His russet hair was thick, and unruly, like a woman's fingers had run through the strands and he'd tumbled right out of bed. His beard was a bit rougher, giving him even more of an edgy look, tamed by the sleek designer clothes he wore with ease. His suit was a chic, tailored charcoal paired with a crisp blue shirt, bending to the will of every lean, hard muscle.

"Sierra."

A shudder racked her. He uttered her name soft and slow, those rich green eyes holding her prisoner. Sierra opened her mouth but couldn't say his name. It was just too intimate. Instead, she nodded. "Hello."

A tense silence fell between them. His gaze narrowed. "Still playing the silent game?"

Her brow arched. "I'm not playing any games," she said cooly. "I'm just getting a donut."

"Which one?"

She blinked. "Huh?"

"What flavor?"

His question came out as a demand, as did most things uttered from those lips. "Chocolate Coconut Dream."

"That's my favorite, too."

Her body softened from his low murmur. Her female parts buzzed with recognition and throbbed in awareness. She wished she could wipe out the memory of that mouth over hers, the way he demanded and controlled and gave so much pleasure. She'd shattered like glass, feeling alive for the first time.

Sierra cleared her throat and prayed her voice worked. "Goody for us. Before I dole out friendship bracelets, you'd better hurry. There's only one left."

He grinned slowly, and shivers raced down her spine. "Still mouthy, I see."

She couldn't do this. She'd combust and embarrass herself, and Kane was already the hottest bachelor the town was fighting over. She refused to go there. "Well, see you around."

"It's nice to see Brick so happy. I'm glad they got back together."

She wanted to ignore him but his tone held genuine pleasure. His support of Brick showed he'd been a decent friend. "Me, too. I was worried they wouldn't work it out."

Kane nodded. "Same. They were meant to be together. It must be nice to have your sister here permanently."

"It is." When Aspen decided to leave New York and move to OBX, Sierra felt as if a space inside her had been filled. Her sister was the only family she had. Having her close by was a game changer.

Kane continued in a thoughtful tone. "I think Brick was just scared shitless to try again."

A humorless laugh escaped. "Yeah, I get it."

"Do you?" His husky voice invited confidence—the same she'd given him that night. "I guess we both do."

She fought his spell. Arched a brow. "Doubt it. Bed hopping is fun, but there's little risk. Just the way you like it."

His lower lip quirked. "Jealous?"

She practically sputtered. "Of course not! I made myself crystal clear—I think it's best we keep our distance and avoid each other. Bed the whole town if you prefer. Just leave me alone."

Instead of jabbing back, he studied her in thoughtful silence. She glared, refusing to squirm. "You're wrong, Sierra. My entire life has been about risk. When you have millions of dollars on the line and one wrong word can destroy it all, you lean in hard. You play with no fear. You go all in. Because halfway ensures failure."

She stood, transfixed, trying to break the spell. "You're talking about work again."

"Yes. Work." He paused. "And now it's time to make a bigger move. One I've been planning for a while, waiting for the right time."

A shiver raced down her spine. Damned if it didn't sound like a threat instead of some type of rambling thought.

It was time to get out of here.

"Thanks for sharing." Sierra squared her shoulders and pushed past him. Her arm brushed his, and his fingers suddenly shot out and grasped her wrist, stilling her. The familiar scents of clove and whiskey rose to her nostrils, an aroma that twisted into her memory.

"You can keep running for now." His thumb pressed into her throbbing pulse at the base of her wrist. "Until I'm ready to catch you."

She made sure not to show fear. Cranking her head around, she met his gaze head-on and slowly tugged her wrist away. "I'm not yours to catch," she said calmly. "Goodbye."

Sierra walked away with slow, careful strides. She wouldn't run.

But she felt his stare burning her alive with each step.

Kane watched her retreat. A flicker of admiration cut through him. The woman he'd fallen hard for all those years ago didn't seem to exist in this polished, distant version. It was the only reason he'd allowed her to hide. He'd needed the time to figure out what the hell had happened and how he wanted to handle things.

Now he knew.

And Sierra Lourde's time was almost up.

He went to the counter, ordered his Coconut Dream donut and a coffee, then took off.

As he drove, his mind flashed through the past few months.

When he made the decision to stay, Kane knew he had shit to figure out before he came hard for Sierra. Her reaction when he announced he wouldn't return to New York had proved all of his theories.

She'd lied.

All those scathing speeches about their night together being just about sex were bullshit. Her cold dismissals and distance had nothing to do with not wanting him. He'd gathered his intel with slow precision, planning to make his big move when it was the right time.

He gave her credit—she'd almost tricked him. If he hadn't deliberately rattled her, Kane would have retreated and believed he meant nothing.

Instead, it was the opposite. Sierra hadn't forgotten him either. He'd begun making a mental list of all the pieces that didn't fit, until he saw the complete puzzle.

Her obvious jealousy over Callie and any other woman he was supposedly dating.

Her desperate intent to avoid him.
The panic she showed whenever they ran into each other.
Her hungry stare when she thought he wasn't looking.
The way her pulse skyrocketed when he touched her today.
Her reaction when he announced he wasn't going back to New York.
Naming her store Flirt.

He understood now why she ran that morning, even though he didn't like it. The timing hadn't been right. With her divorce, and his drive to succeed in the corporate world, the odds were against them.

But the second time?

She'd run because they finally had a chance. And she was scared.

Kane pulled into his rental place and walked in. The small home held two bedrooms, living area, kitchen, and one bathroom. The generous porch sagged and the backyard needed an overhaul. The floors creaked and the walls held some cracks. The shutters were pink with chipped paint.

But it was reasonable and walking distance to the beach. The furniture was comfortable and clean. He was even getting used to all the pink pelicans and seagulls the owner seemed to be obsessed with. Unbelievably, Brick's cranky neighbor had known a guy who'd known a guy and gave him the contact number.

Kane looked around and briefly wondered what the hell he was doing.

Less than a year ago, he'd lived in a penthouse apartment near Central Park, owned a walk-in closet of designer suits, got reservations at all the hot restaurants, and held the respect of some very important people. Everything he'd worked toward had finally come true. Success and money gave him power. He'd made it in the most cutthroat city in the world.

Until everything exploded and he'd ended up in jail.

He grabbed a bottle of water and sat down at the cramped kitchen table. Taking out his donut, he ate it slowly in the quiet. After he got out of jail and crashed at Brick's, Kane spent last summer brainstorming various plans to get himself back in the industry. First, he turned his focus on finding a new opportunity back in New York. But after reaching out to some old contacts, Kane realized the chilly reception from everyone in his old life was a sign.

Especially after he received the text from John that chilled him to the bone.

Remember our deal.

The warning did its trick. Kane left New York and figured he'd create a business here. But all the banks politely declined, especially with no money to back up his ambitious proposal. So, Kane did the next best thing.

He found a job in a small family firm. Kane intended to dazzle them with his skills. Rebuild his name. And make his way back up to success.

This time, he'd do it in a more organic way. He'd go slow, learn the area, and make the contacts needed. In the meantime, he'd enjoy being with his best friend. He'd embrace the beach and horses and his fresh start.

And he'd get Sierra back into his life and in his bed.

All roads had led him here. Kane learned early on never to waste an opportunity. Patience was key with all big wins. He'd given Sierra the time and space needed to lower her defenses and believe she was safe. He was now gainfully employed, settled in, and carving out a place in Corolla.

Kane was almost ready to begin the second part of his plan.

The phone jolted him out of his thoughts. He didn't recognize the number, but picked it up anyway.

"Kane?"

His heart stopped. Every cell in his body surged in a wave of tangled emotions, too intense to try and separate. "Derek."

His half-brother gave a hesitant laugh. "Yeah, it's me. I know it's been a while. Do you—have a minute to talk?"

"I always have time for you," he said quietly. "How are you doing?"

"Good. Really good. I got a new job. I like it."

"Yeah? Where?"

"The teen center. At first, I was just sharing my story and volunteering, but an opening came up and they hired me." His tone turned rueful. "Not as glamorous as Waldorf lunches and high stakes deals, but I come home feeling good about myself."

Kane closed his eyes and rubbed his palms over his face. The past reared up in ugly Technicolor and rattled his insides. Guilt struck, but he was used to it. "I'd say you're miles ahead of most people out there. Fancy jobs are crap if you come home empty. Your heart was always too big for that bullshit, Derek. Got it?"

The glitch in his breath tore Kane's heart. "Got it. Maybe that's why I like working with the kids. I know exactly how it feels to be raw and not know how to handle it."

"You're going to be such a help to them. I'm fucking proud of you."

He pictured his brother's face, so unlike his own. Kane had gotten his red hair from his Irish mother who died before she could figure out the man she married was a monster. Or maybe she'd known and hadn't been able to leave. Kane would never know. He didn't know Derek's mom, but his father never had trouble bedding women. Derek had appeared one day, a young seven-year-old confused and lost after his mother took off. Had she realized her son had been dumped on a monster?

His father informed him he now had a brother and to take care of him. When Kane looked into those teary, fearful Bambi-type eyes, his heart had melted. With curly brown hair, and a small, skinny body, he exuded a sensitive vulnerability that tore at Kane's heart. He'd sworn to always protect Derek, even at the expense of himself.

He'd failed. Kane had been unable to stop the demons from possessing his younger brother. But a promise was a promise so he'd never stopped trying. He'd always been the strong one. It was his responsibility to protect the ones with an open, kind heart like Derek, who felt too much to be safe in this world.

A pause hummed over the line. "I have to say some things to you, Kane. Will you let me?"

"You already apologized. You already made your amends. You owe me nothing."

"Not true, brother. Some thoughts are different once you get out of rehab and begin really working the program. It's easier to keep myself accountable. Does that make sense?"

"Yeah," Kane said softly. "Tell me."

His brother began. "When Dad drank and got mean, I swore I'd never be him. You gave me that goal. Tried so hard to save me, like you saved yourself. I realize now what a liar I was. Not only to you, but myself. Because I loved alcohol more than anything. Just like him."

Kane was falling apart with each word his brother dropped. But he kept quiet and listened.

"I was never able to admit that before. I always thought it didn't matter because my intentions were good. To prove I was worthy of being your brother. To show you I could stand on my own and be a big success. Hell, you were the one to bring me in to Global and give me a job. You believed in me and for a little while, God, Kane, it was everything I dreamed of. Me and you working our way up. Making more money than I ever imagined. I didn't think anything or anyone could change our future."

Kane remembered. For a little while, he'd felt invincible, working side by side with his brother and taking over the world. He just hadn't stopped to look deeper, because he was too focused on achieving more. Always more.

"But I needed to drink. I'd sell my soul to Satan for the bottle, and I did. And this is the hard part to tell you. The part I hate to admit. Ready?"

"Go ahead."

"You were never enough to save me. You spent your whole damn life trying to make things better, I felt I owed you. I stopped trying to find myself in order to follow my big brother. I was terrified of disappointing you."

The confession shot through him like a bullet, shredding through bone and flesh. Pain throbbed in every part of him, but damned if Kane didn't recognize the truth. In his intentions to save his brother, he'd also pushed him over the edge. He'd tried to make everything right so Derek would never need any vices to make him happy.

Both of them had missed the truth.

Derek continued. "That's on me—not you. Chasing my next drink kept me from having to confront that whole mess. But every fucked-up thing happens for a reason, and I'm grateful. For rehab, and this new job, and finally figuring myself out. I need you to know that."

He allowed himself to ask the question that still haunted him. "If I hadn't pushed so hard, do you think things would've been different?"

"No. Because I'd still find a way to drink. I did it all by myself. Don't you ever take that responsibility away from me, okay? Without it, there's nothing but cheap excuses and a drunk at the end of an empty bottle."

"We both made mistakes. And I'm listening, okay? Even if I don't like to hear some of this shit."

His brother's laugh turned genuine. "Sucks, right?

"Rehab helped? You sound good. Solid."

"Rehab was a game changer. Staying in the full year gave me the tools I needed. You saved my life."

Kane dragged in a breath and reset. Once again, he thought of his choices; the deal he'd struck when his life had shattered around him. The rage and resentment eventually quieted. Knowing Derek was sober and safe was worth anything.

"You saved your own life. I just paid the bill."

They both laughed, even as the lie choked Kane.

"Tell me about beach town USA. I'm glad you decided to stay. We both needed fresh starts."

"I think you're right. I'm settling in."

"Catch me up."

He did. Some of the tightness loosened in his chest as he talked with his brother and shared the daily stuff. Too many of their past conversations revolved around them trying to sidestep their past and pretend it was all good. Now, he realized he enjoyed Derek's droll humor and blunt dialogue, stripped to the simple exchange, brother to brother.

They finally hung up, promising to talk soon.

The silence closed around him, along with memories that clawed to the surface. The room faded around him as Kane was dragged back in time, back to his nightmares…

The crash vibrated and echoed through the stale, smoke-filled air.

The pot left on the stovetop where he'd heated up soup. Shit, had he forgot? Kane strained his ears, listening downstairs as each nerve ending prickled with dread.

Lurching footsteps. Muttered curses. The slam of a bottle. The open and shut of the refrigerator.

"Where is it you little shits? Did you take it?"

The roar chilled his blood. He was out of booze. Kane should've kept a closer watch so he could've been out of the house but he'd been up late trying to do his homework and forgot it was Wednesday. The paycheck had run out and now they were gonna pay.

"Kane?"

The small whisper at the door caught his attention. Derek was in his pajamas, the torn batman fleece riding high on his stomach and ankles because it was two sizes small. Kane made a quick note to visit the thrift shop and get new ones. "It's okay," he said, motioning him over. His father liked to boast how well he took care of them since they had their own rooms, but his brother rarely slept there. Not when the monster could surprise him at any time. Kane had told him he could stay in his room, and even though he was five years older, he liked to cuddle against Derek's small, warm body and hear his steady breath. It calmed him enough to sleep sometime.

But there'd be no sleep tonight.

Another smash told him time was running out. Derek's wide brown eyes filled with terror, but Kane kept calm as he guided him inside the closet to his hiding place. "Stay in there and don't make a sound, okay? Remember what I said?"

His brother blinked furiously to fight tears. "Smoosh my mouth in the blanket if I need to cry. Don't worry because you'll be okay because you're like Batman and things don't hurt you."

"That's right. It sounds bad but I'm only pretending it hurts so he stops."

Kane gently covered him with the blankets so he'd be hidden if his father somehow decided to throw open the door. Thank God, he didn't care who the victim was. Derek was so much easier to pick on, but his father was lazy and would take whoever was most available.

Kane always made sure he took on that role.

"I'm coming up and if you don't tell me where my bottle is, I'm going to beat the shit out of you!"

Kane hurriedly asked the final question. "What happens when he leaves?"

Derek's lip trembled but he answered bravely. "I count to one hundred, then come out to help. The Band-Aids and cream are in your nightstand."

"That's right." He forced a smile while his stomach twisted in a knot. "Remember, it's not a big deal and I won't let him hurt you. What song are you going to sing in your head?"

A crash on the stairwell. "I'm coming!"

"I like Dynamite by Taio Cruz," Derek said.

"I like that too. Start hearing it now."

"'kay."

Kane closed the closet door. Stark fear threatened, but he'd learned to be friends with it because at least if it was him, Derek was safe.

His father stumbled through the door. Eyes red. Empty bottle in one hand. Belt in the other. Swaying back and forth, his gaze blurred with rage and need for the liquid in the empty bottle. And they'd all pay for that loss.

"Where is it?"

"You drank it, Dad. Remember?"

He threw the bottle. Kane ducked just in time. "Smart ass shit. I'll teach you to back talk."

Kane glanced at the clock. The beatings never lasted long. His father didn't have the endurance—he just liked to empty his poison on his son quickly and then go to bed.

The belt lifted and it began.

He started the countdown in his head while he sang Dynamite.

The horrific images faded slowly; too slowly. It took him a while to move. Each memory of the past flickered before him, taunting like a deranged jester. His hands shook with the effort to remind himself he was safe. And so was Derek.

Kane turned, catching his reflection in the far wall mirror. The image he presented was polished and confident. A man who owned the room. A man able to charm anyone to get what he wanted.

Underneath, he still felt the stain of poverty and shame. The taint of tattered, borrowed clothes that hung big on his too-small frame. The scent of grease and garbage as they scrounged for food after his father had drunk away all the money for groceries. The creak of the dirty mattress he shared with his brother on sleepless nights where he waited to see if his father would bust through the door and use his fists to take away his demons.

He'd done his best to protect Derek. For Kane, the answer was money. Money was his savior. If he made enough, he'd be safe. Power and money were the thing that kept the monsters away. Monsters like poverty and sickness. Humiliation and helplessness. Hunger and fear.

But maybe that wasn't what his brother ever needed. He had his own path to figure out. Derek had a chance to find the peace that eluded him.

Maybe it was time Kane found the same.

Sierra seemed to be the key. His new job may provide a new opportunity without the stink of his past.

He'd dig in and fight like he was taught.

And maybe this time, he'd win.

Chapter Eight

"Shoes are the quickest way for women to achieve instant metamorphosis."
— Manolo Blahnik

"Brick and I are getting married."

Sierra stared at her sister for one frozen moment.

Then she lost her shit.

"Oh, my God! I'm so happy for you!" she shrieked, allowing herself to express every single joyous, weepy, sappy emotion the announcement gave her. They yelled and jumped up and down together like they were teenagers. Sierra hugged her hard, tears blurring her eyes at the familiar comfort in her sister's arms.

Aspen laughed and swiped at her own eyes. "He surprised me at the place on the beach where the sea turtles hatched. Look!"

She stuck out her hand to show off the gorgeous princess cut diamond that shimmered under the light. "It's perfect," Sierra said, turning her hand back and forth to examine all the angles. "It's made for you."

"I know! Tell the truth—did you help him set this whole thing up? It was almost too idyllic. Everything a romance writer would want in a proposal. He even timed the sunset!"

Sierra wrinkled her nose. "I wish I could take credit but this was all Brick. He asked if I wanted to be involved but I said no. I thought it would be better if it was planned with his vision."

Aspen's eyes danced. "Because you know you're a bossy control-freak and you'd take over?"

"No! I was being respectful." She gave a little huff. "The sunset was my idea, okay? But he didn't warn me when it would happen."

Her sister cocked her head. "And the ring?"

Sierra paused. "I just told him what cut was your favorite and that you liked things…big."

Aspen burst out laughing. "I knew it. I'm glad you were involved. And get ready—because you have a lot of work ahead being my maid of honor. You know I suck at organizing things and I need you."

Her insides turned to mush. She stared at her sister, face glowing with joy, and swore everything that they'd been through was worth it to get to this moment. "I'll be here one hundred percent. I'm so proud of you. Mom and Dad would be, too."

Aspen bit her lip and nodded. "We've come a long way, huh?"

"Us? Let's see, you got left at the altar and my husband cheated on me with a man. I'd say we completed more miles than Forrest Gump."

Her sister punched her shoulder. "Stop! I meant finding our way even with our mistakes. It wasn't as if we had anyone to turn to for advice." Her face clouded briefly. "It was bad for a while. I'm not sure I could have gotten through it without you, Sierra. Have I ever told you that?"

She swallowed back a lump in her throat. "Yes. But I still blame myself for not trying to stop your wedding. I should've fought harder. I wondered if Mom would have known what to do or say."

"It wouldn't have mattered. I had to follow it through so I can get to the good parts."

Sierra laughed. After the heartbreak, Aspen had written a bestselling book that changed her life. And now she was happily engaged to a man who was her soulmate. "Maybe you're right."

"I am."

They smiled at each other. "We have to celebrate," Sierra said.

Aspen's brown eyes lit up. "Yes, I want to do dinner Friday night. Just immediate family for now. Can you keep the news quiet for a little bit? We're not ready to shout it to the world yet. It feels like this big yummy secret we want to enjoy."

"That's so damn romantic. Absolutely, I will keep my mouth shut, and we'll have a simple celebration Friday night with Brick."

"Thanks, Sierra."

"Want me to bring you a new dress from the store? I got a shipment from that designer you adore."

Her sister bit her lip. "Oh, that's tempting. No—let's save it for another occasion. I want to kick back and do casual for Friday."

"Done."

"Awesome. I have to get some writing done. I'm behind. See you later."

Sierra pulled her in for one more hug. "Love you."

"I know."

She cracked up at the Hans Solo/Princess Leia impression and watched Aspen float out the door, wild dark curls bouncing, and drive away.

Emotions struck in wild waves. She stood still for a while and allowed herself to feel them all. Her sister was finally going to marry the right man, and damned if she wouldn't help with every detail so her wedding was perfect.

God, she wished her parents were here. It had taken years to get used to their absence, but somehow, she missed them even more during the good times. She'd just need to make sure Aspen was surrounded by so much love that her sister wouldn't feel the bite of grief.

A sigh escaped as she dropped in the rocking chair. The spark of new beginnings lit the air. A longing for something she couldn't name stirred within her. She craved to do something wild and different. Take a chance on a new endeavor. Leap into the unknown and open herself to risk.

The answer struck home.

It was finally time.

She'd put off the big decision after a brief panic, afraid she wasn't ready to commit to such a relationship. Sierra loved her life, but there was one thing still missing. The type of love she dreamed of to ease the occasional sting of loneliness.

She was definitely getting a cat.

"I'm getting married."

Kane stood outside Ziggy's Tours with Brick. The moment he got the call from his close friend that he had big news, Kane headed right over.

A huge grin curved his lips and he stepped in to give Brick a hug. "Congrats, man. Damn, you finally got smart and put a ring on it. Good thing, 'cause I was ready to make my move."

Brick laughed, thumping him on the shoulder. "Good thing, because I would've had to beat the crap out of you."

"You wish. I was in jail. Learned a few moves."

Brick shook his head, still cracking up. "Only you could call yourself a criminal and every woman thinks it's mysterious and cool."

"Not every woman. Dixie gives me the evil eye every time I go to the bank. Maybe she's

afraid I'm planning to rob them."

"Dixie's mad because you didn't continue dating her daughter, Callie. Not because of criminal rumors that no one in town even knows about."

Kane scratched his head. "Oh. Good to know. Well, since you're retiring your bachelor status, I'm glad I can step in and take your place."

"And I'm glad you can now be the subject of the support group in town." Brick's eyes danced with glee. "Your reputation has overtaken mine."

Kane got a kick out of how things were so different from New York City. There, ghosting was an everyday practice, and you rarely met the same woman again. Here? All of your exes were hanging at the same bar, unless you strictly dated tourists.

At first, Kane had been charmed by the locals, and gone on a few dates, ignoring Brick's warning to be careful. He'd figured out quickly, though, that a promise to call again was taken like a blood oath. Kane had begun to back off, making sure he didn't get involved with anyone he didn't see a future with.

Of course, this was all before he realized Sierra lived here. Afterward, everything changed.

Kane didn't want any other woman but her.

For a moment, the urge to spill the truth to his friend was overwhelming, but he fought it back. No reason to ruin the engagement announcement with his past troubles. He'd held back on pushing Sierra, though Kane made sure he popped up regularly in her presence. The flare of irritation always mingled with a wariness that told him how much he affected her. Watching the woman he craved try desperately to avoid him was an ego buster, but with spring on the horizon, along with a fresh spark of possibility, he was finally ready.

And as much as he wanted to confide in Brick, it wasn't fair to expose their past without Sierra's permission. Best to focus on Brick's obvious happiness, which was way overdue.

His joking air disappeared. "You deserve this," he said quietly. "Aspen is perfect for you."

Brick's face softened. "Yeah, she is. Thanks. You're gonna be my best man, right?"

"Hell, yes! Can I help with the tuxes though? You never did have a sense of style."

Brick grunted. "Fine, but nothing too damn fancy."

"Suspenders are back in and all the rage."

"Fuck no." They laughed together. "We want to have a simple dinner Friday night to celebrate."

"Figured the whole crowd would want to come. Everyone's been rooting for you two from the beginning."

"I know. We'll blast the news soon, but Aspen wanted to have a quiet dinner. Talk about the wedding and be together before things get crazy."

Kane hesitated. "Who's going?"

"Just me, Aspen, Sierra and you."

"Sierra?"

Kane tried not to let any emotion show on his face as his friend studied him with suspicion. "Yeah. She's her sister."

"Of course! Sounds great—count me in. Want me to make reservations somewhere?"

"Already done. Why do you and Sierra never talk? Is there something going on I don't know about?"

His throat closed up but Kane was an expert in pushing through stressful situations. He forced a half laugh. "No. And that's ridiculous, we talk."

Brick narrowed his gaze. "Not really. Whenever we're in a group setting you both avoid each other. Oh, you're polite, but you never have one-on-one conversations. I can't remember a woman you've never been able to charm, yet she's obviously not a fan."

Sweat pricked his brow. He wasn't ready for the interrogation yet. Not until he made his move. Right now, he needed to buy himself time. "I think you're jumping to conclusions. I have nothing against Sierra or vice versa."

He remained calm as Brick studied him. Then, his friend broke into a big ass grin. "Holy crap, you asked her out and she said no!"

Kane blinked. "What?"

Brick let out a howl of laughter. "Hell, I should've known. No wonder Aspen's matchmaking skills failed. Sierra was never interested and was trying to spare your feelings."

He wanted to growl in frustration but figured he'd play the game. At least, until he told Brick the truth. "It was not a big deal."

Brick thumped his shoulder. "Sure. Don't let it worry you. Sierra is a tough one. I've never really been able to figure out what her type is, but trust me. You are not it."

Fuck, this was getting worse. Curiosity won over logic. "Why not?"

"Her asshole husband cheated on her. I think it made her suspicious. She dates now and then, but seems to find something wrong with all of the guys. Aspen said she's looking for Mr. Perfect, who doesn't exist."

He pondered Brick's words. "What's her idea of perfect?"

Brick shrugged. "No idea. Anyway, don't take it personally. You have enough women to handle without Aspen's sister messing up our dynamics. Probably better you didn't get involved with her. Would've been a mess when you broke up since now we're all family."

His stomach twisted as he nodded and pretended to agree. He hated lying to his friend, but Kane took this as a sign. It was time to confront Sierra and fix the mess they'd created.

Brick was in such a good mood, he allowed Kane to change the subject without giving him crap. "How's business? Need any help?"

"Business is finally booming," Brick said with satisfaction. "I just hired another tour guide so I'll get some time off. What about you? How's the new job?"

Kane shook his head. "Different. Let's just say I'm not used to the slow pace."

Brick grinned. "You're a native New Yorker. Gonna take you some time to slow the pace when you're used to building an empire in a week."

"I'd need at least a month."

"Always were an underachiever."

Kane snorted. He figured it would take some time to get back into the world he knew and had once ruled. His job at a small family run firm was a good start. He just needed to be patient. After all, being quietly fired from the biggest firm in New York City wasn't the best thing to put on a résumé. The company hadn't dug deep before hiring him. That suited Kane perfectly. His plan was simple: prove his worth and work his way back up the ladder. He wanted big deals and opportunities. But each time he gave the firm his research on a new possibility, Kane was shot down.

They simply weren't interested in expansion or aggressive deals. Kane tried to convince them to use his experience and get into the higher stake games, but so far, Duncan wasn't budging. He was older, settled in, and liked to focus on easy deals.

Kane wasn't sure how long he could play small. He needed to rebuild his portfolio and bank account. But if he pushed with the bigger firms, it may be too soon. Because they would dig and find he'd been investigated for fraud. It wouldn't matter if he was innocent—the stench was enough to keep him out of the hiring pool.

But he refused to give up or allow frustration to muddle his vision. He'd risen from the ashes before and he'd do it again. Kane would keep researching opportunities and, eventually, he'd find the right deal to put him back on the map.

Brick must've sensed his frustration because he spoke without waiting for an answer. "I know you don't talk about what happened, and I don't want to pry. But I think there's a place for you here, Kane, even if it's not where you started." His friend shook his head. "I thought inheriting Ziggy's Tours was the worst thing to happen, but now it turned out to be the best. You deserve happiness, too."

Damned if he wasn't feeling all mushy after Brick's words. This must be what family felt like—secure you'd be accepted no matter what happened. The hunger for more was no stranger to Kane. He'd just channeled it into his career. Nothing in his personal life had ever given him the same rush or drive that fulfilled him.

The image of Sierra flashed before him. Once, he'd let his walls down, believing there could be more. He intended to give them both another chance.

Kane cleared his throat. "I appreciate it, man. For now, I'm gonna dig in and that means I gotta get back to work. Text me the info for dinner."

"You got it."

"Brick?"

"Yeah?"

He smiled at his friend. "I'm so damn happy for you."

Kane didn't wait for a response. He turned and headed to his car. Anticipation buzzed through him like a hit of caffeine.

He couldn't wait till Friday night.

Chapter Nine

"Keep your head, heels and standards high."
– Lola Stark

Sierra walked into the Grill Room restaurant and spotted Aspen and Brick already seated outside. The deck was crammed with diners but their table was tucked toward the edge, offering a bit of privacy. It was a beautiful day with scattered sun and mild temps.

She kissed them both, slid into her seat, and tucked the wrapped package to the side.

"What is that?" Aspen asked suspiciously. "You better not have bought us a gift already. You'll be broke by the time we reach the wedding."

Sierra laughed. "It's just something small. I wanted to mark the occasion. I'm so excited to talk about wedding plans! Am I still the only one who knows?"

Aspen eyed the gift with a bit of greed before refocusing. "Yep. We're going to allow the news to get out organically now that it's not a secret."

Brick's eyes sparkled with mischief. "We're taking bets who will spread the word the fastest."

Sierra rubbed her hands together. "How fun! Hmm, I'd bet on Mrs. Rossi—she's pretty well connected and nosy."

"Oh, good pick," Aspen said. "I'm going with Marco."

Sierra stared. "Marco doesn't gossip. He sells t-shirts and smokes weed with his friends all day."

Aspen and Brick shared a look. "He's much more than that, trust me. Once he gets a hold of information, he's faster than social media around here," Aspen said.

"That's so interesting," Sierra murmured. Marco owned a souvenir shop next to Ziggy's Tours, so he'd gotten really close to Aspen and Brick. Guess she hadn't spent enough time trying to peel off those surfer dude layers. She was ashamed of herself for judging. "What about you, Brick?"

"I'm going with a dark horse. Someone who's so good at what he does, no one realizes they're being conned to spread the gossip."

"Who?" she asked curiously.

"Me."

Sierra jumped at the male voice behind her. The wicked word was whispered playfully, but shot all sorts of heat in her body. Stunned at his appearance, she watched as Kane dropped into the last empty chair and regarded her with a lazy, sweeping gaze. "What are you doing here?" she shot out.

"I was invited, of course. To celebrate and talk about the upcoming nuptials." Kane grinned. "Are you disappointed to see me?"

His mocking words made her cheeks burn, especially with the pointed stare Aspen was giving her. Sierra sat upright, forcing an easy smile. "No! Sorry, I thought it was just us. It's nice to see you again."

That lower lip quirked in amusement. She knew she sounded stilted and cold, which only made Aspen and Brick more curious. Dammit, why did he have to be Brick's best friend? His appearance had been a shock to her system, but now that he'd decided to stay? It was like he was slowly infiltrating every thread of her life, leaving no safe places. She felt like his prey, and he was toying with his food before gobbling her up whole.

Maybe she should've been a writer. Her thoughts were always so dramatic when it came to Kane Masterson.

Brick broke the humming tension. "Kane is like my brother, and the only family left." His words held no self-pity. She watched her sister slide her hand into his for support. "We thought it would be fun to all celebrate together."

"So fun," Sierra said too loudly. "How about cocktails?"

Thank God, the server appeared and saved her ass. "I heard someone say cocktails," she joked, her high ponytail swinging. "What is everyone drinking tonight?"

"Extra-dirty martini, Tito's vodka, straight up, chilled, extra olives, preferably blue cheese stuffed," Sierra said. She ignored Aspen's eye-rolling at her specific order. Her sister ordered a Chardonnay.

"Great. And you…Sir?"

The mid-twenty-year-old paused and seemed to get lost in Kane's eyes. Holding back an annoyed groan, Sierra watched as the waitress's brain cells melted under so much gorgeousness. It was the same thing no matter where they went out—from bartenders, waitresses, to nice, little old ladies. It was worse when Kane and Brick were together. The two of them were a powerhouse of male sexual energy that scorched every woman in its path.

And…there she went again with her embellished analogies.

Kane smiled. The girl sighed. Clad in a light-gray suit, he'd hooked the jacket over the seat and rolled up his cuffs. His hair was neatly tamed back from his forehead. He blinked in the sun, dazzling with his green-eyed gaze and spicy scent and drool-worthy body.

It was ridiculous.

The memory of him rose up and taunted. Naked, pressed against her, that same gaze blurred with hunger as he surged inside and swallowed her screams with his mouth.

Sierra shifted in her seat as the ache settled between her thighs.

"I'll have what she's having," he said, tilting his head toward her.

"Wonderful choice," the server gushed, unable to stop staring at him. "I love martinis, too."

"The IPA on draft," Brick said.

Now it was Aspen's turn to shake her head. The server smiled with pure giddiness as she basked in the glow of male perfection. "Another great choice. I love IPAs."

Sierra couldn't help feeling sorry for the girl. She was outmatched with the two of them and doing her best. When she finally disappeared, Aspen snorted. "Going anywhere with you peacocks is painful. Can't you paint some warts on your face or something?"

Brick looked uncomfortable but Kane laughed, easily owning it. "Stop discriminating against us. We're so much more than our looks."

"Not arguing against that. Makes you even more deadly," Aspen said.

"Inspiring lust is different from love," Brick said. "You've been collecting hearts since you got here, baby."

Aspen's face went soft and glowy. Watching her sister stare at the man she loved made Sierra's stomach squirm with something akin to longing. Yes, once she dreamed of kids and a man to share it with. But somehow, along the way, she'd lost hope of really finding that type of connection. It was easier to focus on what she did have and love about her life. Now, her sister was a reminder that there was hope.

Sierra turned and clashed with Kane's stare. A shiver bumped down her spine. His face reflected a set intensity that warned he was almost out of patience. The memory of his warning rang in her ears and stirred up a hornet's nest of emotion.

"You can keep running for now. Until I decide to catch you."

Thankfully, their drinks came and they toasted to the engagement. The icy liquid slid down her throat with the perfect bite, exactly as she liked it. Fortified, Sierra grasped control of the conversation. "Okay, tell us what you're thinking for the wedding? Next summer? A beach wedding? We can start with a loose date, and I'm happy to help research reception places or do whatever else you need."

Kane sipped his drink. "I'll jump in when needed. I'm in charge of the tuxes, as previously discussed. And the bachelor party."

"Those are so overrated," Sierra said. "A silly excuse to do what you could any weekend. Hang with friends and party."

Kane shrugged. "Not if we go to Vegas or Rio."

She groaned. "That's so…cliché."

"Not really. I'm sure you ladies will plan an epic celebration. Why are men the ones always getting in trouble?"

"Because you get sloppy. It's a cliché for a reason," she said.

"I doubt Brick would even glance at another woman. It's simply a way for men to bond and celebrate before making a forever commitment."

She snorted. "Bonding in a place known for bad decisions isn't the best idea. I've seen *The Hangover*. All three of them."

"I've seen *Bridesmaids* and *Girls Trip*. You're just as wild."

She glared. He smiled back.

Aspen cleared her throat. "Well, that was fascinating but we have news. There will be no need for a bachelor or bachelorette party so you can stop fighting. Which was…a little weird? Not gonna lie."

Sierra waved her hand in the air. "Sorry, it's been a weird week. I'll behave."

"Please, don't," Kane murmured. "It's nice to see you less in control."

Brick lifted his brow. "You two have to play nice. Because we're moving up the wedding."

Sierra blinked. "Faster than next summer?"

Aspen gave a squeal. "Yes. It's going to be this summer! We don't want to wait. It's ridiculous to plan for a year when we want things simple and fun."

"That's awesome," Kane said. "Why wait when you know?"

"Exactly," Brick said with satisfaction. "We want the ceremony on the beach where the sea turtles hatched. Then we're throwing a party at the Sunfish Bar and Grill for anyone who wants to come."

"Anyone?" Sierra squeaked. "You won't be able to keep track of the food or liquor needed. There won't be enough seating. Dresses can take months to order, Aspen. There are a million details that we need time to plan!"

"Not much to plan if they already have the date and place," Kane said, obviously trying to back their decision.

She was trying not to freak out but the time pressure was too much. Sierra imagined a leisurely year of bonding with her sister, poring over choices and details, and creating the perfect wedding. Once, Aspen had walked down the aisle and found her fiancé had run off with another woman, leaving her stranded and alone. Sierra figured this was the perfect way to wipe out the memory. Create the perfect wedding with the right person. Rushing things could be sloppy and Sierra wanted so much for her sister.

Aspen's voice was both forceful and soft. "Sierra?"

"Yeah?"

"This is what I want." Her eyes filled with emotion and she reached across the table to snag her hand. "I had the big, planned event before, and I hated every moment. It wasn't my dream. It was his. But this time? I want it as joyous and free as I feel when I'm with Brick. I don't want to wait or follow the rules. Does that make sense?"

Her anxiety drained away. She looked at her beloved sister and managed a nod. This wasn't about her. It was about Aspen, and damned if she'd take hostage an event that came from the heart and wasn't hers to choose. "Yeah. It does."

No more words were needed. Sierra cleared her throat and regrouped. The server came back to take their orders, and she settled back in with a new focus. "Okay, the Sunfish it is. Are you doing August or September?"

"Definitely early September so the tourists are gone," Aspen said.

Brick grinned. "Funny how you used to be a tourist and now you're thinking like a local."

"My city sister has gone Southern," Sierra said, joining in on the teasing. "Maybe you can finally learn how to make sweet tea?"

Aspen wrinkled her nose. "I tried. It bombed."

"She tried it out on me," Kane said. "Wanted to make sure it was drinkable before serving to Brick."

"I thought it was good!" Aspen burst out.

Kane shook his head gravely. "It was a crime. Rotted my teeth away."

Sierra giggled at her sister's outraged expression. "She thinks the more sugar the sweeter the tea will be. For a writer, she's extremely literal in the kitchen."

"Did she tell you on one of our dates she pretended to cook for me but ordered all the food from North Banks?"

Aspen threw her hands up. "I didn't get the cooking gene, okay? There can only be one great chef in the family, anyway."

"You like to cook?" Kane asked, swiveling his gaze toward hers.

She tried to be casual, but every time the man focused on her she was thrown off. "Yeah. I find it relaxing."

"Interesting," he murmured.

"You don't cook?"

"No. I rely on the kindness of others."

A snort escaped. "Bet you have plenty of women lined up to cook for you."

His gaze dove deep. "Cooking a meal is intimate. I've never met someone I trusted on that level."

Her fingers clenched around the fork. She tried to keep her voice casual. "Maybe it's because you never wanted that type of relationship in the first place."

"You're right." He dropped his voice. "Maybe I'm ready now."

Heat washed through her. Aspen was still playfully arguing with Brick so it was like they were having this conversation in private. She told herself to remain silent and let the moment pass, but found the words popping out of her mouth. "I cooked for someone once on a daily basis. Trust me, it can turn into a mindless chore that's unappreciated, and amplify the void. Not every meal is a bridge to intimacy."

Her cheeks flushed. Why did she end up uttering her innermost thoughts to this man? Why did even casual topics of conversation turn into something so much more?

His finger tapped against the table. "With your ex-husband?"

Sierra stiffened. She expected to feel defensive but it was simply a fact. "Yes."

"I'm sorry, Sierra. I don't think eating a meal you cooked for me, with my pleasure in mind, could ever turn routine."

A shudder wracked her body and tingles rushed down her spine.

Damn him for doing this to her. Damn him for making her…want.

Thankfully, Aspen interrupted the crackling tension between them. "How's the store doing? Is the new line of jewelry selling well?"

For the last year, Sierra had begun working with local female designers to bring products into the store and give back to the community. She loved the satisfaction of working with other entrepreneurs and found she had a knack for sensing what would sell well. She smiled and settled into her happy place. Business. "Yes, the Jasmine jewelry line ended up being so popular, I put in multiple orders. I think customers appreciated a percentage being donated back to the women's shelters."

"How do you decide what to sell?" Kane asked curiously.

Sierra drained her martini and glanced over. "Hard data like cost versus profit margins. What's sold in the past and what hasn't. Keeping an eye on trends."

"What else?"

Sierra shifted in her chair. "I research new local designers to see when we can collaborate. The networking grows both of our businesses and keeps customers from getting bored. Tourists may be new, but I also cater to the locals."

She began to turn back to her plate, ready to finish their dialogue, but the word shot from his lips in a husky demand. "And?"

Her breath stalled. Chemistry bubbled under the surface with every word they exchanged. God, it was so much easier to avoid him. Being this close was torture. She sensed Aspen and Brick's interested stares and tried to keep her tone jokey. "I think that was enough to dazzle you with my business skills."

His smile was pleasant on the surface, but Sierra caught the sharklike flash of white teeth. "Yes, all those traits are needed to be successful. But I found there's something else that's even more important. Beyond the stats and goodwill. And I bet that's the real key of why Flirt has flourished."

Hearing the name of her store on his lips made her tremble. Sierra knew exactly what he wanted her to say. What he was practically daring her to utter out loud. The word that would drag them both back to the past; to the dark; to what they shared.

She pressed her lips together, refusing.

"Sierra?"

Her name cut through the air and bathed her ears in a velvet bath of sound. She wouldn't say it. She absolutely refused to give him the satisfaction of knowing how much this exchange affected her.

Aspen cut in, having no idea of the undercurrents between them. "Risk. She has the balls to take risks. I think that's what he means, right?"

Kane didn't answer. His gaze probed, pierced, shredded. The silence stretched as Aspen's question hung between them, unanswered.

For the second time tonight, the word shot out of her, refusing to be caged any longer. "Instinct."

The same word she'd uttered when he asked her why she stayed. The same word she'd uttered right before he kissed her and claimed her every way a woman craved to be claimed.

Was that a flash of raw satisfaction or a trick of the light? The awful, throbbing tension broke apart like the rain cooling after the heat of a lightning bolt. "Yes. Instinct."

Her admission allowed escape. With a slight dip of his chin, he released her from his gaze and went back to eating.

Aspen shrugged. "Risk is still important, too."

"Absolutely," Brick said. "Have you thought of expanding, Sierra?"

She forked up a piece of ahi tuna and shook her head. "Unfortunately, the real estate around here is painful. Rents have tripled since everything is getting snatched up, redone, and sold for a huge profit. I'm lucky to have the last reasonable rent in town, let alone try for more space. But my landlord has been avoiding me about re-signing my lease. It's getting me nervous."

Brick squinted into the dying rays of the sun angling through. "Yeah, I heard Dora Young got phased out of her ice cream shop. Rent went up, and she found selling sweet stuff wasn't paying like it used to."

Worry pricked but she tried to push it aside. She figured the rent would increase, but her profits were steady enough to warrant a reasonable hike. Since the location wasn't full mainstream, she hoped it wouldn't be bad. She was going to push for a five-year term this round.

"Flirt is a mainstay, and I'm sure it will be fine," Aspen said firmly.

"Kane, what do you think? Any news from the development side?" Brick asked.

She felt Kane's steady stare on her profile. "My company's been focused on expanding medical facilities. More money and profit in the office buildings or larger lots. I'm sure there will be an increase with the competition but no reason to worry about your lot. Can't see a reason they'd want to sell or convert if the tenants are dependable."

Her shoulders relaxed at his answer. Maybe she was worried for nothing. He was right—there'd be no reason to try and outprice her store when she was a solid tenant. She'd always been curious about his career and exactly what happened in New York.

His shady past made her suspicious. Had he done something criminal in the quest for more money? Greed was a hard sin to avoid. Didn't most big-time execs turn dirty eventually? It was another reason she defended her actions of keeping her distance. She wanted nothing to do with a man who didn't care about anything but himself.

"There you go," Aspen said. She leaned back in the chair with a groan. "That was so good."

Her stomach felt overfull and a tad nauseous. Probably a combo from the stress of sitting next to Kane and one extra strong martini. She could never hold her liquor. "Is there anything we can do now that we've finalized the wedding is September and we have a place?"

Aspen ticked off her fingers. "My dress, your dress, flowers, e-invites—"

She tried not to wince. "No paper?"

Aspen stared.

"Sorry, evites are very cool."

"Aren't they? Just need a local photographer and decide on a place for the honeymoon. Done."

Her face must've given away her disappointment because Brick laughed. "Sorry, Sierra, we don't mean to ruin the planning fun."

"No, it's fine. I'm so happy for you and at least there won't be any stress," she offered. "I guess I'm too excited and wanted to plan a big event. You know how I love that."

Aspen grinned. "And you know how much I hate it."

"What if Sierra and I threw you an engagement party?" Kane asked.

She froze. The words got stuck in her throat. No way was she partnering with her one-night stand to plan an event. That was a no go.

Aspen cocked her head. "An engagement party? Honestly, we figured the wedding is so close what would be the point?"

"It'd be our gift to you and a way to celebrate. Look, once the news is out, everyone's going to be desperate for details and asking a million questions. You'll probably be invited to dozens of dinners to celebrate. If we had a party, you get it done in one shot. Plus, Sierra will be able to create the event on her terms. I'd help, of course. It would be a lot of fun."

Her jaw almost unhinged. Finally, her voice emerged, about to shut down his overly kind and manipulative offer. "Kane, I think that's—"

"I love that idea!" Aspen burst out. Her brown eyes sparkled. "But are you sure two parties so close together isn't overkill?"

"Who doesn't love parties?" Kane responded. Satisfaction carved out his features. "Don't you think it'll be a blast, Sierra?"

She was going to kill him.

Only she was able to see the glint of amusement in those emerald eyes. She better wrest control or this was going to be a disaster. "Absolutely. Aspen, I'd love to plan a party for you and Brick. But I can do it on my own. No need for Kane to be tortured with party planning when I've got it under control."

"Nope, I'm all in." His teeth flashed in a grin. "I'm looking forward to every step. We do this together—a best man and maid of honor gift."

"That's really nice, guys," Brick said.

Aspen gave her a grateful look. "I'm overwhelmed—thank you so much. Just give us the date so we can clear it."

"No problem. With time being so short, Sierra and I will get right to the planning." Kane turned to her. "Just let me know when we can schedule an evening together and I'll be there."

Sierra dug her fingernails into her palms to keep from hitting him. She forced a sickly-sweet smile while her eyes shot murder. "Sure. Can't wait."

"Speaking of gifts, I've been dying to open the one you bought," Aspen said.

"Oh, of course." She took the wrapped box and handed it over. "But you can open it up at home. It's getting late and I better get going."

She hadn't even finished her sentence before Aspen was ripping into it like a toddler on Christmas. Damn, she'd forgotten her sister was like a present junkie and could never wait. Unease shot through her. She'd hoped it'd be opened in private. Having Kane here to be a witness threw her off.

Aspen sucked in her breath as she drew the necklace out with trembling hands. The white gold flashed in the light, illuminating the gorgeous glimmer of rubies spelling out the word *LOVE* in elegant script. "It's Mom's necklace."

A rush of memories overtook her. Standing in the chapel, before her wedding, and deliberately removing one of her mother's most cherished items. Maybe she'd sensed all along her sister was the one destined to wear it. When Sierra decided to marry Patrick, she'd also shut down a part of her heart to protect herself.

Aspen had always loved more like Mom. With a reckless abandon and faith in the end result. Like her stories.

Sierra focused on the present and nodded. "I've been keeping it for you. Mom always believed in a great love, so I've been waiting for the right time for you to have it." They shared a glance, and she knew Aspen understood why it was never gifted when she was engaged to Ryan. Even then, Sierra had known he wasn't meant for her. Tears clogged her throat but she continued. "You found your great love, Aspen. And now the necklace is yours."

Aspen began to cry. Brick hugged her close, then clasped the necklace around her neck. "It's so beautiful. Thank you, Sierra."

She smiled. "Welcome."

Sierra hadn't planned to look over at Kane; she had no intention of sharing such an emotional moment with him. But it was as if her gaze was drawn, and when their eyes locked, she stilled.

Raw emotion shot out at her; a mix of pain and longing and so much hunger it was as if her heart broke open to allow room for him to enter. She fought the urge to reach out to him; lay her hand on his rough cheek and soothe the beast that seemed ready to burst out. She wanted him to share his secrets. She knew there were many untold from their one night, and from his obvious reaction to her gift.

But she said nothing. When she managed to tear herself away and refocus, it was as if the moment was just a dream or a distant memory. His voice was calm and controlled, depicting none of the turmoil she'd glimpsed. "What a thoughtful gift." He paused. "You two are lucky to have one another."

A current of beeps broke the spell. Aspen scooped up her phone with a frown, then began laughing. "And it's official. I won the bet."

Brick shook his head as he did the same and studied his screen. "The news broke. I've got a ton of messages coming in. But how do you know its Marco?"

Aspen shot him a triumphant look. "Because Maleficent told me she found out from Marco, and he's spent the last hour spreading the news. Told ya."

"He should run for mayor," Kane muttered.

Everyone laughed.

The server appeared asking about dessert. They all declined, and Brick paid the bill.

In the parking lot, Sierra hugged Brick and her sister, nodding at Kane, while she lied and promised to contact him about the engagement party. No need to blast out her intention to do it all herself or give suspicion that she wanted nothing to do with him. His gaze was like a physical hold, trying to clutch tight, but she jumped in her car and peeled away before anyone could stop her.

When she got home, she locked the doors and hid in her safe retreat.

She kicked off her strappy platform white sandals with funky chain straps—an oldie but goodie from years ago—and headed to the bedroom. Sliding her shoes carefully into their spot was a satisfying balm to her soul. She took a few moments to gaze at her collection and allowed a few moments of peace to steal over her.

Lovingly, she closed the closet doors and turned to grab her pj's.

The doorbell rang.

Sierra closed her eyes, dreading the confrontation. Because she knew one thing she could no longer escape.

Kane Masterson had finally come to get her.

Chapter Ten

Kane watched her open the door like she was about to face her executioner. Irritation rippled through him, but he made sure to keep his face expressionless. Talk about an ego sting. The woman he was obsessed with didn't even want to talk to him. She'd be happier to pretend they'd never spent the night together and move on as if they were strangers.

He studied her in the porch light. She hadn't changed yet, but her hair was loose, the caramel strands tousled and soft. He remembered how he'd fisted her hair, a tangle of silk against his palm.

White tapered pants snugly hugged her curves. He remembered grasping her hips and lifting her over his body, then slowly lowering her to sink deeply inside her warm, clinging heat.

The silk t-shirt was patterned with yellow and white daisies. The V-neck plunged low in the front, emphasizing the golden tanned skin. He remembered cupping those lush breasts, watching as her nipples hardened and flushed a strawberry red, begging for his tongue.

Those hazel eyes were known to change with her mood, from a misty blue to a brown-green, and every shade in between, accented by thick lashes. He remembered the way her pupils dilated when she was on the edge of orgasm; the yearning intensity in those mysterious depths burning only for him and what he could give her.

Now, they were cool and narrowed in defense. Her aura pricked with edginess. Kane refused to acknowledge the hurt flaring inside at her dismissal. He needed to cling to the facts he'd gathered all these months while he bided his time. Over and over, his research always circled back to one thing.

She wanted him, too. She was just scared shitless.

"Can I come in or would you like to do this for your neighbors' entertainment?"

Without a word, she swung the screen door open.

Kane walked in. It was the first time he was inside her house. He looked about, greedy for more information, noting the elegance and warmth amidst the classic southern beach vibe. Personal accents showed off the things she loved.

Artwork. Canvases of beach photography. Modern watercolors swirled with a free, heavy hand. Black and white photographs of her and Aspen in childhood and through the years. A framed wedding photo of her parents.

Curated knickknacks. Delicately blown glass figurines. Driftwood sculptures. Seashell-encrusted mirrors. Sea glass in colorful bowls.

Comfort. Oversized pillows, thick crocheted blankets, and coffee table books highlighting fashion and jewelry.

The décor matched her—he could easily picture Sierra in this space.

She stood a few feet away, watching him. Kane decided to wait her out, until the silence between them stretched with awareness. "Well?" she finally said.

He crossed his arms in front of his chest. Regarded her with a lazy deliberation he knew affected her. "Don't you think it's time to tell our truths?"

Her eyes widened. "Haven't we done that? I thought we both agreed to move forward in our separate lives."

"No, you did. I just decided to wait until I felt you were ready to stop hiding."

She shook her head. "You're delusional. I'm not hiding from anything or anyone. Especially you. I've been living my life, and from what I've heard, so have you."

He deliberately pushed. "Meaning?"

"Are you kidding? You're dating every woman in OBX. You're certainly not brooding and carrying some torch for me so stop playing the role of victim."

Satisfaction unfurled. Good, she was jealous. Still dialed in to his activities even if she pretended she didn't care. It was time to finally start with a clean slate. "When we first met, the only thing I wanted to do was reconnect. I wasn't the one pretending that night meant nothing. And after that amazing performance where you pretty much laughed in my face and said you barely remembered me except for a few orgasms. How do you think that made me feel, Sierra?"

The anguish that flashed in those beautiful eyes finally eased his own. "I thought it was best not to relive the past," she said stiffly.

"For you, not me. Hell, you treated me like I had the fucking plague. Brick thinks I asked you out and was rejected. I guarantee Aspen believes you think I'm an arrogant jerk. Anyone around us jokes about how we can't seem to be in the same room together without keeping our distance. If you didn't mean to draw attention to us, your plan backfired."

He watched the emotions flicker across her heart-shaped face. Kane sensed he needed to go hard in this confrontation or it would be too easy for her to hide behind neat rationalizations. But he wanted the truth.

She reached up to push her hair back. He noticed her hand trembled. "I was giving you an easy out. This is gossip central around here. If anyone realized we knew each other beforehand, they'd dig and probe until they found the truth."

He arched a brow. "Why would that be bad?"

Her eyes widened. "Are you kidding? We had a one-night stand and didn't even know each other's name. Even my sister doesn't know and I tell her everything. I assumed it was better for us both to move on."

"You assumed wrong. I have no shame about that night. Do you?" Kane held his breath. If she denied it, something precious inside him would break.

The words trembled on her lips, but she couldn't do it. "No."

Relief loosened his muscles. He could work with the rest. "One thing we agree on." He took in her defensive posture and sighed. "Sierra, do you know how many times I thought of you over the years? I woke up that morning thinking we shared something special, but you were gone. It was as if I'd been punched in the gut. You left me without an explanation or a goodbye. You made me question our night together and if it was real."

"I'm sorry." Regret edged her husky voice. "I realized when I woke up that it was impossible for us. We were in two different places in our life. I was a mess and I was afraid if we tried to have a rational conversation over something that was…that was like what I experienced…it may ruin every-thing."

"So, you didn't just fuck me to get revenge on your ex?"

Temper snapped her chin up. "No! Is that what you thought?"

He gave half a shrug, deliberately baiting her. "How would I know? You disappeared twice. Avoid me at every gathering and refuse to speak to me in private. What am I supposed to think?"

Blistering heat shot from her eyes. "Don't pretend you didn't know the rules. We agreed it was one night, and you sure as hell weren't ready for some serious long-distance relationship. I did you a favor. I let you off the hook so we could both have the memory."

"No. You ran for you—not me. I didn't get a chance to make my choice. It wasn't about a few great orgasms for me."

"Me either!"

His voice was like a whiplash. "Then what was it?"

"Magic!" She spit out the word with a gorgeous feminine fury. Over the past months, he'd seen Sierra the ice queen, the professional businesswoman, and the supportive sister. But this was the woman he'd remembered—the wild, free spirit who took what she wanted without apology or fear.

Satisfaction gripped him. He took a few steps forward and closed the distance. The scent of wildflowers drifted from her skin. He locked down his attention before his body shut off his brain cells and he reached for her. "About damn time you admitted it. Because it *was* magic. I've spent months trying to figure out why you refused to even acknowledge me or what we shared."

A shuddering breath escaped her bubblegum pink lips. He tried not to think how those same lips had opened for the thrust of his tongue; how her taste still flooded his senses in his dreams. But that was too much for now. She was like the wild horses, and Kane had no desire to tame her. He just craved the idea of her coming to him on her own terms. "Don't you understand I'd never experienced anything like that night before? I didn't know what to do with it, Kane. I had a life back here; one I needed to rebuild from scratch. You were on the quest to be a Manhattan billionaire and admitted relationships weren't your thing. Did you want me to hang around for another rejection or false promises? Were we going to FaceTime each other a few days per week and have phone sex? What did you want from me?"

"A chance. I wanted a chance because losing you wrecked me, Sierra."

She stared at him, obviously stunned. He didn't give a shit. Finally, he was able to tell her his truth and he wasn't about to worry about a hurt ego or hold back.

Her ragged whisper healed the rift. "I didn't know."

"Now you do. So, what are we going to do about it?"

She blinked. Tilted her head. "I said I'm sorry. I never meant to hurt you, Kane."

"Apology accepted."

"Good." She wrapped her arms around herself in a hug, as if she was trying to draw strength. "I'm glad we talked. We can move forward in a better way. It won't be so awkward with everyone, and I don't want you to worry about the engagement party. I can pull it together easily."

Oh, she was cute. She actually thought they'd move on and neatly button up the past with this brief conversation. His lip quirked in humor. She really had no idea what he wanted. Guess it was time to be clearer. "Are you saying you want to be friends?"

She took a step backward, as if even the thought panicked her. "Umm, I think we can be friendly but it's best not to get…close. I'm not sure being friends is a good idea."

"I don't want to be friends, Sierra." He never got tired of saying her name. It dripped off his tongue like a rich, red wine with complex flavors. It played in his mind like a beautiful mantra and the missing piece of a puzzle he'd always wanted to solve.

"Oh. Okay, I'm glad we agree." She offered a tentative smile. Her shoulders relaxed. "We'll respect each other's space but it'll be less awkward when we're together."

"You misunderstand me. I have no intention of pretending anymore."

He closed the distance one step at a time.

"What do you mean?" she asked, retreating.

He flashed a grin and hoped it wasn't as predatory as he felt. "I don't want to be friends. I don't want to be polite strangers. I only want one thing."

Her back bumped against the wall.

Kane stood a few inches away. He took in the rapid pulse point in her neck, the ragged sound of her breath, the stilled muscles as she waited for his next move.

Slowly, carefully, he reached out and trailed a finger down the curve of her cheek. Heat crackled between them, flushing her skin, whipping up the familiar tension he'd never found with another woman.

"I want you, Sierra Lourde. I want you back in my bed. I want you in my life. I want you to be mine, and I'm going to do whatever I need to get you there."

Her hazel eyes flared with a longing she couldn't hide, even as her voice stumbled over the words. "That's impossible. We can't do this. It's too late!"

A smile touched his lips. He moved his hand into her hair, twining the silky strands in a loose grip, lowering his mouth so close, he felt the uneven rush of her breath and watched her pupils dilate in arousal. He'd forgotten how perfect she felt in his arms, the soft weight of her, the flutter of thick lashes, the lushness of her mouth trembling right before he kissed her. Four years melted away, and it was once again only them together and the unending, seething heat of connection. "No, sweetheart. It's just the beginning."

His mouth dipped, giving her plenty of time to push him away, allowing just enough space between their bodies so she didn't feel trapped.

Sierra didn't move; barely breathed.

His lips touched hers.

Paused. Waiting. Forcing her to be part of what was about to happen next.

A shudder wracked through her. A tiny moan escaped.

"Kane?"

His name ripped past his ears and his patience exploded. With one swift movement, his mouth took hers in a blistering kiss, unable to hold back years of wishing, dreaming, and wanting.

God, he'd wanted to be gentle. He intended to seduce and tease until she was ready, but the hunger stole his breath and he could only devour her whole, his tongue slipping past her lips to dive deep, to take and give and conquer. She gave back everything twofold, arms wrapped around his shoulders, plastering her chest to his, opening her mouth to anything and everything he craved.

He explored the slick, satin heat and gathered her taste, halfway drunk on sheer pleasure. He sunk his teeth into her plump lower lip, captured her moan, and angled his head to consume more. Over and over, he delved and retreated, teasing her into a delicious game. The bite of her nails against his scalp urged him on, taking the kiss to a possessive claiming to prove her words meant nothing against the sizzling chemistry.

Kane never wanted to stop but he knew this was only the first step in his plan.

Pushing too hard before she was ready could cause her to run.

And damned if he'd let her escape him again.

He eased off, breaking the kiss with obvious reluctance. Kane studied her face with a male triumph he couldn't hide. Those beautiful eyes were hazy and lit with arousal, her mouth soft and gleaming with dampness, body clinging to his with a natural ease she couldn't hide.

She blinked. Removed her arms from his shoulders. Regarded him with a growing unease as she began to realize he wasn't about to be neatly dismissed.

Not after that kiss.

"You can't deny what's still between us, Sierra. You just proved we have unfinished business." His gaze raked over her still trembling body. "And I'm not going anywhere until it's settled."

Sierra stared at the man who'd just taken her body to the same extreme heights years ago. How had this happened? How had things gotten out of control so quickly?

Because you haven't gotten over him, the voice whispered. *Maybe that's why none of your dates ever worked out. You've been secretly waiting for Kane Masterson.*

Oh, she hated that he was the one to break off the kiss. With all her denials, Sierra had been the one to whimper and cling to him, obviously having no intention of stopping the embrace from going further. She pushed away the humiliating thought as he studied her and tried to gather her control. "That can't happen again."

A smile touched his lips. "But it will."

Anger was a welcome distraction and she grabbed it with relief. "Who do you think you are? Just because we spent one night together a lifetime ago doesn't give you the right to anything, let alone declaring these ridiculous intentions like we're trapped in one of Aspen's romance novels."

"Thought women liked an alpha male?"

"It's not funny, and I always preferred the beta."

"Good, because I've lost my edge and moved into beta territory."

"Stop! You couldn't be beta if you tried."

"I can be anything you need," he growled, gaze lazily scorching over her body.

She tried to ignore the answering heat between her legs and the impulse to lean back into his embrace. Damn, he was like her kryptonite and she needed to find a cure. "We can't just begin a relationship because you declared it. We're not the same people we were, Kane. Both of us have changed and grown and I don't want to go back. It's better to leave us in the past with a perfect memory. I've moved on and you need to do the same."

"That's what I thought. Until you proved me wrong."

She shook her head. "By what? Avoiding you? Refusing to drag back the past? Not staying that morning or trying to find you all those years ago?"

Sierra waited for the male temper from the sting of her words but once again, he surprised her. His wolfish grin confirmed she was about to be stripped of her last defenses.

"No. By naming your store Flirt." His gaze narrowed with intensity. "You've been thinking about me all these years too, Sierra. So much that you made sure I was a part of the most important part of your life—your business. The store you told me you dreamed of having one day. You may not have known my name, so you chose the closest thing. You picked Flirt with me in mind. Didn't you?"

It was too much. Forcing her to admit the shameful secret was like ripping the Band-Aid off a wound with no delicacy. She trembled under his stare, wishing she could deny it all and throw him out, refusing to speak with him again. She tried to rally and pretend. "It doesn't matter. The name fit the vibe and tone of the store I wanted. You're reading too much into it."

He bent over and pressed his lips to her ear. "Liar."

She jerked away to hide her reaction. "I'm not doing this with you— there's no point. I refuse to be bullied, and you'll need to accept what we had was in the past. Yes, it was special, but I have no interest in pursuing a future."

"May I ask why?"

She gave him a hard stare. "I heard about you being in jail. There'd be no other reason for you to be in this small beach town other than there's nowhere else for you to go. You're not here really by choice, Kane." She nibbled on her lip and asked the question that really mattered. "Did you hurt people?"

He flinched. The flare of pain in his green eyes affected her; made her want to step in and soothe, allow him to explain, and make space for excuses for his mistakes. Still, his response was key, so she waited.

"Yes."

His words broke something inside her. A confirmation that wiped away any excuses. If he hurt people before, how could she ever trust him not to do it to her? It was the perfect barrier to locking up her heart, because this man would annihilate her if she gave him a chance. Her spine stiffened. "I can't be involved with a man who thinks money and power are worth breaking the rules for."

Regret tore through her even as she stayed true to her words.

His face turned to stone. "Fair enough. I have no right to be irritated you didn't come to me for an explanation because we never had the time to get to know one another."

Sierra quirked a brow. "You have an explanation or excuse for hurting people?"

"Does it matter? That conversation is one for later, once we build some trust and learn about each other. Right now, we have to start at the beginning. Create a new one that has a foundation."

Her jaw unhinged. "I just told you we are not getting involved!"

Kane grinned. The boyish mischief was intoxicating but Sierra figured he knew it. "I understand you're scared. I was too, but I'm not about to let a little fear keep me from the one woman I've never forgotten."

Frozen to the ground at his unabashed arrogance, he took advantage by leaning down and pressing a quick kiss to the top of her head. "I'll go slow. For now, let's start with planning a kick ass engagement party."

And while she stood silent, denials stuck in her throat, he let himself out.

Chapter Eleven

"To wear dreams on one's feet is to begin to give a reality to one's dreams."
— Roger Vivier

"I call the Bad Ass Bitches Club to order."

Sierra picked from the cheese and cracker board while she took in the other women gathered at the carved table designed to resemble a corkscrew. The wine bar welcomed them every Thursday night, providing a private room so they could hold their weekly meeting. This past year, they'd all come a long way.

It had originally been a support group to get over Brick, who had no idea women were sharing heartbreak stories and making him out to be a player. Sierra and Aspen had put a quick stop to that ridiculousness, and once the members realized it had just been an excuse to get together, they changed the name to the Bad Ass Bitches Club.

Now, Sierra was a proud member, and they'd welcomed more women into the circle. Riley was the leader. Her bright red hair, smattering of freckles, and killer style allowed her to control the group with ease. Once she'd stopped blaming Brick for everything wrong, she'd actually become a strong advocate for everyone, encouraging sharing and honesty. The topics were wide, but most revolved around everyone's current love life.

Or lack of one.

Sierra sipped her Prosecco and listened to Lacey talk excitedly about her new boyfriend. She was a local waitress with gorgeous curves, white-blonde hair, and a sweet smile. She'd experienced some terrible past relationships. "He asked me straight out last weekend if I was dating anyone else, and when I said no, he asked if we could be exclusive." The roar of approval around the table made Sierra smile. "I know! There's no games. And he pays for shit. He's a real grown-up, but I've been getting in my head and wondering if he's secretly plotting to break my heart for fun. Isn't that screwed up?" Her pert nose wrinkled. "I can't recognize the good ones anymore. But I'm tired of playing games and I just want to be real."

Riley snapped out a response. "Our brains are assholes and try to use past experiences to keep us from getting hurt. But if we recognize it, we can watch our thoughts and move past it."

The comment struck home. Sierra tucked it aside to examine later. Since Kane had stirred up old emotion, she'd been questioning the way she'd set up her life.

Aspen rose up in her chair with excitement. "Yes—I heard Jamie Kern Lima speak and remind us we are all worthy of love and kindness but we need to own our value. We are worthy!"

Maleficent, a new member to the group, tilted her head. Dressed in black leather shorts, open-toed boots, and a t-shirt that said Love Hurts, she was the most badass in the group. Her burgundy braids and elaborate tats boasted confidence, but Sierra had found her heart was tender and hidden behind a wall of rock. Once Brick's rival, she owned a tour company that used to compete with Ziggy's Tours. Now, she'd become a good friend of Aspen and Sierra. "No shit? You think it's that easy?"

"Not easy, but with practice, we get better," Riley said.

Bethany nibbled at her nails; pale skin still seemingly untouched by the sun even living in the beach town for a while. "How'd you learn all this new stuff, Riley?"

Riley sighed. "I'm having some issues with Ian," she admitted. "So, instead of leaning back into my usual ways, where I completely sabotage the relationship, I decided to do a deep dive on fixing some of my crap."

Sierra looked at the hopeful faces around the table. It was nice to know they all struggled with different things. Too many times, female communities tore each other apart to make them feel better about themselves, but here it was different. What had begun as an excuse to gossip and hurt transformed into true support.

Sierra loved it.

They took turns trying to offer advice and encouragement as they went around. The whole time, Sierra longed to come clean to Aspen and her friends about Kane. Just word vomit the entire thing and be done with it. But after that explosive confrontation a few nights ago?

She battled even more confusion.

He actually wanted to pursue a relationship. The sheer panic his declaration caused had bumped up a few of her own insecurities she didn't like to face. And one of them became crystal clear.

She bitched about not being able to find a man that fit. A man who'd take away the edge of loneliness. A man to share her wins and her losses.

But the real truth?

She'd become used to being on her own. Any type of attachment gave her a sinking pit in her stomach. God, who couldn't even commit to a cat? Lately, Aspen had been nudging Sierra to get out of her safe circle. And though she had her business and friends, she recognized those type of relationships were easier. Less risk of being disappointed. Or even worse?

Being hurt.

She'd worked so hard these past years to get into a good place inside and out. There had been so much loss in her life, why bother looking for more when she was relatively happy?

But now Kane threatened her peace. He was a droolworthy, sex-on-a-stick temptation stalking out from the shadows of her past, ready to chase her back into his bed.

Goose bumps broke out at the erotic image.

Dammit, she was doing it again. Picturing herself in one of Aspen's novels. She had to stop.

"Sierra?"

She blinked, refocusing. Everyone was staring at her, awaiting a response. "Oh, sorry. Was thinking about some stuff."

"Great, it's your turn to share," Riley urged.

Sierra shifted in her seat, pinning on a bright smile. "I'm going on a date this weekend," she forced herself to say. The women applauded but she raised her hand. "I'm not excited about it. Another hookup from Brooklyn."

The room quieted. Lacey winced. "She doesn't have a great track record."

"But all you need is one success," Aspen reminded her. "Kiss a hundred frogs and statistically proven, you'll find the prince."

Sierra rolled her eyes. "I'm not even sure I'm looking for one anymore."

Aspen sighed. "But you deserve a guy who will see all the wonderful things we do. You just need to step out of your comfort zone and give it a try."

Sierra looked into her sister's pleading eyes and tried to squash the flicker of guilt. She was going to tell her about Kane. Soon. Lying to Aspen was the worst feeling in the world and once her conscience was clear, she wouldn't have to pretend.

"I'll give this date a solid try," she promised. "But I've decided to do something even bigger." Sierra dragged in a breath. "I'm going to get a cat."

She expected the same hearty applause but everyone just stared at her.

At least, Aspen clapped with enthusiasm. "Finally! Bringing an animal into your house will be so good for you. It's a perfect time to open your life to someone."

Lacey snorted. "I'd rather have a naked male animal in my bed, but what the hell. Cats are cool."

"Are you going to the rescue shelter?" Maleficent asked. "My friend works there—I'll tell her you're coming."

"Yes, that will be great. I know exactly what I want. A sweet, smaller sized rescue with a chill personality. Maybe a kitten so we can immediately imprint on one another? I'd love to bring her into the shop so she could become Flirt's mascot."

The group warmed up to that idea, offering help and saying how great it would be for marketing. "Maybe you can even put the cat on your graphics," Aspen suggested. "Marco has seen some great growth for his store. Bet he'll have some ideas or help out."

Sierra lifted a brow. "He's doing marketing now? Marco's come a long way, huh?"

Aspen grinned. "From the pot-smoking, carefree, hippie type to a real business person? Yep. It's amazing, right, Maleficent?"

Sierra watched Mal freeze up, staring back at them with a touch of defensiveness. "Why are you asking me? I don't know Marco that well."

Aspen hadn't seemed to catch on to Maleficent's unease. A laugh escaped her sister's lips. "Marco thinks you're the smartest businesswoman and is always talking about you. Poor Brick is a bit jealous, I think. He likes being a mentor to Marco."

Maleficent picked up her bold Cabernet and sipped. She took her time with her answer. "Marco's a nice kid but I keep telling him he's better off learning from Brick. Or Sierra—you both own a shop. Maybe you can reach out and give him a few tips. I'm really too busy to play mentor."

"Sure. I can reach out." Something felt off about her friend, but Aspen interrupted.

"Marco's harmless. I just think he's got a crush. Who can blame him?

You're a smoke show," Aspen said.

Maleficent's cheeks flushed. Fascinating. Sierra had never seen the woman crack under any type of compliment, bawdy suggestion, or challenge. Was there something else going on Sierra didn't know about?

She would have liked to dig deeper but Bethanny's comment made her fingers clench around her wine glass. "Anyone know who's dating Kane?"

Lacey's head whipped around. "No! My friend saw him at Sunfish alone and tried to hook up but he said he was busy. Bought her drink, though. Think he's with someone but trying to keep it a secret?"

Sierra's gut clenched. She hated sitting quietly while her friends all discussed Kane on a revolving weekly basis. She didn't blame them for being obsessed. He was the hottest man in Corolla and charmed everyone he met.

"Who would keep him a secret?" Bethanny scoffed. "I can't figure out why he's not dating anyone."

Riley cut in. "Is there someone back in New York no one knows about?"

Aspen sighed. "No, I can confirm he's fully single. Brick said he suddenly pulled back and said he only wants to focus on work. But it's weird to me, too. It's been months and he hasn't dated anyone."

Sierra refused to allow herself to blush while her mind scrambled to make sense of her sister's statement. Was it possible Kane had been holding back because of her? It was a damn long time for a man to remain celibate when they'd barely saw each other, let alone promised anything. But the idea gave her a rush of satisfaction that made her almost as tipsy as one lousy glass of wine.

Aspen shook her head. "He's like the male Sierra. Too bad you both never clicked. Maybe you would've balanced each other out," she joked.

Oh, God.

Sierra felt the culmination of female stares. "Yeah, I think Sierra is the only one who doesn't go on and on about Kane," Lacey said.

"Well, I'd be whatever that man wants," Bethanny said with a laugh. "I bet one night with him would be enough to live on for a lifetime."

Sierra choked on her wine, which thankfully broke up the conversation. The topic turned to the best lip stain for kissing without smearing and before long, it was time to go.

Aspen walked out beside her and linked arms. "Hey, you know I don't mean to give you a hard time about dating, right?" she asked, a slight frown creasing her brow.

"Yep."

Aspen shot her an exasperated look. "I'm serious. I don't want to be one of those awful sisters who's pushing love and joy on you just because I'm getting married. That's horrible."

"You were always horrible. I'm used to it."

She laughed as Aspen bumped against her. "I like the cat idea."

"Me, too. Childless cat ladies are popular, at least."

"Stop." A laugh bubbled from her. "How's the engagement planning going with Kane?"

Sierra tried not to react. "Good. We're, umm, working on it. There really is no reason for him to be involved. I'm happy to do it myself."

Aspen tapped her lip as she seemed to ponder. "I know he's a peacock, but he was really there for Brick. He stepped in to help with Ziggy's Tours, and he's tried hard to become a part of the community." A tiny frown creased her brow. "Can you give him a chance? Let him be a part of the planning? He doesn't have any family and sometimes I—"

Sierra stopped at her car. Heart beating furiously, she looked at her sister. "What?"

"I feel bad for him. I think he's lonely."

The words tore through her and caused more damage than she admitted. She took the opportunity to dig. "Yeah, but is it because he did something terrible in New York and now has to pay the price?" she asked. "He was in jail, Aspen. That's a big deal. Do you know anything about what happened?"

Aspen sighed. "Not really. He hasn't even told Brick all the details. We just know he was arrested, but then they dropped the charges, and he was out of a job. He seems to want to rebuild his life. We've spent a lot of time together and I trust him."

Dread pooled in her stomach. She didn't want to think of Kane being a victim. Her sister hadn't met the man he was years ago. He admitted ruthlessness in getting what he wanted and the way he looked at money as his only goal. Sierra knew he had demons—but didn't everyone have some crap from the past they needed to transform?

Kane admitted he hurt people. She wasn't okay with letting someone like that in her life. Someone who would only choose himself when the stakes were high.

Someone who found it easy to leave.

The thought confirmed her decision to not get involved. "Just be careful. You were always easier to trust than me," Sierra said.

"Will you try, though? To be nice to him and let him do some stuff?"

Ah, crap. Normally, it would be a loud no, but Aspen looked so eager, she decided to give in. "I'll try."

"Good enough." They hugged. "Want me to go with you to the shelter?"

"Nah, I'd like to do this on my own. It's a big decision, and I want to be guided to the right cat naturally."

"Okay. Call me after your date to give me the deets!" Aspen called, walking away.

"Will do!"

Sierra drove home and tried not to think about the kiss with Kane. His departure reeked with a warning he'd only gotten started in his pursuit, and now with Aspen's plea to involve him, Sierra was completely mixed up.

Best to take one step at a time. Brooklyn had been pushing hard to set her up with this guy, and after the confrontation with Kane, she'd decided it was a good time to declare boundaries. It would firmly show she wanted to move on in a new direction. She'd get a cat and open her home up to a new family member. And she'd invite Kane to a few vendor appointments, then call it a day.

She could handle it.

No problem.

Kane walked into his office and sat at his desk. Once, his view had been the skyscrapers of a powerful New York City skyline. He'd sat in a designer leather chair, stared at walls covered in expensive art, and had a private wet bar for cocktails.

Now? His chair hurt his back; the space was cramped and held a bunch of file cabinets, a battered desk, and a lone dorm refrigerator. The plaster walls had dings and dents and was painted a sad Eeyore gray. His view was a parking lot.

His lips twisted in a rueful half-smile. It was another reminder not to count on anything for too long. Not money, security, or power.

The thought was depressing so he pushed it out of his mind and focused on what he could control. His comeback. The big return to the property world in the Outer Banks. There were endless opportunities to make a splash. He'd been scouring the landscape and trying to put something big together to make an impression on his boss. It only took one deal to change everything. He knew, because he'd done it before.

And he was going to do it again.

On cue, Duncan strolled in. He was an older man with neatly combed back white hair and blue eyes that were too kind for this type of business. Silver glasses perched on his broad nose. His suit was gray like the walls and off-the-rack, the hem of his pants dragging a bit on the floor for his average height. Kane tried not to judge. He had a thing with designer clothes and the way they made him feel. Funny, he understood Sierra's passion for fashion. It was amazing how the right outfit could center someone and give them power. It was just another bond they shared. "Morning, Kane. I've got something for you."

His boss took a seat in the cheap fold-out across from him. He was a good guy but lacked vision. Then again, he didn't seem to have the hunger to make his own business bigger and better. "Stealth Property contacted me, asking to scope out a space to build one of their resorts. They have certain specs I sent over. I thought you'd be interested."

"Yeah?" His brow climbed. This is the stuff he did in his sleep at his old job and gave him the biggest buzz. Grabbing a deal and flipping real estate for profit was a gift. Somehow, his brain clicked in all the right ways to get what his clients wanted. Stealth was well-known in the industry and a power player. "I'm surprised they came to us."

His boss grinned. "Yeah, me too. We're small potatoes but seems someone found out you were working here and thought you could get the job done. There's a hefty bonus in there, too."

"You didn't want this one?" he asked carefully. Usually, the owner claimed all rights to these types of opportunities.

"No, I have enough crap to deal with. Plus, the last time I tried something like this, I ended up being the villain in town. No one likes to hear their mom-and-pop shops are going to be bulldozed. You have less connections."

Kane laughed. "I'm the bad guy, huh?"

His boss laughed. "Take it, leave it, doesn't matter. I'm happy with what we've built here, but I sense you're not. Stealth wants a conference call this week." He paused, his gaze shrewd. "If you succeed, Stealth may want to hire you."

Kane cocked his head with amusement. "Why do I get the feeling you won't be fighting to keep me?"

His boss stood from the chair. "'Cause I won't." His gaze held a hint of sympathy that startled him. "I recognized your talent immediately, and

I'm grateful to have you. But being in business for so many years allows you to see the bigger picture." Duncan hesitated. Kane waited, curious. "I have nothing left to prove. But I think you still do. Let me know if you have questions. Good luck."

Kane was firing up his computer before his boss hit the door. The old zap of adrenalin hit full-force, and soon, he was lost in the new proposal of possibilities. He put together a networking plan and fell down the rabbit hole of research until he surfaced late that day.

Before he got home, Kane decided to stop in for a beer at Sunfish. He texted Brick to see if he could join, but he was busy with Aspen and asked for a raincheck. Kane found an empty stool, ordered a whiskey, and enjoyed people watching. The place was kicking with tourists, bringing a revelry and chaos that amused him. It was as if everyone used their weeks off to cram as much fun into the hours as possible, and Sunfish was always a popular spot.

He chatted with a few drinking neighbors, waved to others he knew, and settled in.

Until he saw Sierra.

His body tightened with immediate awareness as his gaze locked in. She sat at one of the tables, her caramel hair shiny and curling down her back. A bright red sundress splashed with white flowers showed off her tanned shoulders and hugged her generous breasts. His gaze automatically swept down to check the shoes.

Yeah. She'd come out to play. The sexy red sandals held a sassy bow in the front with an open back. Kitten heels about an inch. She was afraid to look too tall so the whole thing screamed blind date. She leaned across the table, obviously trying to hear her companion over the noise, then offered a smile.

Jealousy ripped through him. He fought the urge to get up, cross the room, and haul the guy she smiled at off his feet and out the door. The primitive roar inside him ached to rip free and bellow the truth she refused to accept.

Sierra belonged to him.

The scene around him faded away as he studied the guy she sat with. Average looking, with a too-short haircut and roving gaze. His hand covered his phone like a cherished girlfriend's hand. Even worse? He was wearing flip flops. Kane was embarrassed for him, but relief also hit full force.

She'd never be into a guy who didn't even try.

His chest loosened and he was able to watch their interaction with calm. Oh, she was trying, he'd give her that, but the guy seemed more interested in the cut of her dress and his next text.

She'd barely get to dessert if she wasn't rescued.

With a grin, Kane gripped his beer, got off the stool, and decided to save her again.

Just like he had four years ago.

 The flare of awareness in her pretty hazel eyes struck him full-force, before a wall shot up to hide her emotion. But it was too late. He'd caught her interest and it was enough to jump into his role with delight.

"Sierra! It's wonderful to see you," he said, interrupting their obviously flat dialogue. He bent over and kissed her cheek, watching them redden. Kane knew it was temper, but at the moment, he didn't care. Any type of response from her was a win. "I've been waiting for you to come over and see Pedro. He misses you."

Her companion cleared his throat. Sierra glared, her teeth gnashing together. "Umm, Kane? What are you doing here?"

"Well, you mentioned you may be coming here tonight and we've been so busy, I hoped to catch you. Oops, sorry, don't mean to interrupt." He stuck out his hand to Mr. Flip Flops. "I'm Kane."

The guy nodded and tentatively shook. Kane deducted more points for a limp shake that held no power. Sierra would eat this guy for breakfast. "Hi. I'm Gary."

"Gary and I are on a date right now," Sierra said, her mouth twisted in a painful smile. "We can talk another time."

"Oh, I'm sure Gary doesn't mind. You believe in co-parenting, right?"

Gary jerked. His brown eyes widened. "You're a parent?" he asked.

"No! Don't listen to—"

"Sierra is the best mom. I know we just broke up, but Pedro hasn't been sleeping well. I think we should take him to the park tomorrow together, don't you?"

"No! There is no—"

"How old is Pedro?" Gary asked, obviously concerned about being thrown into a sticky ex situation.

Kane gave a smile. "Just turned one year old. Right, honey?"

"What are you doing?" she hissed.

Kane held up his hands. "Do what? It's not Pedro's fault we settled most of our arguments in the bedroom. Neither of us were ready for such intensity, but Pedro deserves our full support."

Gary began to cough. "I-I didn't know about this situation."

"Of course not, it's relatively new," Kane said cheerfully. "You mind if I pull up a chair real quick? What are you drinking, Gary? I'll buy the next round."

Sierra opened her mouth to take control but it was too late.

Gary jumped up from the table with his beloved phone. A sick smile curved his weak mouth. "Uh, sorry, but I'm not ready for this yet. And I, uh, forgot that I need to get home to let the—uh, my dog out. Take my seat, Kane. It was nice to meet you, Sierra."

Sierra blinked. "But—"

Gary took off.

Kane dropped in the seat across from her, wrinkling his nose at Gary's choice of cocktail. "An apple martini? Really? How did you manage to stay beyond the intros?"

"I am going to kill you."

He sipped his whiskey, put his elbows on the table, and grinned. "Trust me, I'll be better company than Mr. Flip Flops."

"What are you even saying? Have you gone insane? Barging over here and ruining my date? You have absolutely no right!"

"Maybe not, but I saved you from a worthless evening. Don't even try to lie and tell me you found anything in that guy valuable enough to stay past appetizers."

She pressed her lips together, obviously pissed, but there was another spark in her eyes that kept him in his seat. *Interest.* When was the last time this vibrant woman had a man who'd not only meet on her level, but challenge her? "My opinion has nothing to do with it," she said primly. She could've left, but instead she reached for her wine glass. "Stay out of my personal life, Masterson. This is your last warning."

"Duly noted." He tipped a finger and the waitress ran over. "Can we get a bucket of oysters, an IPA, and a"—he glanced at her glass—"Prosecco?"

"Of course. Be right back."

Sierra gave a snort at her rushed retreat. "You're so damn bossy. The only reason I'm staying is I didn't finish eating and you might as well pay. But if you ever pull a stunt like that again, I'll out you in public."

"Flip Flops didn't stick around to hear Pedro was our dog." He regarded her across the table with a glittering gaze. "Any man who runs that fast isn't worthy of you, Sierra."

She shifted in her seat but refused to give him an inch. "Neither are you."

His lip quirked. "You're right. But I'll get there."

He heard the slight intake of her breath. She fiddled with her napkin. "Why do you keep calling him flip flops? Is this shoe discrimination?"

"Definitely. You had a flicker of hope tonight, which pisses me off. He didn't even try."

"Are you basing this all on shoes?"

Kane ignored her surprised tone and pushed. "Shoes are important. They show your mood or mental state. Kitten heels and bows are about flirt and hope. I hate that you wasted any effort on him."

Shock crossed her face before she managed to gain back control. "I didn't realize you noticed my shoe fetish."

"I notice everything that's important to you," he said quietly. "What do you think I've been doing these past months while biding my time?"

She shifted her gaze and their eyes locked. The room faded away under the familiar sting of electricity, but then the waitress dropped off their oysters and drinks, breaking the moment. Kane reached for one, expertly squeezing half a lemon and a dash of sauce like she preferred, then offered the oyster. She paused before taking it, and he watched her bubblegum lips part and suck the tender flesh into her mouth. She chewed, eyes half closed, as if enjoying the sharp tastes on her tongue. Kane savored every flicker of expression with greed. Sierra taking her pleasures in any aspect was an incredible treat.

He hardened immediately. Kane's vision blurred with the crack of desire exploding through his body. The woman had some witch-like power over his dick, even though they'd only spent one night together years ago. He'd tried to tell himself if they ever met again, it could never be the same intensity.

Now, they'd both proved the lie.

When she'd swallowed and opened her eyes, he reached for his own oyster. She snapped back to her sassy self. "How'd you know about my date tonight?" she asked suspiciously. "Did you plan this whole setup?"

He took his time answering. "Nope. Call it Fate. I stopped for a drink after work. Didn't take long to assess the situation and formulate a rescue plan."

"And if I looked like I was having a great time?"

He grinned. "I would've interrupted sooner."

Temper steamed from her pores. "This thing between us has to stop. I already told you it's best we move in separate directions."

"Funny, I think the opposite. Here, eat this one."

God, she was sexy when she was mad, but he figured she was still hungry enough to snatch the oyster from his fingers. Kane decided to change the subject to keep her at the table. Being alone with her was rare. He wanted to do everything to extend his time.

"I've been thinking about the engagement party and have a few suggestions," he said.

Her brow arched. She patted the napkin to her lips. "Oh, really? I'd love to hear them."

He swirled his glass. "I created a spreadsheet with all the places that have private rooms and would be a good fit for the theme."

"You came up with a theme?"

He gave a half shrug. "Not exactly. I just figured casual elegance would fit Aspen and Brick. They don't like formal, but we want good food, good staff, and good décor. I'll email you the list and we can each call half to speed up the process. The alternate idea is to rent tents and create a beach engagement party but we'd be more dependent on weather."

Satisfaction unfurled at her look of surprise. "Wait—you did all of this alone?"

Kane shrugged. "Sure—it didn't take long. I also created a vendor list but I'm sure you know more people and may have already decided who you want to work with. I did think something with sea turtles would be nice for a favor—maybe handmade soaps in that shape? Oh, and I'd say a DJ is key and they'd prefer it over a band. Maybe Taylor Swift can be a theme song for them to walk into? That could be fun."

Her reaction was worth all of those sweat-worthy hours figuring this shit out. Once he began climbing down the portal of engagement parties, Kane admitted it wasn't so bad. Just like putting together a deal. Get your stats and numbers, find who you want to work with, create the scene needed to close, follow through. Who knew event planning could be satisfying?

"I don't believe it," she muttered. "Why are you doing this?"

He opened his mouth to answer.

"Don't lie."

He shut it. Considered. Damned if he was going to lie to this woman ever. "Two reasons. I like the idea of us working on something together for people we both love. Second, I wanted to impress you and show you another side of me."

She gave a long sigh. "Crap, that was a good answer. Even though I don't like it."

"Have another oyster."

She glared but ate the third one while he tried not to grin. "I'll look at your spreadsheet but I don't pride myself on working well with others.

This is my sister—the most important person in my life. If you're going to try to mansplain crap or push your agenda, I'll push back. And I don't care if I sound bitchy, it's just the way it is."

Delight lit him up. "I like the way you are. I really want an opportunity to help. For Brick. Okay?"

Her tongue slicked over her lower lip. Kane almost bent over as if sucker punched. He'd give up anything to taste her one more time.

"Fine."

"Thank you, Sierra." Her name danced on his tongue. He noticed she stiffened slightly, as if trying to fight her reaction. "Maybe we should meet tomorrow after you've gone over the spreadsheet?"

She snorted. "Nice try but we can text. Besides, I'm going to the animal shelter."

"A cat, right?"

She stared back at him.

Kane smiled gently. "Brick said you were considering it a while ago, but never pulled the trigger. I'm glad you decided to adopt. You deserve to have a companion who loves you unconditionally. You'll be a great mom."

She blinked rapidly, as if he'd surprised her with his words and she didn't know how to process. Too bad. She deserved to have consistent compliments and appreciation from a man she invited into her life.

But it must've been too much. His question made her slam down a wall between them.

Damn. One of his faults was going too hard, too fast.

She looked down at her lap, as if gathering her thoughts. When she lifted her chin, the mask was back in place. "I have to go."

He nodded. Kane realized she needed space from him to process. "I got the bill. Drive safe, Sierra."

Gratitude shone in her hazel eyes from the easy escape. "Thanks. You, too."

She walked out of the restaurant, her heels tapping across the floor. But the encounter only proved things between them had only just begun.

Kane smiled as he settled up and headed home. Sierra wasn't interested in dating anyone else. He just needed to be patient and wait out her stubbornness. There was no real reason they couldn't be together now. Yes, he needed to gain her trust, but with Brick and Aspen's wedding, they'd be forced to spend more time together.

He was in a damn good mood. Finally, he was rebuilding his career, and Sierra was back in his life. Things were finally on the upswing.

At this point, what could go wrong?

Chapter Twelve

"Shoes are the quickest way for women to achieve instant metamorphosis."
— Manolo Blahnik

He knew about shoes.

The thought kept dancing in her mind as she drove to the animal shelter. Sierra went over last night's encounter and poked for specific reasons Kane Masterson was a con man.

After all, he'd interrupted and ruined her date. Fed her oysters like he was her lover. Complimented not only her personality, but her worthiness. Created a detailed spreadsheet most men would never try to embark on.

And knew exactly what shoes meant to her.

God, it was awful. Even worse? She was terribly attracted to the way the man wore his clothes...and footwear. There was a pride in his appearance, and the way he seemed to realize fashion didn't have to be about ego or money, but personality and choice. Kane could come out of a second-hand shop and still look as delicious as he did in custom designer suits, because he wore his clothes—his clothes did not wear him.

It took a mighty ego and confidence to own such male potency.

Sierra shook off her thoughts as she pulled into the Dare County Animal Rescue. She'd called for an appointment and was excited to hear they had a new litter of kittens to consider. Yes, a kitten would be a lot of work, but the idea of being the first to shape their infancy was enticing. Of course, she'd consider an older cat if she was friendly and well-behaved. Her new companion needed to fit into her shop well and not intimidate her customers. She imagined one of those bookstore cats, quiet and unassuming, prowling around the shelves with dignity and restraint as people browsed.

And of course, she did not want a male cat. Flirt was female driven, which was important to her.

Colette greeted her with a warm smile. "It's so nice to meet you, Sierra. Mal told me you'd be coming in, and I'm really excited for you meet all our cats today. Your application was approved so we're all set to find you a forever fur baby."

Sierra smiled back, loving her energy. With a messy ponytail, make-up free face, dusty jeans and work boots, the young woman gave off vibes that screamed animal love. They chatted a bit as she was brought across a small field to the main cat shelter. Crates were lined up, stuffed with blankets and various toys. A main play center with towers, balls, and tunnel mazes was in the rear, and Sierra saw a couple playing with a tiny gray kitten.

"This is our cat room. We have the kittens out in the play area so you can spend some time and see if you bond with any of them. And of course, we have various ages to pick from. Some were strays. Others were given up by their owners." Colette's brown eyes filled with sadness. "So many families just can't afford pets, or to spay their cats so they go on to have multiple births and the population explodes."

Sierra nodded. "I can imagine how hard it must be nowadays."

The woman's face cleared. Freckles sprinkled her nose. "Yes, but you're here today and will make a big difference. The names are on their cage. Do you want to see the kittens first?"

"Yes, please." Excitement and nerves sparked. She wished Aspen was here, but Sierra had wanted to do this herself and rely on her own intuition. She entered the cat room and Colette spent some time pointing out the various kittens, citing names and sexes. Sierra sat down on the rug while eight small balls of fur mewed and tumbled over one another in obvious joy. She nodded at the couple, who seemed to have fallen in love with the charcoal one, cuddling to their chests. Sierra got choked up when she spotted tears in their eyes, as if they were adopting their first child.

Damn, she was getting emotional herself.

She took her time with the kittens, getting to know each of their personalities as she watched them play. Patsy—a black one with white paws kept to herself, surveying the wildness with a touch of worry. Sierra tried to coax her over but the kitten quickly hid in one of the tunnels.

Colette came in to check with her but Sierra still wasn't sure. They were all adorable, and any one of them would probably be a lovely addition to her life. But there was no gut pull to one particular feline.

Maybe it wasn't supposed to be like that? Maybe she was silly to think picking a cat could be like her one night with Kane, when she was guided by a primitive instinct she couldn't fight?

Sierra left the kittens and perused the other cats awaiting rescue. One by one, she looked into their faces and watched them. A few she took out and spent some quality time with. Her heart ached to take them all, but she was only ready for one.

She just wanted to find the right one.

Sierra was about to go back to the kittens when her gaze caught on the last crate at the end of the row. There was no card displayed with a name. Curious, she walked over and stared through the spaces of the metal.

Her eyes widened.

A gigantic garish orange cat sat toward the back, staring at her, goldish eyes unblinking. One ear was cocked forward; the other ear fell limply to the side like it no longer worked. She was like any other TikTok user and loved a good cat video so she knew about grumpy cat, but this one raised the stakes. The frown from its odd mouth was intense, as if the world had not only disappointed but destroyed. Massive paws made him look like a lionfish, but Sierra couldn't tell if he was fat or just overly large.

If it was even a him.

Sierra kept staring at the odd creature, waiting for him to dismiss her or hiss and try to creep back into the shadows. A light touch on her arm made her jump.

"Sorry!" Colette said. "I was saying your name but you didn't respond. Everything good? Do you want to see any of the cats?"

She pointed a finger at the crate. "Why doesn't this one have a name?"

Unbelievably, Colette looked a bit uneasy. "Oh, well, he's newish and a bit…difficult. Of course, he must've had a hard time out there on his own. He was a stray. Found him limping on the side of the road but he put up a wicked fight. We've been calling him Garfield for now. Jamal's been working with him—he's our cat handler."

Garfield didn't fit at all. The cat seemed to agree, because he suddenly sprang forth and hissed at Colette in a temper tantrum.

Colette stepped back. "He's temperamental. Doesn't seem to like many people" She seemed to realize she wasn't being positive and a flicker of guilt crossed her face. "But I'm sure Garfield will be a great cat once he feels safe."

"Hmm. Can I see him out of the crate?"

Colette looked like she swallowed a sharp object, but smiled gamely. "Oh, sure. Let me just get some help getting Garfield...out."

Sierra knew if this lovely woman was afraid, she should forget this whole meet and greet and move on. But she stayed silent as Colette got one of the other cat handlers, who wore long gloves to protect his arms, and tried to coax Garfield out of the crate.

"Come on, buddy, we're just going to have a quick play session with someone nice." The handler seemed more comfortable than Colette, first offering a small treat, and moving with slow but firm movements. He expertly faced the cat away from him, lifted, and brought him calmly to the small meet and greet room. "Garfield is a tough one. He hasn't liked anyone yet and may hiss at you. Don't look him in the eye or you'll seem confrontational. Don't try to move too fast. He

needs some patience."

Colette gave her an apologetic stare. "Sorry, I'm not familiar with Garfield like Becker is. He's like the cat whisperer around here."

"You're doing great," he said kindly.

"How long has he been here?" Sierra asked.

Becker scratched his head. "We picked him up a while ago, but he needed to be neutered, get his shots, and be socialized a bit. He's had a hard time. Definitely not comfortable with people. Temperamental. Jamal has been working with him, and he's now able to be handled from the crate without a problem. But I always had a soft spot for Garfield. You don't have any other animals, do you?"

"No."

"Good." He smiled. "I can stay if you want."

Sierra watched Garfield shake out his orange fur and stalk around, getting the lay of the room. Fascinated, she shook her head. "No, I'd like to be alone with him if that's okay?"

"Of course, just yell if you need us."

Colette and Becker closed the glass door behind them. Sierra knew they'd keep a close eye but she felt like they had the space to themselves so Garfield could be who he wanted. She took a cross-legged position on the floor from a distance away.

Up close, he was even more intimidating. He seemed to grow bigger as he stretched out, giant paws investigating his surroundings, nose twitching, limp ear hanging crooked. His tail swooshed and his mouth curved in pure displeasure and disgust.

No wonder everyone was afraid of him.

"I bet you're pretty misunderstood," she said quietly. "Everyone wants a cute kitten, right? Or a sweet, untroubled soul who didn't have to deal with any of the bad stuff yet. That's the type I wanted, too. Uncomplicated."

He pawed at a rubber ball, then swatted it to the side. Prowled back and forth as if thinking about something important which had nothing to do with her.

Sierra sighed. "I'm not even sure why I'm here. You probably wouldn't be happy with

me. I think we're complete opposites."

He twitched, turned, and paced some more.

"I need a shop cat, like one who looks good in a bookstore. I own a boutique so I also wanted a female cat. You'd scare people and that's not good for business."

He gave her side eye. Swatted at something that moved on the floor. His fur bristled.

"My house is really nice and I'd want you to live inside. No going in and out dragging creatures in as gifts. I think you're too old and set in your ways to be trained. I should get a kitten."

Finally, he pivoted and sat on his rear. Blinked. Those gold eyes fascinated her, but she remembered not to look at him directly because it was confrontational and she didn't want to piss him off.

But Sierra couldn't help it. She tried to use her periphery but this cat stared so intently, she literally felt the command to meet his gaze head-on.

She did.

Time stopped. In a flash, she saw things in those eyes. A knowledge of the outside of this shelter and the things he'd seen. Done. Experienced. A stubborn pride that overcame the world weariness most animals would succumb to on the street. A beautiful fuck-you to the masses who tried to break him into something and someone he was not.

Understanding passed between them.

"You're perfect," Sierra whispered.

Slowly, he unfurled his legs and stalked over. She held her breath, not sure what to do, and then the giant cat went straight to her lap. Using his paws, he kneaded her legs as if trying to shape them into the perfect pillow.

Then dropped to her lap. The gesture screamed arrogance. He was making himself comfortable on his terms, not bending to her whim. Her heart began to speed up and she lifted a hand, gently petting his fur. The thick softness under her palm was the perfect antidote to any worries. Her mind eased, and the low rumbling of a purr filled the quiet room.

And in that moment, Sierra realized they were twin souls and this was the cat she was looking for.

He wasn't the best one. He wouldn't have been her pick.

But he chose her. And he was now hers.

Colette popped her head in. "Everything going—oh, my goodness!" Her jaw seemed to drop, then snap shut. "I've never seen him do this before."

Sierra smiled, refusing to look away from this magnificent creature before her.

"He's the one I want."

The cat stretched his neck to glance back. He seemed smug, as if promising her she made the right choice but he wouldn't make it easy on her. Love never was.

For now, Sierra was okay with it.

"I'm so happy for you and Garfield."

"His name is Montgomery," she corrected.

She knew no one with that name. It wasn't from a famous celebrity or leader; it wasn't picked from a beloved book or movie. But it was a name that screamed dignity. A name that spoke regalness. A name that was meant to be remembered.

Montgomery cocked his head as if considering. Then began licking his paw, obviously not giving a crap what she decided to name him. As long as it wasn't a copycat of a cartoon who ate lasagna.

Sierra began to laugh, looking forward to her new adventure as a cat lady.

Two days later, Sierra stared out the side window, caught between astonishment and a betraying excitement she hated admitting. What was he doing here?

She looked down at her stretchy pants, oversize t-shirt and sock-clad feet. Sunday nights were reserved for cozying up to prep for the rest of the week. Not hosting hot men at her place while eating Chinese straight from the cartons.

"I'm bearing gifts!" he shouted from the porch, obviously aware she was hesitating about letting him in.

Sierra blew out a breath and opened the door.

Kane held two giant tote bags in his hands. A devastating grin curved his full lips. "Congratulations on your new addition. I can't wait to meet him."

She rolled her eyes. "Really? You're here to see my cat? Are we suddenly besties who come over each to other's houses for late night visits?"

His face fell. The expression only gave him an adorable charm difficult to resist. "Not yet, but I'm hoping. Aspen told Brick who told me so I figured it'd be nice to stop by."

Damned if her lips didn't twitch in a smile, but she kept her tone firm. "You can come in for a minute. I don't want to overwhelm him since this is all new to both of us."

"Got it." He stepped through the threshold, sniffing the air. "Is that Chinese?"

"Yes."

"Any leftovers? I didn't get to eat today—too busy."

A suffering sigh escaped. "Why are you reminding me of a stray cat yourself?"

"Because I know how they feel."

His answer gave her pause. Sierra wanted to ask further questions but he was already setting the bags down and looking around. "Is he hiding? Poor thing. I don't want to intimidate him."

"Montgomery likes to sleep in the sunroom but he'll come out when he's ready. What did you bring?"

"Montgomery, huh? Very distinguished." Kane began pulling items from the bags with an enthusiasm that amused her. She hadn't seen this side of him, like a kid excited about giving gifts to please. "I did some online research and found these were the best food and treats to give. It's made with real ingredients and not that fake crap manufacturers try to push." He placed everything on the coffee table in a neat line. "These toys are good for giving mental stimulation. These have catnip, but there's a lot of disagreement on if it's good to use but I figured you'd decide what's best." He wriggled a large box from the bottom. "This is a cat tower I can build for you. It's got the highest reviews for safety. And this thing is motorized so he can play chase." The cute mouse was on roller wheels and made little squeaking sounds when Kane pressed it. "I already put batteries in it. What do you think?"

Crap. What she thought led to danger. He was being sweet and a bit nerdy and her silly heart softened to mush. Once again, she realized how nice it was to have a man take an interest and care about something in her life. Sierra had Aspen and a ton of girlfriends but no men stayed in her life once she shut down the romance.

She stared at him with a new outlook. From the first, she'd been wary of getting her heart broken with this man. It was easier to keep the past firmly in her memory and not spoil the perfect night.

But right now? Sierra wondered if she was playing small in order to keep things in control. What if she gave Kane Masterson a chance? What if she opened herself up to the possibility of not only a great affair, but a great love? Was it just her stubbornness that made her believe they couldn't try out a real relationship, with morning afters and dating? Could she navigate these type of feelings without constantly wondering if she was going to end up hurt and alone again?

She'd changed over the years. Achieved her dreams of a fulfilling career and independence on her terms.

Wasn't it possible he'd changed, too?

The questions flooded her with confusion. She needed time to sort things out. One thing was clear—if she was ready to go down that unknown path, she wanted to tell her sister and Brick the truth. And she needed clarity on his actions that led him to jail and fleeing New York.

"You don't like them?" Kane frowned. "I can return them. I didn't mean to push. I tend to do that, huh?"

"We both do," she said quietly. "But this was really nice, Kane. Thank you."

Their gazes locked. Understanding mingled with the familiar heat, but instead of retreat, Sierra held her stance. "Want some lo mein while we wait for Montgomery? You just can't judge me for not using plates."

"I'd love some. No judgment zone. Ever since I moved to my place, I barely put on clothes, let alone use plates."

A jolt of awareness zapped her. The image of him striding around naked, all those ridged muscles on display for her gaze, made her falter. His wicked grin told her he knew, so Sierra refused to let him win this round. "Me, too. Funny, a few minutes earlier and you would've caught me climbing out of my bubble bath. I like to walk around without a robe so my skin air dries. Much healthier."

She hid her smug expression as she headed to the kitchen. The strangled sound from his lips was satisfying. "That was cruel," he said.

"You started it. Drink?"

"Sweet tea, please. One day, I'd like to finish it."

She shot him a look and handed him the pint of noodles. Safe across the granite countertop, she poured two glasses, took out a fork, and slid them over. His green eyes heated but he nodded his thanks and began to eat. Sierra watched in silence for a few moments. "If I let you finish it, what should I expect?"

He choked, placing the carton down quickly and drinking some tea. Kane shook his head and stared at her. "Woman, are you trying to kill me?"

Feeling bold, she gave a half shrug. "You're the one doing the chasing. Showing up at my house, declaring it's only a matter of time before you catch me. I'm simply asking what would happen next. Or is it the game that gives you the adrenaline rush? Just like closing one of your big deals?"

It was a fair question, but his menacing frown said he didn't like it. "Do you think this is a game?" he asked softly.

"I don't know." She crossed her arms in front of her chest. "I don't know you enough to make that call."

"Because you wouldn't give me a chance. You ran." He paused. "You denied me."

A shiver squeezed through her. He was right, but she hated thinking of herself as a coward. "We don't have to make this complicated. If we want to put some ghosts to rest, we can go into my bedroom right now. Maybe a few good orgasms will break the spell and we can both move on with our lives. No one has to know."

He shook his head. "God, you're such a flirt."

Her jaw dropped. "Nothing I said was even close to flirty!"

"You're so damn direct and bold, you can annihilate a man with one blast of that sharp tongue. It's the hottest type of flirting imaginable."

Was it wrong to feel a rush of satisfaction that this man seemed to know her? Oh, sure, she knew how to be soft and approachable around men. She loved the give and take; the dance of male and female that pulsed with possibilities. But few knew the woman behind the façade. Her ex-husband, he told her she was too intimidating, and that she'd do better if she was less edgy. Sierra hadn't thought to question his opinion. Instead, she spent too much time trying to mold herself into the perfect wife, so she could have the perfect life.

When that had all blown up, she'd finally said fuck it. But all her dates made her nervous. She worried she'd come on too strong, too fast and scare any potential relationships away. She got in her head and couldn't seem to pull out. Until this moment, she hadn't even realized she'd been policing herself or trying to be someone she wasn't.

Not with Kane.

He didn't seem the least intimidated or turned off.

He looked exactly the opposite, jaw clenched, green eyes roving over her body with every dirty thought boldly crossing his face. Every part of her trembled to step forward and give in. Let him drag her to bed so this tormenting tension could break and either split her apart…or put her back together.

"Sierra?"

She tilted her head, waiting.

"I think you want me to push. Sex is easier to pigeonhole us, because we both know once I get you naked, you won't be leaving that bedroom for a damn long time."

Her mouth went dry. He continued.

"But I'm playing for bigger stakes. I want to take you out on a date. I want to help you plan the engagement party and stand beside you while we celebrate the two people we love. I want to tell the world the truth— that four years ago I fell hard and I haven't stopped dreaming about you. That's so much more than a few orgasms."

She had no spit left. Sierra cleared her throat, body tight with tension. "That's a lot to process."

The wolf retreated. His lip quirked and his face gentled. "It is."

She faced him from across the counter and over lo mein noodles. "You want a relationship with me. Not just sex?"

"Yes."

"Have you ever been involved with someone long-term, Kane? Said I love you? Compromised and given up things you wanted for that other person? Put someone else first over your career?"

Direct hit. He jerked back as if slapped. Triumph mingled with regret at the truth on his face. This man had never thought of anyone but himself. He'd been in jail. He'd hurt people. Both Brick and Aspen knew very little of his past. Kane Masterson was a mystery. And though the connection was always there, Sierra was terrified he was full of words but no action.

"No. You're right. I haven't done any of those things."

Disappointment hit, but she didn't flinch. At least, he was being honest. She needed all of the ammunition to keep her heart safe. Sierra nodded. "I thought so."

"But it's only for one reason, Sierra." His gaze crashed into hers, lit with a fire that stole her breath. The silence pulsed around them, stretching, as if knowing his next words would change everything.

"I was waiting for you."

She shuddered at his stark tone, stripped of smart banter or pretty prose meant to entertain and seduce. No, this was spoken from the deeper, darker places in his soul, and her insides melted with the need to go to him, slide her arms around his neck, lean her head against his chest, and ask for his secrets; for his trust.

Frozen in place, a rush of emotions hit full force. Her fingers curled into fists. All she had to do was walk around and give in to the moment, and Kane Masterson would be hers.

Suddenly, a low hiss filled the air, startling them both.

Sierra blinked and focused on Montgomery, who'd finally made his way out to meet the new visitor. She'd been careful about giving the cat space and time to settle into his new home, but found after a few hours of exploration, he settled in like he belonged. She was able to handle him without issues, and after only two days, Sierra was already smitten with her new companion.

Aspen came over to meet him, and after a bit of hesitation over his size and demeanor, they'd taken to each other easily. If things continued, Sierra planned to bring him to Flirt and get slowly acquainted with the space and being around people.

But right now?

He looked like a demon cat ready to rip apart his greatest enemy.

Fur prickling, massive body crouched as if ready to attack, the hiss sounded deadly and made Kane still immediately.

Kane raised his hands in surrender. "Umm, Sierra? Is that your…cat?"

Startled at the reaction, she frowned and came around the island. "Montgomery? It's okay. He's a friend."

She figured he was protecting her and once she showed Kane wasn't threatening, the cat would relax. With slow, careful motions, she knelt down, putting herself in between them. "He even brought you toys and treats. Did he scare you, baby?" she crooned.

The cat's giant golden eyes met hers, as if needing reassurance. Sierra's heart melted.

"Mommy's okay. Kane won't hurt me. Wanna meet him?"

She reached out and patted Kane's knee. Kane grit out in a whisper. "That's not a cat. It's a monster."

Sierra shot him a glare. "Don't say that about him. Montgomery was a stray and had a hard time of it. He just needs to know he's safe."

"What about my safety? 'Cause he's going to try to kill me."

She rolled her eyes, putting out her other hand to stroke the cat's prickly fur. Slowly, Montgomery began to settle, but his gaze stayed on Kane with a blatant warning. "You're being ridiculous. He's been a sweetheart. He just needs time. Some relationships aren't love at first sight."

Kane snorted. "Nice analogy. He must've had to be drugged to get him into that shelter. He's a Cujo in cat form."

"He was hurt by a car, and the shelter got him medical help. He was alone in a crate for a while so he's not used to people." She arched a brow. "I'm surprised at you. I thought you liked animals."

"Domesticated, cute, furry animals. Brick's got a rat creature masquerading as a dog, and now you have a pet who looks like the orange gorilla from *Jungle Book*."

Montgomery crouched back and hissed again.

"Don't say things like that. He doesn't like it," she said.

"Sorry. Umm, listen, Mo, I'm not here to cause trouble. Wanna take a look at some of your presents?"

Sierra rose the same time as Kane. Moving carefully, they eased into the living room where the bags and boxes were spread out. The cat turned to keep him in sight.

"Try giving him a treat," Sierra suggested.

"Here you go, buddy. These are amazing. The most expensive ones on the shelf." Kane opened the pouch, knelt to the ground, and held out the tidbit. "What do you say? Wanna give it a try? I've got more where that came from. Anything you want."

Montgomery took a tentative step forward. His ears and nose twitched. Regarded the man and his treat before him, offering the bribe. Then with a sudden leap through the air, he landed in front of Kane's outstretched hand. With one swift movement, the cat's giant paw smacked out with a mighty strike.

Kane fell back, the treat falling out of his grip.

Montgomery gave a threatening hiss, then turned away, swishing his tail in dismissal at the whole charade. Nose stuck up, he stalked away and settled in front of Sierra as if guarding her from a man unworthy of her attention.

Kane's jaw dropped. He stared at the cat in confusion, and the entire scene began to strike her as hysterical.

Holy crap, Montgomery had completely dissed him.

Sierra started to laugh as Kane tried to regather his composure and get off the floor. Swiping at his pants, he glared at the cat.

Montgomery glared back.

Yeah, it was officially war.

"He won't let you buy him off," she said. Humor danced in her voice. "Has there ever been anyone in your life you couldn't charm?"

"No," he admitted. "But I don't think Mo is normal. Why couldn't you get a cute, cuddly kitten?"

"They were boring," she said. "I like complexity. He's definitely an alpha and doesn't like being challenged."

"Sierra, you have to be careful. Don't bring Mo to the shop. He'll threaten the customers and cause issues."

She looked down at her protector, who had settled and was nicely licking his paw, haunches firmly planted on her sock-clad feet. "His name is Montgomery. And I think he'll be great."

Kane groaned. "You're enjoying this, aren't you?"

Sierra grinned. "Yep. Kane Masterson has finally met his match. You can't buy him, charm him, or intimidate him."

"Very funny. Can we go back into the kitchen and finish our conversation? Maybe close Mo—umm, Montgomery—off in his room until we're done?"

She regarded him thoughtfully, then made her decision. "No. I think it's time you went home. Montgomery's still getting situated, and I don't want to force him to spend time with someone he doesn't like."

Kane blinked. "You're throwing me out for a cat?"

Sierra smiled with satisfaction. "Absolutely. There's a reason he doesn't trust you and until that's settled, I'm not ready to dive into any type of relationship. When he's comfortable in your presence, we can discuss our next steps."

Those green-gold eyes widened. "You want Mo to make the rules for us? A stray cat you picked up in a shelter two days ago? An animal that doesn't know me or you or what we shared years ago?"

"Sounds good to me." She scooped Montgomery into her arms and walked to the door. "I appreciate all the gifts, Kane. More than you know."

It was the most she could give at the moment. She prepped for an argument, but he only followed her out, pausing on the threshold. His gaze took in the cat firmly held against her chest, then rose to her face. His voice was a husky murmur of sound, wrapping around her like a seductive cloud of darkness. "I hope you feel safe tonight, sweetheart. Tucked in your bed with your feline guardian. But if you believe I'd back down from any challenge to keep you from being mine, you don't know me. You bought a little more time. Time means nothing after years of waiting, so I'll do what you need. Prove myself. Make that damn cat love me. Wait on the sidelines until you decide the reward is bigger than the risk to give me a chance."

A smile touched his lips and then he turned, disappearing into the shadows.

"Good night, Montgomery."

His sentence drifted in the humid air, as much a warning as an endearment.

Sierra shivered and stepped inside, shutting the door behind her.

Damn that man.

Chapter Thirteen

He'd been cockblocked by a cat.

Kane drove home, still off-kilter from the way the evening ended. He'd been ready to take Sierra's offer and rid her doubts in the bedroom. Words could get twisted and tangled in context and intention. But his body couldn't lie—the way he craved to hold her, to not only bring shattering pleasure but a safety he knew Sierra desperately needed. She pretended to be open to love, but Kane clearly saw her skills of protecting herself. The easy way she placed distance between any interaction or experience that could hurt.

Loss did that to a person. First her parents, then her husband. Each event forced her to dig deep and restart, stronger than before. The problem was with each rebuild, she'd lost a piece of her trust and confidence.

He knew her heart because his was the same.

They'd just gone different ways to deal with the crap. He'd avoided all romantic relationships, choosing to put his effort into work and chasing security. It was cleaner. Kane had never been left, but betrayal had been a cruel teacher.

It had been easy to fall for Sierra without walls, because she was the first woman he'd ever wanted with his heart and soul. All the ones before her were a blurred line of trophies; beautiful, hungry women who wanted the same thing—money and first-class experiences. The sex was satisfying and easy. He'd never formed any attachments, though many had tried. Kane believed his heart was simply not built for any deep emotions.

Until Sierra. When he was around her, the dirt from his past didn't matter. He felt…clean. Seen. Alive.

Dragging in a breath, he went over his next options. If it wasn't so frustrating, it'd be hilarious. The way Mo sat in front of her, his fuck-you gaze shimmering with male challenge, was something Kane had never experienced. It both pissed him off and gave him mad respect for the cat. He was scarier than a damn German Shepherd protecting his master from a break-in. Lord knows, he seemed almost as big.

He'd rejected both his advances and his bribes, but Kane loved a hard trial. The prize of winning Mo's trust and loyalty held bigger stakes than normal. Because with the cat's approval, he'd prove something to Sierra.

That he wasn't afraid of hard things. That he didn't intend to walk away.

That she meant more to him than anything else.

He didn't blame her for being wary. When she asked if he hurt people, it had wrecked his insides to tell her the truth. Because even though he'd been betrayed and set up for fraud, his actions had still hurt everyone around him.

He'd trusted the wrong person because he'd been greedy for more. He'd ditched his brother in the pursuit of power. He'd betrayed Global Enterprises by refusing to do his job correctly, when he may have been able to catch the truth earlier on. Before his ass got thrown in jail and he was stripped of everything, he'd fought for.

Most of all?

He'd hurt himself.

No, he couldn't lie and pretend he was guiltless. But it also meant showing her the man he was today. And telling her the truth.

About Derek. About his past.

About everything.

He needed to take that chance and put it all out there so she could make her own decision.

He'd never shared those pieces of himself, and it was a risk. If Sierra was disgusted, or refused to accept his choices, it was over before things had even begun.

But if she was going to leap, Kane would need to go first.

The road forward began with truth. Truth about how and when they'd originally met. Truth about their past and their intent for the future. Truth about their feelings and what that night had begun between them.

It had to start somewhere.

Good thing he was ready to take the leap.

But not yet.

He still had work to do with her heart. In the meantime, they had an engagement party to plan. She'd mentioned her top picks for the party and vendors but nothing was booked. He could use this upcoming week to lean in to planning and make appointments. She'd probably be pissed he was trying to lead, then step in.

So, he'd just show up beside her, offering his support and help.

Kane grinned. She hated not being in charge so that would set her off, but her temper was a turn-on and an important insight into how she worked. On what she needed.

On what made her happy.

Kane spent the rest of night doing research for Stealth. The challenge juiced him up, and he was eager to get back into the game and make some big money. He wanted to prove to Sierra that he was a sure bet and could easily provide her everything she could want. She was a strong woman who'd built her own legacy. Since New York, he'd had to start over, and it was important to show his own ability to rise and pivot to meet any challenge.

Therefore, Kane could not fail.

The week passed, and Sierra admitted it was getting harder to pretend Kane was a man to be politely kept on the sidelines.

She stared at him from across the event space where they gathered to fine tune the food and flowers for the engagement party. After going over Kane's spreadsheets, she'd quickly set up appointments with two places that were frontrunners, eager to get a date nailed down and the party quickly planned.

For each meeting, Kane showed up with a broad grin and an enthusiasm that charmed everyone around him. Both owners—females—gushed about how sweet it was he took such an involved part in his best friend's engagement, until Sierra was tempted to wave her hands in the air and remind them she was the one in charge.

He came with lists of helpful suggestions, and asked questions that managed to even impress Sierra. It was annoying as hell to be jockeying for leader position in her own sister's celebration.

They decided on the Currituck Club, which offered a coastal view and was situated on a golf course. It was a generous space with elegance and good food and had been Kane's top choice.

Sierra had to agree, even though she hated the idea a non-local made the pick. When she'd grumpily admitted it, he asked how long it took to move to inner circle status. Then laughed when she advised him to lose his New York accent as the first step.

Now, they were picking out details and here he was again, in the middle of the afternoon where she'd figured he couldn't leave work. As Alicia laid out stations of menus, centerpieces, and décor, Kane chatted with her while Sierra simmered with annoyance. The woman was completely turned toward Kane, basking in his attention and…

Giggling.

With a shudder, Sierra took control. "Alicia? We'd appreciate it if we could take some time to look over these options and chat alone?"

The bird-like woman jolted in her chair as if Sierra had ripped her out of a fantasy. God knows, she probably had, one where Kane asked her out and began a romantic fantasy with a twist of erotic romance thrown in. "Oh! Of course, of course, I'll just be in the back and will check in if you have questions." With a last longing look, she hurried away, her sensible beige heels clicking across the floor.

Silence fell. Sierra crossed her arms in front of her chest, leaned back in the chair, and glared.

He threw his hands up in surrender. "What? I didn't do anything."

Sierra gave a snort. "Don't you ever get tired of sprinkling your fairy dust around to unsuspecting women?"

He blinked. "Honestly? No."

A laugh escaped her lips. "Why am I not surprised? How'd you get the time off to meet me today?"

"I never take a lunch break. Today, I did."

"Lucky me."

That lopsided grin appeared and made her heart beat faster. "Look at how much progress we made in just a week? We make a great team."

Sierra didn't want to admit it, but he'd definitely brought his A-game. She figured he'd be pushy and treat their appointments like running a business meeting. Instead, Kane let her make most of the decisions without complaint. When he disagreed, he had a way of offering up his own suggestion without arrogance, allowing her to bend without feeling she lost something.

No wonder he was a master negotiator. When you left the table, you felt as if everyone won.

"You're staring with that mulish expression. Which means, you're trying to analyze me again."

Surprise bubbled up. She shifted in her seat, suddenly aware of his intense interest. She'd never had a man study every reaction, trying to dig into her thoughts. Not even her ex had tried that hard. "Nope. Just trying to focus on what will make Aspen happy. I'm thinking the seafood package with the dessert buffet. She loves her sweets."

He followed her lead, allowing her the space. "Great choice. But do you think the dessert buffet is overkill if we get them a cake?"

Damn, he was right. She wanted a kick-ass cake and it may get lost with the other desserts. "Yeah, you're right," she said a tad grumpily.

"You could add some of those Italian pastries in case someone doesn't like cake?"

"Good idea." She circled it on the sheet and moved on. "They offer all this other décor stuff but I want simple elegance. Fresh flowers in creams, white, and a touch of bright blue will soften things up. No bows or hearts. They have a butterfly garden option?"

Kane shuddered. "Brick would hate that. Too cheesy."

"Agree. These centerpieces are nice but nothing calls to me. It's all so standard."

Kane fished out his phone. "I found this item on Etsy and forgot to send it to you. What do you think of these?"

Sierra stared. "Etsy?"

Were his cheeks getting red or was it just her imagination? "I heard it was a good place to find creative solutions to parties."

Her phone dinged. She looked up the link and studied the delicate fish bowls in blue sea glass. "These are beautiful. We could fill them with water and floating candles."

He nodded. "Sounds good. Want me to order them?"

"We need the final guest list, don't we?"

He shrugged. "It may be backordered so I'll order extra and people can bring them home."

Sierra took in a deep breath. "Okay. Umm, remember when you mentioned those sea turtle—"

"Soaps? Yep. Want me to get them, too?"

She couldn't begrudge him the win. "Yes, please. I thought that was a great idea."

Sierra prepared herself for the smug satisfaction she deserved but instead, the man practically beamed with happiness. "Thanks. I think Brick will really like it, too."

And that's when it hit her. He may have wanted to spend time with her, but Kane was actually enjoying being involved in each step. Curiosity stirred. "Did you ever plan events for your company?" she asked.

Those tapered fingers danced across the phone. The scent of clove and spice hit her nostrils and she fought the urge to take a bigger breath; to gather his distinctive fragrance into her lungs so she'd have it later. Now, she was the one blushing from the intimate thought.

"No, we had people on staff for that. I guess I never got to throw a party for anyone before. It's more fun than I thought."

Her heart stopped, then beat faster. She kept her tone neutral. "Hmm, no birthday or holiday parties for friends or family?"

"Nope."

He didn't seem concerned from the lack of that experience. "What about you? Do you like having parties thrown for you or no?"

"Never had those either." He looked up and flashed his famous grin. "I saw the way Aspen ripped open your gift. She seems to love surprises."

Sierra tucked away the facts he'd shared to analyze later. "Oh, yeah, she's like a kid when it comes to that stuff."

"But not you."

She tilted her head. He said it like a statement, not a question. "I'm not big on them, no. What gave it away?"

A shrug lifted his shoulders. "You were surprised too many times before." His gaze lifted to drill into hers. "And most of them weren't good. Makes sense you'd try to avoid those experiences again."

Her defenses shattered. His words cut right through bullshit and told her he saw all the broken pieces. And that he didn't care. Hell, he was there for all of it, and suddenly, Sierra needed to give him back something.

"I'm going to tell Aspen tonight. About us."

Kane stilled. The connection between them tightened, burned, sparked. His direct stare ripped away the barriers and dove deep. They both knew it was a turning point and there would be no going back. His voice was a rough mix of velvet and gravel. "You sure?"

No. But she nodded. "Yeah. It's time."

His muscles relaxed. Emotion flickered over his carved features, but quickly smoothed out. "Good. I'll tell Brick. I'd say we could talk to them together but I know you'd rather do it in private with Aspen."

Sierra winced. "I'll need some time to explain why I've kept this from her. Better to have our privacy. Sisters can be complicated."

"I can imagine."

She cleared her throat, not sure what to do with this sudden intimate moment. "Well, I think we're set and can call Alicia back in."

"Sierra?" She cocked her head. "Thank you."

There was no need to pretend. They both knew she'd made the first step admitting they were moving toward something together. If he'd been arrogant or pushy, it would've been easy to pull back or run. Instead, his green eyes glittered and her hand trembled and everything inside of her softened into surrender.

"How are we doing?" Alicia chirped, breaking the sacred moment.

Kane didn't break eye contact, gripping her gaze like a tight hold, taking charge. "We're fine."

"That's great! I'm happy to sit with you and go over all the choices you both—"

They didn't respond. Just kept staring at each other while the sexual tension hummed and sang wildly in the air.

Alicia cleared her throat. "I'm just going to give you a bit more time!"

The woman hurried out. A smile touched Sierra's lips. "I think we scared her."

"Don't care." He deepened his voice and his spell. "Just care about tasting you again. Everywhere."

She tried to speak, but nothing came out. Her skin flushed and every part of her grew sensitive and achy. She wanted this man just as badly as that initial night, in the rain, in the dark. She wanted his tongue and his cock and his dirty mouth. And she wanted him in the bright morning light, with no more shadows or secrets.

"But after tonight, there's one more barrier."

She frowned. "What?"

"Mo. Did you bring him to Flirt?"

"Yes. Brought him yesterday for an hour to test things out. He liked it. Brooklyn and Prim love him."

"Not surprised. He definitely has an affinity toward females. He'll be a tough one to crack."

Humor danced and played with sweet erotic sensation. "Think you can?" she teased.

"Yes, my sweet flirt. Because once I do, I'll be buried deep inside you, swallowing your screams and your pleasure. That's worth walking through damn fire."

She was already on fire, her flesh heated and stretched too tight, her core wet and needy. He took a breath, as if he scented her, and a primal greed flickered over his face, reminding her of a fierce, predatory, protective...

Wolf.

A sliver of panic set in. Things were moving fast, and she needed space. Sierra jumped from the seat and hitched her purse on her arm. "I have to go."

He blinked. "Do you want me to—"

"Tell Alicia I'll call her with payment and details to get it booked. I have to go," she said again.

Damned if the man didn't turn a bit arrogant. His eyes flashed with a knowledge that showed he knew exactly why she was running, but he'd allow her escape.

This time.

Without hesitation, she headed out, not afraid to admit this was one time pride had to take a back seat to her innate instinct to flee.

Chapter Fourteen

"The right shoes can make everything different."
– Jimmy Choo

"Why am I getting a weird feeling you're setting me up?" Aspen asked, frowning over her glass. They'd just finished a meal of shrimp and grits that Sierra was known for. She'd sprung for a good bottle of white, which was perfectly chilled, dry, and fruity. The dessert was simple but satisfying—chocolate chip cookies.

Sierra had always enjoyed cooking for her sister, even as she teased about Aspen's lack of talent in the kitchen. After their parents passed, it was a way Sierra made sure they bonded. A good meal was a purpose to chat and share; to linger and spend time with one another. It became an important part of their relationship and a way to continue taking care of her sister.

"Why? Because I want to spoil you a bit and update you on engagement plans?"

Aspen took a sip of wine and narrowed her gaze. "No, because you haven't insulted me once tonight which means you're saving it up for a confession."

Crap. Nothing was worse than a sibling who knew all your secrets. Sierra pushed over a cookie and gave a dazzling smile. "You're paranoid. Try the cookie."

Aspen regarded the tray like it was laced with poison. "Hell, no. I'm not about to let you hypnotize me with your sugary treats. I want to be sober for this."

"These aren't pot cookies, Aspen. I'll leave that move to Marco."

Aspen laughed. "That was a trippy book signing, right? Funny, Marco hasn't been doing much weed anymore. I think he's still trying to woo Mal."

Her jaw unhinged. "What! That's ridiculous—there's a ten-year age difference! Maleficent would never date Marco."

"Why not? Age gap is the hottest thing in the romance genre right now, and Marco is more charming than you give him credit for."

"Now my mind is officially blown." Montgomery strolled in to check on leftovers and circled Aspen's feet. "No, baby, you ate already. I'll give you a treat later."

Aspen knelt and gave the cat some love. He allowed her to stroke and pet him, crooning how handsome he was, and when his ego was full, he flicked his tail and prowled out. "He's the sweetest thing. It's as if he knows you saved him, and he'll do anything for you and the people you love."

"Right? He did well in Flirt so I'm bringing him in a few more times to test things. Some of the customers jumped at first, but he didn't hiss once! If he becomes a regular, I'll post a sign so people know to expect him around."

"Love it. Did Kane end up dropping off those gifts he bought? It was so cute—he seemed excited for you."

She dropped her gaze. "Umm, yeah. I think I'll have one of these cookies." She took a few bites and decided to dive right in since Kane was mentioned. Why drag out her misery to the end of the night? Better to get it over with. "You were right about me having something important to tell you."

"Finally. Tell me."

"I slept with Kane."

The ear-splitting shriek made her almost fall off the chair, but she should've been prepared. A combination of shock, temper, and marvel flickered over her sister's face. Sierra glanced over at Montgomery to make sure he didn't get upset, but he'd already disappeared into the sun room. She braced herself for the next outburst.

"Are you fucking kidding me? Oh, my God, I should've known you two were hiding sexual tension behind hate. I should retire as a writer for not recognizing what was right in front of me the whole time. When did this happen? This week? A month ago? Are you having a secret affair? Was it good? Forget that—I imagine it's the best sex you ever had in your life. Why didn't you tell me?"

Sierra bit her lip and spoke carefully. "Well, do you remember when I visited you in New York right after I got divorced?"

Aspen scrunched up her face. "What does that have anything to do with this?"

"Humor me. Do you remember? You had that book event and left me alone one night and suggested a few bars for me to go and have a drink?"

"Umm, yeah. I guess?"

"I met Kane at the bar, and we had a one-night stand."

The second round of screaming commenced. This time, Sierra expected it and covered her ears until the noise died down. "Are you fucking kidding me right now? You met Kane before and never told me?"

Sierra sighed. "Yeah. I thought it was just a one-night stand and decided to keep it a secret. We never even exchanged names. I was such a wreck after the divorce, and we connected, and one thing led to another. I ran away in the morning and never thought we'd see each other again. Until you introduced me to him here."

Aspen's brown eyes were so wide that they were about to pop out of her head. "This is too trippy. Wait—I don't understand. Why didn't you just tell the truth when you met each other? You raced out of the room with a headache! And Kane left right after and seemed like a mess! And I can't seem to stop yelling in exclamation points!"

Sierra couldn't help it. She laughed and then began to tear up after realizing how hard it was to keep a big piece of her life from her sister. How it almost didn't seem real because Aspen didn't know. "I panicked. I never thought I'd see him again, and I wanted to run away and not deal with it. Later on, the idea of sharing something so personal that I'd tucked away and tried to forget was overwhelming."

Aspen shook her head hard as if to clear it. Then stared at her for a long while. "You pretended not to know each other for *months*? This isn't like you, Sierra. You're the most direct, let's-deal-with-this-shit-now type of person I know. Which means..."

Sierra winced. She sensed what was coming.

"Which means you have real feelings for Kane! You never got over him. And you don't know how to handle it!"

The truth more than hurt. It irritated the crap out of her. "Maybe," she said grudgingly.

"Not maybe. Definitely. How does he feel about you?"

She squirmed in her seat. "He wants to give us a chance."

Aspen blinked. "Why don't you look thrilled by that? A guy you fell for blasts back into your life and wants a second chance to see what you could be to each other, and you look like you lost your best friend?"

"I don't know! When we first met, I realized we were two different people. He was obsessed with money and power, and I needed to rebuild my life. We lived in separate states. There was no way it could work. Am I supposed to just drop everything and open my life to a possible chance with a man who was in jail and may not have changed? A chance to get annihilated and hurt for no reason? A chance to make things even worse with all of us if it blows up and will be awkward and awful forever and ever when we're all together?"

Aspen smiled. "Yes. Exactly that."

Sierra jumped from the chair and took a few steps back, as if her sister was about to pounce on her. "Why? That makes no sense!"

"Because love doesn't make sense, babe. It's a prickly, painful, agonizing mess. But if it works the way it's supposed to, love is the best damn thing in the world. And you know this. Which makes me want to ask another question."

Sarcasm dripped from her voice. "What, oh, wise one?"

"What's really holding you back?"

But Sierra wasn't ready to face her sister's question. Or answer it. Instead, she shoved another cookie in her mouth to stop any words from leaking out. Aspen watched with those wise owl eyes she'd seemed to have inherited after she went through her own journey with Brick. Great. Now, Sierra would always be fighting to prove she still knew more as the oldest. "I don't want to talk about it," she mumbled in between chews. "It's not love, and you're trying to drag me into one of your books. I refuse to become a character to make you more money."

Aspen grinned. "Okay, I'll let you off the hook for now. But this is a lot to process. I don't have to keep this a secret, right? I'm assuming I can tell Brick?"

"Kane's telling him tonight."

"Good. Are you both going to begin dating? Or at least pretending not to hate each other any longer?"

Sierra blew out a breath. "I guess? He wants to date and move forward to see what happens. If we do, I need you to back me up when the gossip hits town. It'll be a lot for me to handle."

"Got it. I'm pretty much an expert at being the center of gossip around here after dating Brick. As for the jail thing, it's a pretty simple solution. Ask him the hard questions. Be open. Don't bullshit yourself anymore because you're scared."

Sierra rolled her eyes. "Stop trying to be the wise mentor in this scene, okay? I just want my sister."

"Fine."

"Aspen?"

"Yeah?"

"Do you forgive me for not telling you?" Sierra meant it to come out jokingly, but it didn't. It was as if telling the truth opened up another piece inside of her that needed space and breath. Like it was the next step on a journey of risk. Because once Aspen knew anything, it became real.

Aspen seemed to ponder the question for so long, sweat began to prickle her skin. "I think I need some time to sit with it. I'm really hurt. You broke our trust."

The gasp escaped her mouth the same moment Aspen burst into hysterical giggles.

"I'm fucking with you! Of course, I forgive you. You're allowed to screw up, too, you know."

"You suck!"

Aspen got up and gave her a hug. Sierra leaned into the comforting warmth, breathing in the vanilla citrus fragrance of her shampoo, the strength in her arms wrapped tight, the feeling of being with the one person who knew all of you and loved you completely. She blinked back the sting of tears.

When they pulled away, Aspen grabbed her wine and settled back in. "Now, let's get to the good stuff. Tell me everything. A blow-by-blow account of your sexual escapade that night, you big slut."

Sierra bit her lip. Repoured her wine. And leaned forward. "Fine. He did this thing where—"

Kane sat on the couch and faced Brick. Dug was snuggled in his lap, snoring loudly, drool pooling on his nice pants. He thought about moving him but the rat monster creature seemed too deeply happy, so Kane left him alone.

"So, I gotta tell you something."

"Yeah? What's up?" Brick had one eye on the baseball game. They'd shared a pizza, had a beer, and spent the last hour bullshitting. Even though he considered Brick not only his best friend but family, it was uncomfortable sharing secrets. He'd grown up used to not confiding in anyone, with business and his personal life, so opening up was difficult. He hadn't even told Brick the real story about Derek being in rehab. But he had to start somewhere, and he might as well start tonight.

"I slept with Sierra."

Brick's head shot around. Shock crossed his face but he held his tongue. Seemed to think about it. "No shit? When?"

Kane dragged in a breath. "Four years ago. We met at a bar in New York. She was visiting Aspen. We never exchanged names and she disappeared in the morning. I didn't see her again until we met here, and you introduced us."

He waited. He knew it took Brick some time to process. "Wait—you knew each other but pretended to be strangers for this long? Why the hell did you do that?"

"She panicked and wanted to keep it a secret. I let her. But now things have changed."

Brick scratched his head. "How?"

Kane dove in. "I have feelings for Sierra. Have since that first night, but she ran and there was no chance. Now, I want us to date and see if we can have a relationship."

"Did Aspen know all this?" Brick asked, frowning.

"No. Neither of us told anyone. But Sierra is telling Aspen tonight, and I wanted to do the same. I know this complicates things. Not sure how Aspen is going to feel about it."

His friend gave a quick grin. "Aspen is a hopeless romantic so she'll be wishing for the best. How bad you got it? You want a serious shot?"

"I do. I never felt like this before. Beyond the crazy chemistry, I'm pulled toward her all the time, and she fascinates me. Half the time it's as if I got clubbed. Some of it's not pretty."

Now, Brick laughed. "Sounds about right. No wonder you haven't been dating anyone. The rumors are running around that you're hiding a secret relationship. They'll have a field day when you come out in public. Both of you ready for that?"

His jaw tightened. "I'm ready. I'll protect her if she gets any heat."

"Not worried about Sierra. More worried about you."

His brow shot up in astonishment. "Me? Why? I can handle anything."

"In business, sure. But—" Brick trailed off, a worried glint in his blue eyes.

"Just tell me."

Kane waited, knowing he'd be getting some hard truths. "You're like a castle with a fucking moat around it, man. You know how long we've known each other, and you still barely tell me anything about your past, or the jail thing, or even these feelings for Sierra? I'm not asking to hang every weekend and braid each other's hair, but maybe you let some people in? Me, Aspen, Sierra. We care about you, no matter what ends up happening."

It was the most heartfelt speech his friend had ever given him. The hard armor inside his chest softened, and Kane wondered if maybe it was time to make some changes. Especially if he wanted a relationship with Sierra. She deserved more of him.

So did Brick.

"I'm sorry. I'll do better."

Brick nodded. "Good."

They sat in silence for a while. "Sure you don't want to try that braiding thing, though? Aspen does love your thick, sexy hair."

"Fuck you."

They both laughed. Kane pet Dug and breathed easier. "You can ask me any question you want. Other than you and Derek, anyone I trusted made me regret it. I'm sure you're wondering about the backstory."

Brick scratched his head and looked intrigued. "Hmm, tempting. Aspen talks a lot about backstory being the key to a good character. There's one thing I always wondered about."

"Shoot."

"You ended up at my house broke, except for those designer clothes you were carrying. But dude, you closed million dollar deals for a while. Where did the rest of the money go?"

Kane winced. It was a damn good question. "My mentor, John, convinced me to put every dime into a long-term, high-risk annuity. Said I'd be making big money for years, and if this paid off, I could pretty much be a billionaire."

Brick shook his head. "Those things rarely pay off and they're locked tight for any emergencies. What an asshole."

"I was the asshole for listening. When everything blew up, I had empty accounts. I think that's exactly what he was planning so I didn't have anywhere to go afterward."

"I'm sorry, man."

His words touched deep. "Thanks. Anything else you want to know?"

A few moments of silence ticked by. Kane waited to get ready to spill his guts since he expected Brick had a ton of questions.

"Nah. Want another beer?"

"Yeah. That'd be cool."

Brick got up and went to the kitchen. Kane relaxed and continued petting Dug. Friendship was pretty bad ass. It meant not having to explain every action because there was trust.

Since he got to OBX, he'd been hit with all sorts of challenges, but he had more hope for the future than he had in a long, long time.

Chapter Fifteen

Kane walked into the meeting prepared with a hot list of properties ready to be flipped.

It had been a challenge. This wasn't a big city where deals lurked around every busy corner. No, with the beach as the main draw, prime real estate was gathered close to the water or in the heart of shopping towns lining Main Street. Sometimes, it was a game to dig deep enough to find the real owners to buy from. He'd seen a ton of shade in NYC but hadn't really found too many red flags in OBX.

Kane was focused on moving fast and keeping things clean. His past experiences had pushed him into grayer areas to walk the legal lines, and though he did it for the goal, the twist in his gut confirmed he wanted a clean slate. Looking back with a safe amount of distance, he clearly saw how greed played into too many deals. Hell, his mentor had been his greatest teacher. Each lesson was primed to show Kane the end justified the means, and if you weren't first, you were last. Last meant ruin. Last equaled failure. He'd learned to dull his emotions and sharpen his instincts for winning.

Until he landed in jail. Lost everything. And finally realized the truth about the fake world he'd once believed in.

But this time was different. Kane learned he couldn't trust anyone but himself, and doing this deal with Stealth was his way to get back in the game. This time, on his terms.

He studied the two men at the conference table with an expert ease. One was in power, and the other was here to make Kane feel more valued. Todd Fletcher—CEO of Stealth—was well-known in the South and was slowly making a name for his company as a major player. He dressed in designer lapels but his conservative black suit wasn't custom tailored, and fit him poorly. The shoes were a knock-off of a famous Italian designer, and he smiled a bit too broadly at Kane, making him seem nervous. He peered from behind thick-framed glasses that gave off a cover model vibe rather than power.

The guy to his right, Jack, knew his place. The simple white shirt and red tie were classic. His features held no strong emotion, and his brown eyes stared back with a simple clarity that told Kane he probably knew more about the nuts and bolts of Stealth than Todd. Kane had been trained early on to court the approval of the quietest guy in the room, not the loudest.

Jack would be in Todd's ear and Kane needed to make a quick, solid impression.

"I was happy you could meet with us," Todd said. "We're looking to grow our team and your past experiences in New York are impressive. Unless you intend to return home?"

Kane smiled, easing back into his chair. He shot his cuffs, and his last good set of links caught the light. Once, he'd had a drool-worthy collection but it had all been left behind. "New York served its purpose, and I was honored to get my experience with Global. But it was time for a change. A close friend of mine lives in Corolla, and after a much-needed vacation, I decided to make the move permanent."

Todd boomed out a laugh. "Nice to know we can still run with the big dogs. We're looking forward to seeing what you came up with. I'm sure it was a challenge not knowing the area."

"I thrive on challenge. And you were smart enough to hire me for my outside opinion. A fresh perspective is needed with these beach towns, especially when rents are increasing and available property is shrinking."

Kane felt Jack's gaze on him, but the man remained silent, absorbing the conversation. "Exactly," Todd said, jabbing his index finger in the air. "Jack and I need someone fresh to round out the team—one with less connections to the community. There can be a certain sense of…upheaval we hope to avoid with a new face."

A strange unease settled over him as he felt the energy shift. Was this a test? Sometimes, companies threw out bait projects to see how things were handled before giving out the real prize. Not that he was worried. He'd been playing these games for years, and he never minded sharpening his claws. "Understood. I think you'll appreciate these properties to house an exclusive resort."

Kane spent the next hour sifting through his top choices, going into a detailed prospectus for each. He leaned into his innate confidence and used his past experience to show he'd handle whatever came at him.

They pulled his proposals apart with hard questions Kane appreciated. And when all was said, he waited with patience until they spoke first.

Jack and Todd shared a knowing glance. Slowly, Jack nodded.

A pleased smile curved Todd's lip. "Kane, thanks for the presentation. You hit all the marks we were hoping, and we'd love to hire you for this deal."

His blood sung with adrenaline. He'd figured they'd play harder and let him sweat so they'd have better negotiation power. But this looked like a straight win. "I appreciate your confidence," he said with a tip of his chin. "Which property do you want me to move on?"

"None of them," Jack said.

He cocked his head, a question in his gaze.

Todd cleared his throat. "We had a property that came up for our consideration but it's a bit delicate. It houses some local businesses which can become a bit of a challenge, so we wanted to see how you'd handle this type of deal. And you impressed us, Kane. You're the one we want."

"But not for these properties I worked on? You need me to close on something else?"

Jack slid over a stack of folders. "Correct. I'll send you all the stats, but that's some old paperwork you may find useful. The new landlord has gotten himself into some trouble, and we can buy out the lease, then flip the building. He just needs some convincing. The specs and price are better than the others."

Kane nodded, still finding it strange they didn't just be straight with him. But who cared if he got the job? He was a master at negotiation and maneuvering and would get it done. "Then I'll handle it."

Satisfaction carved out Todd's face. Jack kept his expression neutral, but his gaze probed as if checking to see if Kane was the real thing or a bullshit artist. "Reach out with any questions. We're counting on you."

Kane grinned. "I won't let you down. But I haven't seen your offer yet. I've been happy where I am."

Todd practically rubbed his hands together in glee, giving too much away. "Not getting bored over there closing medical office deals? You could do that in your sleep."

"I came to OBX so I'd have more time in my schedule. I don't want to give it up for nothing."

Jack remained mute, but Todd laughed. "Of course. I think you'll be very happy with our generous offer." He outlined the terms of the contract, plus bonuses for each step in the deal. He didn't even have to wait until closing to get a nice chunk of money.

All he had to do was close this one deal, and he'd be set.

"HR will send everything for you to look at. In the meantime, go over the Sunrise property and let us know ASAP. We need to move quickly."

They shook hands, did the goodbye bullshit, and Kane left.

Holy shit. He'd gotten it.

Satisfaction coursed through him, along with the familiar thrill.

He was back.

Kane wanted to dive in and get started, but he had something more important to do.

He drove to Flirt and parked in the lot. Sierra's car was there. Admiring the bold, yet inviting window displays, he almost laughed when he realized he was more excited to see her than go back to the office and work. No woman had ever been able to compete with the lure of a new deal.

Until now.

Kane got out and entered. The bell tinkled in welcome. Some delicious scent warmed the air, making him immediately relax. He stood in the entrance and scanned the space, taking in the store she'd named from his memory and that he'd never visited before.

God, it was like the essence of the woman permeated every inch of Flirt, and he wanted to sink himself into the experience. Loose groups of females roamed around, chattering and laughing as they fingered beautiful fabrics he immediately wanted to touch. Displays of jewelry scattered throughout with signs of local female designers proudly displayed. Miniature crystal chandeliers hung from the ceiling and the palette reminded him of her home, creams and butter and bright whites blending with sea-blue, yellows, and lavender. A line for the fitting rooms snaked toward the back, smartly edged with impulse buys like scarves, trinkets, and candles.

A young girl with a nose piercing appeared with a dazzling smile. "Welcome to Flirt! I'm Prim, let me know if I can help you in any way!"

"Thanks. Can you let me know what that scent is?"

Her face lit up. "Oh, that's our best-selling candle, Beach Love. Let me show it to you." She led him to a beautiful table of various candles and picked up one in beveled glass with jeweled tone shells embedded in the top. "Not only will the scent relax you, but it's a piece of art for your room. Tangerine, black pepper, and oakwood give it that scent. Only $19.99 but if you buy two, you get one free." Prim handed him the candle and eased away. "I'll let you browse but I'm here for anything you need."

Kane gave her credit for a great sales pitch. People hated sales teams to hover or spy, but they were also pissed off if no one was around to help. Prim immediately began hanging clothes, but he sensed she'd be available the moment he sought out her gaze.

Sierra did well with her training.

Kane spent some time as a shopper and threw himself into the experience of Flirt. He picked up items, ran his hands over fabrics, and eavesdropped on conversations that held the joy and mystery of females bonding over shopping. Brooklyn was manning the counter and then the familiar husky tone of Sierra's voice cut through the air.

He turned his head and once again, experienced the jolt of recognition he'd had that very first night they met.

She wore a playful, white eyelet dress with a bouncy hem that showed off her gorgeous bare legs. Hair tied up in a fashionable ponytail, her multiple silver link chains roped around her neck and ankles gave off a fun vibe, and showed off her perfect cleavage. His gaze dropped and a smile automatically curved his lips.

White flats covered in elaborate lace with a rounded toe. Simple and flirty. She was feeling good today after telling her sister the truth.

Every part of him clenched with the need to touch her. He wanted to be the one allowed to cross the store and take her into his arms. He wanted to claim her with his mouth and hands so the world knew she belonged to him. It was a primal instinct that made him clench his fingers and not move until he was under control.

It had been two days since he'd seen her last. They'd spoken after their dual conversations with Aspen and Brick but he'd given her some space to settle. The engagement party was officially booked and sending out invitations was the next step. Sierra had all the addresses and said she could just print out labels, so Kane had been officially dismissed.

Good thing he had a few last-minute proposals to offer.

It was time to take the next step together.

But first, he wanted to make himself comfortable in her second home. So, he roamed incognito waiting until Sierra recognized him.

Unfortunately, Mo came to him first.

Kane reached out to examine a tapestry bag in an interesting patchwork design when a blur of fur jumped out. A blistered curse escaped as he staggered back, heart beating from the scare. In seconds, the cat managed to squeeze himself in between the bags and take center stage, unfurling his massive length to full capacity.

Golden eyes squinted with menace. His fur prickled.

Damned if Kane didn't feel a tiny bit intimidated. "Umm, hi, Mo. Remember me? I brought the great treats."

His whiskers twitched and that grumpy mouth parted to show teeth.

"Montgomery!" Pru came to his rescue, stepping in between them with concern. "What are you doing? We need to be nice to the customers."

Immediately, the cat softened, ignoring Kane and sitting down like a perfect, docile cat.

"That's a good boy. I'm sorry, Montgomery is new to Flirt but he's extremely friendly. Aren't you, sweetheart?"

Damned if that menace didn't let out a purr and look completely harmless.

Pru smiled. "There we go. I'm sure you made a move that took him by surprise."

Kane shook his head. Sure. Guess it was his fault he was about to be eaten by Cujo Cat. Then he noticed Mo was now sporting a fancy collar with the store's logo hanging from a chain. This cat moved fast. If Kane didn't gain favor, he'd be out on the street instead of in bed with Sierra.

"I must've," Kane said smoothly. "He looks like an amazing cat."

"Pru, is Montgomery causing a prob—"

Sierra trailed off as she spotted him. A myriad of emotions flickered across her face but Kane lasered in on the most important.

Pleasure. There had definitely been a glint of it in her expressive hazel eyes, and that mattered more than the others. Or the current frown tugging at her brow as she glanced back and forth between him and Mo. "Kane, what are you doing here?"

"Buying candles," Pru cut in with a big grin. "It's so nice to meet you. I've been wanting to introduce myself for a long time."

He cocked his head. "Nice to meet you, Pru. I'm surprised you've even heard my name. Unless Sierra has been talking about me?"

Sierra crossed her arms in front of her chest and shook her head. "No. It's because you belong on the cover of *Southern Hotness* magazine. You're hard to miss around here."

He laughed long and loud, drawing a curious crowd who were currently staring.

Kane decided it was the perfect time to make his stand.

"Thanks, sweetheart. I always appreciate a compliment coming from you."

And then he leaned over and kissed her.

Take that, Mo.

Chapter Sixteen

"If your hair is done properly and you're wearing good shoes, you can get away with anything."
– Iris Apfel

Sierra was in shock to find Kane Masterson in her store.

It was the one place he'd never tried to invade. Months of silence and pretense had thrown a wall between them, and as if he recognized Flirt was as personal as her home, he hadn't overstepped boundaries.

But with one bold move, he claimed not only her space, but her.

His mouth took hers in a firm, possessive kiss that gave no doubt they were involved. Caught off guard, Sierra was about to push him away, but the moment those warm, talented lips met hers, she was a goner.

She kissed him back, and when he pulled away, those green eyes were dancing with satisfaction. And something else. Something that stopped her from lashing out at the chauvinistic male move. Something that lit up her insides and made her giddy.

"Thought it was time I visited your sanctum," he said in that sexy, rumbly voice. "How's your day going?"

She couldn't help shaking her head. "Well, after that performance, it's going to get a lot busier. We have an audience."

Kane didn't seem to notice the greedy stares and delighted smiles from every woman in the shop. Numerous gazes sharpened, and low murmurs drifted in the air. He grinned and whispered in her ear. "Should we give them another round?"

"No. Pru and Brooklyn will already torture me enough. Plus,

Montgomery still doesn't like you."

"I'm working on Mo. I thought it was time we make it official."

Her brow lifted. "Are you always this pushy?"

His face fell. "Yes. When I want this badly, I'll do anything to get it."

"I'm not an IT."

Damned, if he didn't reach out and gently cup her cheek, staring at her like she was the most precious thing in the world. "Exactly. You're the only woman I've ever wanted like this. The stakes are even higher."

Her cheeks flushed. More tittering. They were really putting on a show. As the owner, she should put a stop this whole spectacle.

So, why was it impossible to move from his orbit?

Sierra stared at his perfect masculinity. He exuded an innate confidence and sensuality that hummed and followed him everywhere, kind of like Pigpen and the cloud of dust. Full lips hugged by scruff. Emerald eyes with gold framing his pupils gave his gaze an extra kick to her heart. Thick russet hair tamed back from his face. He must've come from a meeting because his navy-blue suit was impeccable, emphasizing his lean muscled length and broad shoulders. Even worse?

He smelled so good—that intoxicating mix of clove and spice that made her woozy. Kane Masterson was literally a weapon to all females and she was not immune.

Sierra cleared her throat. "Well, this was a fun interruption. I have to get to work."

"I want to take you on a date. Will you go to dinner with me this Friday night?"

She hesitated. Not because she didn't want to.

Because she did. She wanted to claim this man for hers in front of everyone, and that need was dangerous. Sierra wasn't a possessive person, but the idea of telling the world he was taken gave her a sharp stab of sheer satisfaction. He waited for her answer, and she knew he was forcing her to stop denying him, in front of everyone, in the store she'd built and named after him.

"Yes!" Pru shouted, breaking the crackling silence. "Yes, she will go out with you!"

Brooklyn screamed from the counter. "Hell, yes! Her answer is yes!"

And then the rest of the store began adding their own approvals, until there was a crescendo like a wave rushing through the space. A young voice shouted, "If she doesn't I will, Kane!"

His lips quirked. "We have fans. Can't disappoint them."

Happiness unfurled within and Sierra didn't want to fight it any longer. Didn't want to fight him and these feelings she had that had never settled. "Yes, I'll go out to dinner with you."

A loud whoop echoed from the crowd. She laughed and Kane gave a high five to the crowd. When was the last time she experienced actual giddiness?

He dropped another quick kiss to her lips, winked, and turned on his heel. "Thanks, everyone. I gotta go make some dinner plans."

As applause erupted, Sierra realized this was going to be one long-ass afternoon while she explained herself.

Kane stared at the screen. Dread slithered through him as he read the details surrounding the property he needed to close.

At first, he thought it was a mistake. He assumed he'd gotten the wrong address and it was all a big joke.

Instead, Kane learned the joke was on him.

Because the property Stealth wanted belonged to Flirt.

It took him a while to process the nightmare he'd just scored a starring role in. Flirt was on the lot that the current landlord could no longer afford. Digging deep, Kane discovered it had been hidden for a while, and now neared bankruptcy. Of course, if Stealth stepped in now, this idiot in charge—Benny—would grasp the opportunity and sell. This would keep other hungry vultures from swooping in and competing when it finally went into foreclosure.

The move was cold-blooded but Kane had done it before. A bargain deal could be made if they closed in quickly, and got Benny to believe they were a savior. Which was Kane's job.

But this was bigger than grabbing up a property to increase lease prices for the tenants. Stealth intended to bulldoze the entire site and create their resort. Another thing Benny didn't see—the land behind it was the real profit. He was sitting on a real estate gold mine and no one had figured it out.

Yet.

Kane's mind raced. This was bigger than being outpriced out of her rent. This was a complete demolishment to cater to the unending tourists and their lust for bigger, better experiences.

And he was the one who had to lead the charge.

Kane popped up from his chair and began to pace. His gut twisted as he tried desperately to figure out his next step.

What were the literal odds on this shitshow? This one deal was the gateway to his old life. He'd have a job, money, and be able to rebuild his reputation. There were a million properties out there but no—he was specifically guided to target Sierra's store, the one she'd built from her own sweat and tears. Flirt, the store she'd named in memory of him. Flirt, her pride and joy and the only thing she loved.

The universe had a hard-on for him.

He was used to doing difficult deals. He'd become cold to owners' pleas; owners with big dreams and no funds to buy out the big, bad corporations gobbling up all the mom-and-pop stores.

But this was different than anything else he'd faced.

He'd be deliberately hurting the one woman he wanted. The one woman he believed was his soulmate. The one woman he had to convince he was worthy of.

He was so fucked.

You could walk away...

The voice rose inside him and offered up a solution. Kane knew there was always a choice.

Find a solution.

The same mantra rose up and repeated in his head. There must be a way to figure this out. Because there was no way Sierra could forgive him if he did this. He'd be the enemy. But if he didn't, he could kiss this job and his future career goodbye. Stealth wasn't stupid. They probably knew about his jail time, but were using his experience to their benefit. If he walked and refused, Duncan would fire him, and Stealth could get mean and choose to dredge up his murky past.

Start at the beginning.

Dragging in a breath, he went back to his laptop. He needed a meeting ASAP with Benny to gather more information. He'd also do another analysis of the first three properties to see if he could persuade Stealth in that direction. Maybe if he got the deal of a lifetime, they'd be willing to let Sierra's property go.

In the meantime, he wouldn't say anything to Sierra. They were finally moving in the right direction and had a date. For now, Kane would keep the two worlds separate and find a way out.

He had no other choice.

Sierra glanced around the crowded restaurant and sighed. "We couldn't have started out with a quiet place two towns over?" she asked.

He flashed that trademark, lopsided smile that made her tummy flip. The crooked tooth was key to keeping him from looking too perfect. It was like having a mole on a supermodel's face. It should've balanced out the unfairness, but instead made them even more gorgeous. "Ashamed to be seen with me?" he asked, voice teasing.

Sierra rolled her eyes. "Hardly. But it seems we'll be eating in a fishbowl." The restaurant held some tourists, but there was also a ton of people she easily recognized—from staff to the crowds lounging at the bar. They murmured together and glanced over with a mix of curiosity and delight. There was nothing everyone loved more than an exciting new hookup.

"Good. Maybe your friends will stop trying to match you with blind dates."

"I never tagged you the possessive type," she said, quickly perusing the menu.

He waited until she lifted her gaze to meet his. "I never cared this much before." His stark words made her still. Things were changing between them fast. It was as if Kane decided not only to pursue her, but also smash down barriers.

Sierra had expected some initial games. Some attack and retreat, with flirting and a bit of foreplay. She hadn't counted on being thrown right into the deep end, where Kane seemed unafraid to say how he felt. As if the time apart had spurred the need to move quickly rather than slow down.

Her head spun but she tried to be open to this new chapter. She'd tried to forget him. Tried to ignore him. Tried to pretend their one night was a fantasy that couldn't become real.

She'd failed in every category, and Kane wasn't allowing her the safety of retreat. It was time she gave this a fair chance, even though she was scared of getting hurt.

Sierra decided to be just as honest. "I'm trying not to freak out."

Delight flickered across his face. "Who's afraid of little ol' me?"

She sighed and gave her response. "*I* should be. Thought Brick was the Taylor Swift fan."

"He is. Always blasting that song in the car when I ride with him. Got in my head."

They were interrupted when Katie, a Bad Ass Bitch club member, stopped by their table to take their order. "Oh, my God—you guys look so cute together!" she gushed, grinning widely. "I cannot believe you kept this a secret. Sierra didn't even hint at this during any of our meetings but how can I blame you? Everyone's always talking about how hot Kane is and how they want to bang him. I would've felt awkward, too!"

Kane laughed. "I'm flattered anyone in your group would deem me worthy."

Sierra snorted but Katie gave a dreamy sigh. "You have no idea. Sierra, you're so lucky. I heard you asked her out officially in Flirt, which was adorbs." She lowered her voice. "Just watch out for Maddie. She's feeling a bit rejected since you always chat her up when you get your coffee, so she thought you were interested. The news crushed her a bit."

Kane frowned with concern. "I'm sorry she feels like that. I like to talk to her because she makes me comfortable, like a good friend. Can you explain that if you see her?"

Katie lit up. "I definitely will. You're such a sweetie." She patted him on the shoulder. "What can I get you to eat?"

They both ordered crab cakes, mashed potatoes, and green beans along with a bottle of Cabernet. He shot her an amused look. "I didn't know you talked about me."

She refused to inflate his ego anymore. "I don't. Some of the others do."

"Why do I doubt you'd admit it?" he asked. Katie dropped off the wine, and he took over, pouring the ruby colored liquid into two wineglasses. "Did you tell anyone else we met years ago?"

"No! Just Aspen. No one else needs to know."

He lifted his glass. "A toast. To our official first date."

They clinked glasses. He locked eyes with her as she took a sip. "Were you born with the magical fairy dust to charm women?" she asked curiously. "Or was it something you learned?"

Shadows gathered in his eyes. She was immediately sorry she asked the teasing question. Kane seemed to pick his words with care. "It was only my father and half-brother so I think I was always grateful to be in a woman's orbit. I sought out their presence."

Sierra craved to ask a dozen more questions, but didn't want to push. Her voice gentled. "That makes sense. I'm guessing you're not close to your dad?"

"No." A shutter slammed down. "He wasn't a good man."

Her heart ached. So much emotion simmered behind the short answer. "And your brother?"

The light came back on in his eyes. "We were very close. Kind of us against the world, but some demons got him. He's an alcoholic like my father."

Her hand slid automatically across the table to entwine her fingers with his. "I'm sorry, Kane. That must've been hard on you both. Is he okay?"

"Yes. He got out of rehab, found a job he likes, and is making a new life for himself."

"Good."

He tightened his grip, brushing his thumb across her palm. Shivers raced down her spine. He continued. "I'm not used to talking about myself or my past. The first night we spent together? I felt as if I was already connected to you—like you saw a part of me I'd always hidden. I want more of that. As much as I want to strip you naked, dip my fingers inside, and watch you come all over my fingers, I also want us to be vulnerable to one another. Is that possible?"

Sierra blinked. God, had he just given her a visual that lit her insides on fire? Her nipples tingled. She fought to focus on the latter part of his question. "Umm, I think?"

His lower lip quirked. "You'd like that, huh?" Kane leaned in. His gaze hot. "I promise to do that and more when you're ready. Just say the word."

"Bathroom. Now."

His jaw tightened, and a flare of shock lit his green eyes. Sierra couldn't help the quick splutter of humor that escaped, making him shake his head in frustration. "Are you trying to kill me?" he complained, taking a long sip of wine. "I won't be able to get out of this chair for a while."

Sierra laughed. "I'm sorry—it popped out before I could stop myself. You were due for a little payback."

He gave a slow, smug smile. "That's okay, sweetheart. I have my own ways of payback."

Thank God, Katie came over and dropped their plates on the table, saving her from answering.

They ate and conversation flowed easily. They finalized details for the engagement party which was coming up quickly. Sierra had to admit having Kane as her partner wasn't what she'd thought. It had actually been fun to share ideas and she enjoyed his enthusiasm. The more he seeped into the day-to-day details of her life, the more she realized how much she liked it. And even with the gossip buzzing around them, Sierra was able to relax over the meal and enjoy his company.

"I'm meeting with a fabulous designer in Charleston next week," she said, blotting her mouth with a napkin. "She makes these hand-beaded bags with a special insert for your phone and wallet. The patterns are gorgeous—they're really unique."

"I'm surprised she's not selling them at the shops in Charleston? That's a tourist city."

"She is, but she's looking to expand, and I think Flirt would be perfect. I'd do a custom window display. I can picture the sun sparkling on those beads and catching attention." Sierra tapped her finger against her lip. "But she's looking for a high cut. Not sure it would be profitable enough, so I'm heading out for a face-to-face meeting. I think she's been burnt before. I need to show I'm all in."

"You've really built your dream business," he said slowly. "The night we spent together? You never mentioned that was one of your goals."

"I didn't know it was," she admitted. "I only knew I had to find my own voice and identity. It was as if I was always stepping into a role I wasn't prepared for. A guardian to my sister. A wife to my husband. A community member and friend in a new town I desperately wanted to fit into. Once I began paying attention, I followed the bread crumbs and took a chance."

He scratched his head. Seemed to consider his next words. "Would you ever think of…expanding? Opening up a newer store in a more dynamic location?"

She laughed. "No. I like where Flirt is, and I don't need a second store. I'm happy where I am."

"Right. Makes sense." A frown creased his brow. "You mentioned the lease. Have you heard back on a renewal?"

"Not yet. But my landlord is a bit flaky. I'm sure there will be an increase, which I can handle. I'm going to track Benny down next week."

Kane stiffened. His gaze narrowed with intensity. "And if he refuses to renew the lease for some—strange reason?"

"I can't imagine. It just won't happen. There's no reason to think anything has changed."

He nodded but there was something in his face that concerned her. Like he was worried.

"Kane, what is it? Anything going on I should worry about?"

He relaxed and smiled. "No. Sorry, I got distracted. Want dessert?"

"No, thanks."

"Then let's get to the second half of our date."

Sierra raised a brow. "It's a two-parter, huh?"

"Yep. The public is over. Now it's time for the private."

He paid the bill and escorted her to the car. As they walked out, the stares lasered into her back, but at this point, Sierra was amused by all the attention. She'd never done anything to rivet the town's interest before. Her divorce earned her some gossip, but nothing like dating Kane Masterson, the hottest bachelor in town.

She finally knew how Aspen felt.

Sierra relaxed as he drove, navigating the crowded streets of downtown, and heading out to the beach. The hazy colors of sunset streaked the sky. He parked and turned. "Will you watch the sunset with me, Sierra?"

Pleasure shimmered. It was one of the things she adored; watching the sun sink while she gazed out from her front porch, sitting in her rocking chair, drinking sweet tea. His question was both considerate and romantic, as he stretched his hand out with invitation.

"I'd love to."

They grabbed a blanket from the trunk, kicked off their shoes, and made their way down the curvy path to the boardwalk stairs. A few people lingered on blankets scattered on the sand but there was plenty of empty space. The white powder crunched under her feet and the hot wind tossed her hair. The ocean roared before them, stretched out in a vast expanse that caused both wonder and humbleness. Puffy white clouds floated in a pale-blue sky, slowly morphing and darkening into the familiar colors of fire.

They sat together on the blanket and watched in companionable silence. Kane took her hand, playing with her fingers, chin tilted up as he gazed at the sky. She studied his profile. The ache in her chest grew; the familiar hunger growing more with each day. Not just for his body, but for more of the man he hid from the rest of the world. She was greedy to be the woman he shared his soul with.

"I never appreciated a sunset until I came here," he said. "The buildings block most of the view in the city, and I was too busy to stop and look. When Brick first showed me what I was missing, I couldn't believe it happened every night and I'd never thought to watch."

She nodded. "Things are slower here. There are more reminders of how days pass, which I love." A dreamy smile curved her lips as the blazing ball of orange began slowly sinking. "There's something about the end of a day that inspires me. Sunrise never motivated me the way it does so many others. Too many unknowns ahead out of my control. But this? I can look back on the hours I spent and take account. I can learn to accept what the day brought. It's completely satisfying."

Kane glanced over. His gaze drilled into hers, diving deep with curiosity and fascination. "I never knew that," he murmured. Lifting her hand, he pressed his lips into her palm. "Yet, it makes total sense to me."

She ached to move closer and let him hold her. Lay her head on his chest while he stroked her hair. She missed the simple comfort of companionship with someone you loved; the sensation of being completely full because all the empty spaces were shared. Emotion struck her hard, so she broke her stare and focused on the dying sun.

"What about you? Sunrise or sunset?" she finally asked.

The light faded and shadows danced across the beach. Only a shimmer of fire glowed in the distance, inches away from oblivion for another day.

"Always sunset."

"Why?"

Sierra waited, gripping his hand, as the sun finally disappeared.

"Because it means I survived another day." His face tightened with memory. "It was a big fuck-you to my father and anyone else who doubted I'd make it."

Chills gripped her body. She reached over, touching his rough cheek, and he jumped slightly before pressing her hand against his.

"It was very bad?" she whispered. He nodded. "Then I'm grateful you not only survived but thrived. And you're here with me right now."

Startled by her words, he muttered her name, then pressed his forehead to hers. They sat there in the new darkness, sharing the vulnerable moment as the waves crashed in the background. They didn't move for a very long time. When he finally got to his feet, he took her hand and they walked back to the car.

He drove her home. The car pulsed with awareness and what they both wanted. Sierra didn't know if she was ready. Once Kane was invited into her bed, there would be no more barriers between them. And she was only beginning to build trust, to know the man he'd become in these past four years.

Still, she didn't stop him from escorting her to the porch. The light flickered and the bugs flew around as he faced her. "Thank you for coming out with me tonight."

It should've sounded awkward, but instead she was charmed by his politeness. "I had a great time. Thank you for dinner."

She paused, a bit jittery, and he gave her a smile. "I'm not coming in, Sierra. I want to. Badly. But you're not ready yet."

For just a second, she wanted to rebel and reach for him, forcing him to bend to her rules, not his. Instead, she nodded. "Probably a good idea."

"Good night."

He leaned down to brush his lips across her cheek.

At the same time, she moved, so his mouth slid over hers, the contact electrifying.

Sierra gasped. Stared into glittering emerald eyes. Every inch of her body poised for flight or fight, waiting.

At once, like that first night, their mouths crashed together in a wild primal need for more. She stepped into his embrace and his arms wrapped tight around her, a low moan exploding as his teeth nipped, gaining entrance, then plunged his tongue deep.

His taste and scent swamped her senses, and she gripped at his shoulders, meeting each thrust with her own demands. Her hips arched, and her body wept for more, the ache so deep inside she'd go mad to slake it.

Fisting his hand in her hair, he held her still as he ravaged her mouth, bending her back so she was helpless under the sensual assault. Sierra hooked her leg around him, opening her thighs with invitation for more. Nails biting into hard muscles, she savored every stroke of his tongue and the slight pain in her scalp as her blood heated and the last of her rational thoughts slid away.

"More," she demanded, sinking her nails into the cotton of his shirt. "Don't leave me like this."

"Fuck, sweetheart, you feel so good. I'm going to give you what you need so bad," he said in between long, drugging kisses.

Thank God, she hadn't locked the door. With a quick turn of the knob, they stumbled in a tangle of limbs into the house, kicking it closed behind. She tore at the buttons of his shirt while he backed her up toward the couch, fingers frantic to find naked skin, mouths clinging to one another. His chest finally bared, Sierra ran her hands over his rippling muscles, down his abs, cupping his erection through his pants, tracing the hard ridged lines of his cock.

Kane pressed his mouth to the curve of her neck, biting down as she broke into shivers, wet between her thighs. "Perfect. God, you're burning up for me." He pushed her skirt up as his mouth found one breast. He teased her nipple through the lace of her bra, scraping his teeth over the sensitive nub, playing the edge of light and dark, of pain and pleasure, in all the ways she'd fantasized.

He gripped the edge of her white lace panties and pulled them down, leaving her throbbing and needy. Twisting up, she grabbed at his hair in greedy demand. "Please."

"Are you wet for me?" he growled, sucking hard on her nipple.

"Yes. I need—" she broke off, almost sobbing. Her body was aching and on fire for a release she wanted more than she'd ever wanted anything. His wicked chuckle told her he loved every moment.

"Let's see if you're ready for me, beautiful."

His fingers traced the flesh of her inner thighs, then moved up in one swift motion, parting her lips and sinking in deep. He sucked in a breath as she gripped him tight, pleasure rippling through her limbs as he stroked.

"Oh, fuck, you're dripping for me. Do you know how long I dreamed of having you like this? This sweet pussy on fire for what I can give you?"

The dirty words were making her crazy and desperate. "Damn you, Kane, stop teasing!"

Another low laugh. His thumb rotated over her clit, each teasing brush wringing out another shudder. So. Close. Just. Right. There.

He backed off, fingers deftly playing her like his own private instrument. He watched her face with a mad intensity that got her hotter—jaw clenched, green eyes blazing, every feature concentrated on memorizing her reaction with each slow slide of his fingers.

Finally, ready to explode in frustration, his thumb hesitated over her clit, fingers still inside of her weeping channel. "Sierra."

She blinked, in a daze, staring back at him.

"Say my name. Tell me who's going to make you come. Tell me who makes you feel like this."

She caught something in the demand of his words, dragging her back to that night when she'd insisted on keeping her name a secret. Kane wasn't allowing her to hide any longer, and his voice throbbed with a need that met hers.

The answer spilled from her lips in a heartfelt plea. "You, Kane. Only you. Always you—please make me come."

He took her mouth in a savage kiss as his fingers plunged deep. His thumb pressed, rubbed hard, over and over, and then she was falling apart, piece by piece, caught in one of the most intense orgasms.

Her body shook and he pushed her to ride out every second,

extending her pleasure. "So beautiful," he crooned, studying her face. "I can watch you do that all day and never get tired."

Trembling, she lifted her arms, offering herself up. "I'd happily let you."

He laughed, nuzzling her neck, moving lower. "And now I want to—fuck!"

With a ferocious roar, he fell off her in a tangle of limbs, twisting around with eyes wide in pain. Sierra shot up and took in the scene before her.

Montgomery had jumped on his back and sunk his claws in. Kane managed to shake him off, and the cat jumped lightly to his feet, hissing in warning as he stared back in shock. "Holy crap—he clawed me! Ah, that hurt!"

"Montgomery!" she yelled, flying up from the couch to go over. "Are you okay, baby? Did you get scared Kane was hurting me? Mommy's fine, it's all okay," she soothed, motioning the cat over. He took up the invite and walked into her arms, allowing her to cuddle him.

Kane's jaw dropped. "What about me? That psycho could've caused permanent damage!"

"I'm sorry, he didn't mean it, Kane. He was scared and tried to protect me. Are you okay?"

He shook his head, obviously still in shock from the attack. "I'm not sure. I may need a minute to transition from making you come to getting my back slashed by crazy Mo."

"Montgomery," she corrected. Guilt reared up. Pressing a kiss to the cat's head, she patted him gently and eased to her feet. "Let me look. Your shirt probably protected you."

He blew out an annoyed breath. "Lucky me."

She pressed her lips together and pulled off his shirt, examining his skin. "You have some scratches but they're not deep. Let me disinfect them."

He grunted but allowed her to go into the bathroom and emerge with supplies. She smoothed antibiotic gel over the cuts and carefully bandaged them. "Good as new."

He turned and gave Montgomery the stink eye. "He did it on purpose."

"That's ridiculous. You're mad because he took you by surprise."

"I'm mad because I could be buried deep inside of you right now."

Heat flushed her cheeks. "Maybe it was a sign. We got carried away."

Kane tipped her chin up and studied her face. Then gave a regretful sigh. "Yep, the mood is officially ruined. You're back in your head."

"Kane—"

"It's okay. I understand." He brushed a kiss across her lips but it was casual and an obvious goodbye. "I'll call later."

She nodded. He got dressed and headed to the door. "We're not done, Mo. Not by a longshot."

The cat tilted his head as if considering the words. Then he spun around, twitched his tail in dismissal, and stalked away.

Sierra tamped down on her laugh until Kane was safely gone.

Maybe her cat was smarter than she was. She had a feeling she'd wake up in the morning with a sated body and a regretful mind. Neither of them deserved any regrets when they finally spent the night together.

But Sierra knew it was coming soon. Because she didn't know how long she could fight these feelings for Kane Masterson. They were too intense and growing rapidly every day.

Soon, her time would be up.

Chapter Seventeen

Kane shut his laptop and buried his face in his hands.

Was he Fated to never achieve happiness? Was he cursed or meant to get close but never close enough? It was as if his life was one big deal he couldn't close. Frustration simmered in every cell.

He was trapped.

The past two weeks with Sierra had been a game-changer. They'd been growing closer, regularly sharing meals or going on simple dates where they could talk and get to know each other. Kane had backed off again, keeping their physical contact to hugs and kisses, giving her plenty of time to feel comfortable before the next step. The woman of his dreams was falling for him. He experienced the knowledge in every gentle touch, every lingering stare, and every delighted laugh.

Brick mentioned he'd noticed little birdies flying around his head when they'd met for a beer. He'd denied and quickly retaliated by saying Brick's eyes got wide like a cartoon character when Aspen walked in the room, but his friend just laughed.

Kane was happy. Believed he could have it all—success in both his work and love life.

Until that damn deal.

Dread twisted his stomach. Kane was running out of time. After a lengthy meeting with Benny, a deep-dive into other property deals he could tempt Stealth with, and a conference call with Jack and Tim, he'd gotten his final answer.

They were moving forward on the property and Kane was in charge. He'd looked into every alternative, even going as far to see if he could find Sierra another similar place to move, but came up empty. The deal was going to be done. Stealth was just offering him the opportunity first.

If Kane said no, they'd move ahead with someone else, and he'd be cut out of a prospective future. He doubted another job would appear if he tanked this opportunity.

It was time to lean hard on Benny, work his magic, and get the contract signed.

A breath shuddered from his lungs. The landlord was a true asshole. Benny had already said he'd been dragging on renewing the leases, and had used the last six months of funds to go into debt with the maintenance. It was a matter of time before everything blew up.

And Sierra had no idea.

There must be a way to explain to Sierra that he was just a tool Stealth was using. He'd help her with every step, vow to find her another place. She would understand.

She had to.

His mind skipped over the next steps. The engagement party was coming up. He'd tell her afterward, and they'd find a way to deal with the fallout together. He'd be right by her side and though he knew she'd be furious for a while, he'd eventually get her to forgive him. She'd have no choice.

Because he already knew he was in love with Sierra Lourde.

He always had been. Since the morning he woke up and found her gone, a part of his soul had been searching for his missing piece. He'd just have to convince her this betrayal didn't have to break them.

Kane wouldn't let it.

Sierra squinted through the windshield and held a death grip on the steering wheel. Dammit, the storm was getting worse and the roads were already flooded. Cars with their headlights slowed down as they navigated giant puddles. Streamers of fog surrounded the landscape, making it even harder to go faster than a crawl. At this point, she'd never be back in Corolla before midnight.

Biting her lip, she made an executive decision to take the next exit and find a hotel. She'd been gone one night already, so Montgomery couldn't be left alone another night. Aspen had checked on him yesterday for his food and water, but Sierra worried he'd believe he was abandoned again. In just a few short weeks, she admitted the cat had stolen her heart. If she'd known how wonderful having an animal was, she would've gotten him sooner.

Then again, Sierra knew Montgomery was special. They were twin souls. No other cat would have been such a perfect fit.

She pulled into the parking lot of a Holiday Inn and let out a sigh of relief. Racing through the rain, she made it to the lobby, grabbed a room, and took the elevator up. Her clothes were soaked and she had nothing to change into, but she could dry them out overnight.

After she got settled, she sat on the bed cross-legged and made the phone call.

"Hey! How was the trip?" Aspen asked.

"Awesome. We made a deal that's good for both of us. I already grabbed a few samples to start with, but I think they'll be a huge seller."

"I knew it. You're such a badass businesswoman. Are you home?"

"No, that's why I'm calling. There's a big storm and the roads are flooded. I stopped at a hotel for the night but I need you to look in on Montgomery for me again, if that's okay."

Her sister groaned. "Babe, I'm in New York with Brick and Dug. I had to see my new editor and do a local signing at B&N. Did you forget?"

"Crap, I did. Sorry, my brain is elsewhere nowadays."

Aspen snorted. "Yeah, with your hot new lover who's giving you a thousand orgasms. You're probably brain dead."

"Stop. We haven't slept together yet."

"What are you waiting for? God, you must have cobwebs in your vagina!"

Sierra burst out laughing. "Bitch."

Aspen laughed with her. "Call Kane. I'm sure he'll love to babysit."

"Doubt it. Montgomery scratched him up the last time we were together."

"Ouch. Well, maybe a bonding retreat will be good for both of them. I'm glad you're safe, though. Gotta go!"

"Okay, love you, bye."

She hung up. Then called Brooklyn, but one of the kids was sick so she couldn't do it. Inez was out on an overnight date. Which left...

Sierra scrunched her nose in thought but made the call.

"Hi, beautiful. How did it go?"

She shivered at the sound of his deep, sexy voice. Tingles exploded between her legs as she remembered their last hookup. God, the way he'd stroked her and brought her to orgasm. The expert way his tongue and teeth and fingers played her body, forcing her to the edge and keeping her there. Demanding she say his name.

Sierra cleared her throat. "Hi. It went well." She repeated the details and they chatted a bit. "I actually have a favor to ask. I had to stop at a hotel because of the storm. And I forgot Aspen and Brick are in New York. Inez and Brooklyn can't do it either. So, I was wondering—"

"If I can take care of Mo?"

"Montgomery. Yes, if that's not a problem? He needs fresh food and water and maybe you can stay overnight so he's not lonely?"

There were a few beats of silence. "Are you trying to get me killed, Sierra?"

She swallowed a laugh. "He's not going to hurt you. He sleeps in the bed with me now and is really sweet. I swear."

"Sure. He'll have even more opportunity to claw at my sensitive body parts. One specific one I really need in good working order."

"Kane, you just can't give him a hard time. He'll probably stay in the sunroom if you're there anyway. I doubt he'll even try to sleep with you."

Kane sighed. "I really wanted another pussy in my bed. But I don't want you to worry so I'll do it."

She giggled. "Clever. Thank you—I appreciate it."

"How much?"

"A lot."

She heard his tongue click over the line. "Hmm, I'll collect later. Let me head out. Talk tonight."

He hung up and she stared at the phone in surprise. What could he possibly want from her when they were in two different states?

Sierra shrugged. Guess she'd find out later.

She grabbed a sandwich from the downstairs café, showered, wrapped herself in a towel, and hung her clothes up to dry. With the television in the background, she worked for the next few hours on the new contract and the financial spreadsheets for the upcoming quarter.

When Kane called back, she was cuddled in bed, relaxed and already a bit sleepy. "You on your laptop?" he asked.

She frowned. "No."

"FaceTime me there."

Click.

Okaaaaay. She retrieved it and brought up FaceTime. The picture came up. He was in her bedroom, propped up against the cream headboard. Immediately, her heart raced. He looked lazy and sensual, hair damp from a shower, simple white-t-shirt stretching over those broad shoulders. Those green eyes drilled hers right through the screen.

Her gaze softened. How sweet. He wanted to prove Montgomery was safe. "How is he doing?" she asked.

"Mo's great. We made a bargain. I stay out of his way and he'll stay out of mine."

"Did you give him a treat? He likes the ones you brought him."

"I tried but he refused to take it from me. I'll leave one in the sunroom for him later."

"He'll come around. Where is he? Isn't that why you wanted to FaceTime?"

A slow, wicked grin curved his lips. Her breath caught in her throat as his eyes darkened. "No. I wanted to see you for my own personal enjoyment. Where are your clothes?"

She squirmed on the bed. Heat gathered in her core at the sensual predatory look. "They got wet so I had to hang them up to dry." She paused. "Why are you in my bed? Are you ready to go to sleep?"

"Not yet. I thought I'd be more comfortable here while we…talked."

A buzz of electricity shot through the air, connecting them through the screen. Her breasts tingled with sheer anticipation. Something was about to happen and she couldn't wait to find out. "Kane?"

"Are you ready to show me how grateful you are, sweetheart?"

His voice poured over her like warm, sticky honey. Her fingers clutched at the knot in her towel. It took her a while to untangle her words. "What did you have in mind?"

Transfixed, he leaned close to the camera. That sensual mouth quirked in a hint of a smile.

"Drop the towel and I'll show you."

God, her expression was everything.

Kane drank in the combination of innocence and lust glittering in her hazel eyes and was immediately hard. He figured seeing her through a screen would give him a bit of control, but it was as if she was right here. The same electricity exploded in the air, tightening with a sweet, familiar tension.

In fact, his control was ready to splinter. Wet hair tumbling over her bare shoulders. The white towel barely clinging to her full, heavy breasts. Her nipples poked against the fabric, ready to play. Her face was clear of makeup, pink lips pursed in thought. Not being able to touch her was the biggest punishment of all but he'd take the sting for the payoff of watching her pleasure.

Those teeth reached for her lower lip. Pondered. "You want me to drop the towel?"

Oh, she wanted to, but something held her back. His voice soothed. "Yes. I want to see you naked for my eyes only. I want to enjoy looking at you while I'm lying in your bed, imagining all the times you touched yourself while thinking of me."

A gorgeous blush tinted her cheeks. His dick pressed painfully against his jeans. He could study her face for a thousand years and never memorize all of her expressions; all the flickers in her gaze.

"I've never done it. Had…phone sex."

Primal satisfaction unfurled. He was glad. The thought of her being with anyone else made him want to roar, even though it was both outdated and chauvinistic. He practically growled the words. "I'm glad you waited for me."

She seemed to make her decision. "What do we do?"

Her usual snappy banter faded under the unknown. Kane was so turned on he felt like an overexcited teen. He dropped his voice in command. "Drop the towel, Sierra."

He waited one beat. Two. Three.

The towel fell from her body.

Kane sucked in his breath at her perfect, naked body on display for him. He greedily devoured every generous curve and sloping plane, taking in her tight nipples and the rapid rise and fall of her chest.

"Like this?"

He loved the teasing pitch as she spoke. Her hesitancy seemed to disappear, as if she liked the drool-worthy stare he was giving. "Oh, yeah. You are everything I ever wanted in a woman. I could spend all night studying that gorgeous body."

Her brow slowly lifted. "I hope this isn't a one woman show."

Kane grinned. "I'm here to please, sweetheart. Tell me what you want"

"Shirt. Off." She paused. "Slow."

He obeyed, peeling the tee up over his stomach and taking his time removing it. She licked her lips and damned if he didn't almost preen at her obvious appreciation. He'd never been so damn happy to work out as he was right now. "Better?"

Her gaze touched every inch of his bared chest. "Yes. You're beautiful, Kane."

His gut squeezed. He wished he could touch her and show his own admiration, but he had to work with the limitations. "You deserve to be taken care of, even if I'm not there. So I want you to lay back on the pillows and relax. Adjust the camera. I want to see all of you."

Her rapid breathing showed her obvious excitement. She moved the laptop and stretched back, her beautiful caramel hair spilling over the white pillowcase. Kane groaned at the intoxicating display. Her thighs were slightly parted, giving him a hint of her bare pussy.

"Are you wet?"

She shuddered. "Yes."

"Show me."

Her hand coasted over her full breasts, down her stomach, and stopped. "Kane?"

"Yes, sweetheart?"

"Take off your pants."

A low chuckle escaped. He discarded his jeans, lingering over the snap and taking his time lowering the zipper. Kane didn't wait for the command to remove his black briefs. He was barely able to hold it together and they hadn't even gotten to foreplay. This woman tested his control on a regular basis.

He enjoyed her gasp of breath as his cock was freed and already painfully hard. "This is what you do to me." He stroked himself, enjoying her fascinated gaze as he tightened his palms and worked his hand up and down in a slow rhythm.

Kane didn't have to ask again. She continued coasting her fingers over her mound, parting her legs a few more inches. He gave a vicious curse as she teased her clit, rotating in a clockwise circle, then dipped inside her pussy. Her head arched back and a moan escaped as she got caught up in chasing her pleasure.

"Oh, you're such a bad girl," he said. "Look at how wet you are. If I was there, I'd spread those thighs wider and press my mouth against your sweet pussy. I'd use my tongue to tease your clit real nice, and no matter how hard you begged, I'd wait until you were going crazy."

"Kane!"

"Eyes on me, sweetheart."

Her drunken gaze fastened on the screen, where he stroked a bit harder and faster, matching her pace. He continued with his dirty talk, pushing them both to the edge, until their breath mingled together in pants and the tension cranked to a torturous threshold.

His command was like a whiplash. "Let yourself go, Sierra. Now. Come for me."

Her heels dug into the mattress and then she was screaming his name as the orgasm took her. Kane held on for a few more precious moments to enjoy her surrender—the pleasure washing over her in waves, shaking her body.

Then he reached his own orgasm, shouting roughly as he was shoved over the cliff. Her eager gaze only emphasized his gratification as he jerked his hips in brutal satisfaction and spilled himself over sheets that smelled like her.

Boneless, it took him a while to refocus. Sierra was sprawled out on the bed, a smile curving her lips. "God, is that what we would have done with a long-distance relationship?" she murmured dreamily. "I've been missing out on a whole new aspect of sex."

Kane laughed. "Watching you was hot, but nothing compared to being able to touch and kiss you. Kind of like having cheese and beer instead of caviar and champagne."

She lifted her head. "Did you just compare our Face-sexing to food?"

"My brain is mush. It was the best I had."

Her soft laugh filled him up. "Well, at least it was creative. Aspen would approve."

"Please don't tell your sister about this."

"Of course not." She winced at his stare. "Well, only if she asks. I don't want to lie to her ever again."

"And they say men brag about their sex lives," he muttered.

"Do they?" she asked, obviously interested.

He grunted. "Only if they don't care. The moment they get to girlfriend or wife status, we close the vault of info."

"Wow, I never knew." Mischief flickered over her face. "I guess I'm open game."

Kane shot up and glared at the screen. "Hell, no. You're my damn girlfriend, Sierra. There's no one else I'd ever want to be with." A horrible thought entered his mind. "Wait—don't you feel the same? You don't think you're still going on blind dates, do you!"

Her languid smile was full of amusement. "Usually, I don't like possessive claims on my freedom, but I won't torture you any longer. No. I only want to be with you, Kane."

Relief poured through him. "Exactly what I thought. You're my girlfriend." The word seemed barely enough to contain all the things Sierra was to him. The woman he loved. His soulmate. But she wasn't ready for such declarations yet. He'd be patient.

"Well, you didn't officially ask, but yes. I'm your girlfriend."

"I'm glad you see it my way."

She giggled and his entire being lit up. He'd do anything to keep things like this, but the threat of the Stealth deal kept shadowing his happiness. Each step he took to earning Sierra's trust could be blown up once he told her about the store. For now, Kane clung to the hope that every moment spent together was a tightening of their bond. It had to be strong enough to sustain the fallout.

They talked some more and said goodnight. He closed his laptop, cleaned himself up, and headed to the kitchen for a bottle of water.

Then found Mo blocking his progress.

The cat was like a massive orange ghost in the shadows, looming with threat. Damned if Kane didn't take a step back. Golden eyes glinted with warning. When he first arrived, the cat had stayed away, as if sensing his arch enemy was in the house. Kane figured he'd eventually surface, so he took care of the water and food, and minded his own business.

But now, Kane sensed a confrontation was coming. Trying to compete with being alpha male was his first instinct, but Mo had probably fought even harder than Kane in his ability to survive. Nature was cruel and Mo held the scars. Kane had to be the one to bend.

He held up his hands in surrender. "I get it. You hate me because you're afraid I'll take away Sierra. But I don't want to do that at all. Because she loves you, Mo. You make her happy. You give her someone safe to love, and she's not there yet with me."

The cat squinted. Waited.

"What if I promise never to come in between you? Hell, she's already picked you over me so you're the front runner. All I want to do tonight is make sure you're fed and have what you need. I'm asking that you don't jump on my head tonight and try to strangle me. Please."

A swish of the tail. A cock of the head. Was he listening or planning Kane's murder?

"Sierra will be happy if we get along. No woman wants to see a who's-dick-is-bigger competition. Okay? Can we have a truce?"

Quiet settled over the house. The clock ticked. Silently, Mo retreated back into the darkness of the kitchen and disappeared.

Kane let out a breath. He grabbed his water and two cat treats, leaving one on the floor by the sunroom, and the other right outside

Sierra's door. Maybe if Mo was feeling generous Kane wouldn't die of smothering tonight. He didn't want to shut the door just in case Mo needed him.

Kane changed the sheets and got settled, enjoying being surrounded by Sierra's sanctuary. He fell asleep easier than he had in a while and had no dreams.

Until something woke him hours later. A sensation of being watched.

His gaze met the glowing gold eyes staring from the pitch black. His heart galloped and he barely stopped himself from jumping up with an unmanly scream.

Mo was here to hurt him.

He refused to whimper. Tightening his body, he prepped for the claws to attack and prayed he could defend himself without hurting Mo.

Seconds passed. He held his breath and waited.

Finally, the glow faded. Kane heard the rustle of sheets as they were rearranged. Then the soft sigh of Mo as he settled.

It took him a while to relax and realize Mo was sleeping next to him and, so far, had spared his life. Eventually, he went back to sleep, a slither of satisfaction curling in his blood. Mo must've believed him. It was definitely a first step between them.

Kane slept with a smile on his face.

Chapter Eighteen

"Kane, can we talk?"

He looked up as Duncan came into his office and shut the door. In Manhattan, he was used to being dragged into his boss's luxury office for a game of intimidation. With Duncan, he came to you, and no matter what deal you closed, treated each employee as an equal. As Kane watched him settle in the chair opposite his desk, white hair neatly combed back, gaze peering over his silver glasses, he was struck by a sense of ease he rarely experienced in his career field.

"Of course. Is everything okay?"

Duncan's smile was gentle. "That's what I came to ask you. Stealth called. Said you'd delayed the contract meeting and they weren't happy. You haven't responded?"

He fell back into the familiar role, masking his features into a calm ease. "I had some issues with scheduling but it's already on the calendar for tomorrow morning. Apologize you got dragged into it. I'll call Todd ASAP."

Duncan studied him for a long moment. Kane held his smile, used to the mask he wore after so many years of being forced to use it. "I'm not mad, son. I actually wanted to chat about a few things."

He relaxed. "Sure. What can I help you with?"

"Do you want to do this deal?"

He jerked. Tried to focus. "Of course. Are you having second thoughts about me taking the job at Stealth?"

Duncan shook his head "No, you misunderstand. I've been watching you and became concerned. Not only did you delay meetings, but my contacts say you've been inquiring about other properties in the area to lease. Is there something else going on you'd like to discuss?"

Kane wondered what it would be like to trust Duncan and tell him everything. That he was desperate to find a place for Flirt. That he was suddenly questioning how badly he wanted this new job. To be dragged back into a competitive, cutthroat business where the job demanded twenty-four-hour care and commitment suddenly sounded empty. Not when he could spend quality time with the woman he loved and his friends and the horses and the town he'd come to care about.

But he couldn't. Look what happened with John. Hadn't that taught him the most valuable lesson of all? That he could trust no one but himself? If he confessed everything to Duncan, it could all be held against him.

Better to keep his secrets tight and close this deal. Then fix the fallout. It was what he'd always done before.

"Thanks for the concern, Duncan, but things are good. I'll get this deal finalized and transition over to Stealth. I'm so grateful for the opportunity you gave me to work here. I'll never forget it."

The man tipped his chin. "Understood. I was happy to have you here. And if things ever go sideways, your job is always open."

Surprised by the kindness, Kane tried to ignore the tightness in his throat. "Thank you."

He watched his boss walk out and wondered why he felt so lost when he'd just gotten back in the game.

Things were moving too fast now. He had to get ahead of it and be the one to tell Sierra before she found out and it was too late.

Sierra watched her sister enter the room and gasp in delight. Her hand flew to her mouth as she took in the crowd gathered together to celebrate the engagement. Brick stood beside her, grinning widely, while Aspen took it all in, glancing around as if searching for someone.

Their gazes met and locked across the crowded room. As only siblings could, they spoke to each other in thoughts and responses.

I cannot believe you did this. Everything is so beautiful.

I enjoyed every moment. You both deserve it.

I wish Mom and Dad could be here. To see this party you threw for me and know

I'm happy. For them to know we're okay.

Me, too. But I'm sure they know.

They both teared up and started laughing. Sierra closed the distance and gave Aspen a hug, savoring the embrace. "Thank you," Aspen choked out.

Brick leaned down to give her a bear hug. "You should've been a party planner, Sierra. Everything is perfect."

She turned and smiled at Kane. He hung back, giving her the spotlight, but she motioned him forward. "I had some amazing help from your best man."

He reached her side and greeted both Aspen and Brick. "Congratulations. You look stunning."

Brick preened, smoothing out the lines of his fancy paisley cuffed shirt that Kane had bought him. Sierra admitted he looked even more handsome with the polished outfit. She'd rarely seen him outside of shorts and a t-shirt.

But her sister wowed in a little black dress with lace and a plunging neckline. A gold cuff bracelet, chandelier earrings and a lariat necklace from Flirt elevated the style. Aspen had tried to stuff her feet into Sierra's black Louboutin's but after hobbling for five minutes, her sister gave up. Fortunately, Sierra surprised her with some classic Miu Miu slingbacks she'd discovered on sale, and they looked divine.

Aspen beamed. "Thank you. Seems you survived co-planning with my sister and lived to tell about it." Her eyes danced. "If Sierra is impressed, I can't imagine how much effort you put in. You're a good friend, Kane."

Unbelievably, red flushed Kane's cheeks. Brick must've seen it too but he just slapped him on the shoulder, eyes shining a bit bright. "Thanks for doing this. Means a lot."

Kane cleared his throat. "No problem. I'll grab you a drink so you can start mingling." He walked toward the bar and disappeared into the crowd.

Aspen grabbed her hand and lowered her voice to a whisper. "Did he just blush or am I hallucinating? Oh, my God, he's got it bad for you!"

"Stop! It's your engagement party which means the subject all night is you. Not me." With a gentle push, Aspen moved forward into the throng all excited to talk to the couple. "Have fun."

Brick guided his fiancée with a hand to her lower back, and soon they both got swallowed up in celebration.

Sierra grabbed the signature champagne cocktail called The Romantic, and sipped the light pink bubbly as she wandered and made sure it was all running smoothly. She chatted with various groups, hanging for a while with Inez and Brooklyn, then went to check to make sure more oysters were brought out. She was about to enter the kitchen when someone grabbed her from behind and elegantly spun her around.

Kane gave that heart-stopping mischievous grin. "You are not allowed to go in the kitchen. They have it under control, sweetheart."

She gave a huff. "They ran out of oysters so I was just—" she trailed off as another server popped out holding a new tray. Sierra bit her lip. "Oh. Well, I wanted to make sure they knew."

He took her hand and gently tugged. "You worked your ass off and now it's time to enjoy. Did you try the Cynic drink? The hint of sour mix is brilliant. Reminds me of Brick's grumpiness."

She couldn't help laughing. "Remember I didn't approve that drink. It was all you."

"And I'm proud of my brilliance in creating it." His gaze slowly morphed into a heated stare. "Have I told you how sexy you look? How I keep making excuses to put my hands on you?" He lowered his voice to a growl. "You wore those shoes for me, didn't you?"

Sierra tilted her chin up in challenge. She loved bantering with this man, who seemed to combine the perfect allotment of humor, wit, and sexual innuendo to keep her sharp. "I hate to break you of illusions, but women wear shoes for other women. Men rarely notice."

"I do." Those green eyes roved over her figure with masculine appreciation. "Red is bold. Unapologetic. A bit rebellious."

Sierra had chosen a simple wrap dress in lipstick red. The sexy slippery material was usually too flimsy for her curves, but she'd wriggled into the perfect undergarments to pull it off with support. Manolo Blahnik stilettos matched the dress in pure classic lines with a square buckle of sequins glittering in dramatic fashion.

And yes. She'd worn the shoes for him.

"I wore them because they matched my dress. You're overthinking."

Most men would back down. Not Kane. "No. You knew exactly what you were doing." His lower lip quirked. "Those shoes promise me something."

She took a step forward so they were inches apart. The crowd and lights and music faded away to a dull roar under the sting of his gaze and the spicy scent of his cologne. The crisp black shirt and perfectly tailored pants screamed confident masculinity. A wayward curl fell over his high forehead. She ached to brush it back, press her lips to his, and lean against all those hard muscles.

"What do they promise, Kane?" she drawled, lowering her lids to half-mast.

He sucked in a breath. Coils of sensual tension slithered around them, pulling tight. "What I've been wanting since the moment I saw you. They promise I get to fuck you tonight. In all the ways I dreamed of for four long years."

Every smart-ass retort died on her lips as her voice disappeared. She swayed on her stilettos, but he caught her, gently squeezing her arms. The crude declaration should have made her stalk away but he'd out-gamed her.

Because she wanted the same exact thing.

His smile widened with pure satisfaction. "Cat got your tongue?"

Somehow, she rallied. "Nope. I simply have nothing to say to such an outrageous statement."

He put his mouth next to her ear. "Stop flirting with me, Sierra. I need to focus on this party, and then, I'll focus on you."

Her jaw dropped as he pressed a kiss to her temple and walked away.

"I. Do. Not. Flirt!"

But he was already stepping into a conversation with Marco and Brick, leaving the words hanging in the air.

Damn the man. He was impossible.

Inez and Brooklyn immediately swarmed her. "You sneaky slut," Inez teased, grabbing her hand. "That was the hottest scene I've ever eavesdropped on. You were practically melting over each other."

Brooklyn had a dreamy look in her eyes. "That man hurts my eyes with his sexiness. And you look sensational—all glowy and hot. Oh, my God, the Manolos! You are serious tonight!"

Sierra couldn't help laughing at the remark. He'd definitely won that round.

Her friends peppered her with questions. She answered some, dodged the others. But confessed they still hadn't slept together yet and they were figuring things out.

"Not much to figure out," Inez said. "Things look pretty perfect from over here. He's your sister's fiancé's bestie. The town loves him. He's into you. All the checkmarks are there."

"Things do seem to be going well," she said with a hint of worry.

Brooklyn sighed. "I know it's hard to believe it won't all fall apart. After your divorce, you grew in so many ways but you also kept yourself locked up tight. When I see you two together, it's like your light is back on, Sierra."

Inez nodded. "It's totally okay to go slow and have doubts. That's how trust is built. Just don't create obstacles when there aren't any to keep yourself safe."

Sierra smiled. "I love you, guys. Thanks for the therapy session, I think I needed that."

The next hour flew by as the buffet opened and everyone mingled.

She was on her third Romantic cocktail when Deanna and Carlos motioned her over. Deanna owned the café and Carlos owned the toy store next to Flirt. After casualties were exchanged, Deanna gave a frown. "We wanted to ask if you'd heard anything about Bernie getting you a lease renewal. I know yours is up before ours but there have been some rumors flying around that are freaking me out."

"No, he's not answering my calls. I just figured he was busy and would get it to me soon. What have you heard?"

Carlos and Deanna exchanged a look. "My friend works for a real estate place. Has connections with some developers and it seems they're looking to put in a luxury hotel. Our building may be up for sale."

Sierra tried to process. "Wait—you think we'll have a new landlord? Are you worried our rents will go up or something worse?"

Deanna shrugged. "Don't know. Depends on who it sells to and what Benny wants. I mean, the place has been falling apart lately—he hasn't made any repairs to the lot or the roof. Maybe it's his way of getting out of expensive repairs. Property values are crazy high."

Sierra nodded. "To be honest, I was trying not to worry but Benny has kind of disappeared. Crap. Isn't that property too small to convert to a hotel? I doubt we'd be prime real estate for that move."

Carlos took a sip of his beer. "Probably right. They'd have to own the land behind to do anything of value. We're trying to get a meeting with Benny together. Want to join us?"

"Definitely. Let's get ahead of this instead of being surprised. Maybe we can hire a lawyer to look over the lease or our options?"

"Good idea," Deanna said.

Sierra tried not to worry during her sister's party, so she tucked the information aside for tomorrow. The cake was rolled out, and she couldn't help feeling proud of their choice when everyone oohed and aahed over the multi-tier sugar concoction. Kane checked on her, bringing her a slice and making sure she sat to eat. His gentle scolding was like a warm blanket wrapped around her. As the oldest and always in charge, it was rare anyone tried to mother her. Having him so attentive fed her hungry soul.

The DJ began to play and people started to dance. Inez and Brooklyn gave a shriek and dragged her out, refusing to listen to her protests. Soon, Aspen joined them and Sierra let herself go, allowing her body and mind and soul to be free. "Dancing Queen" blasted out and women flooded the floor, joining together to loudly sing the lyrics. There was something about dancing with other women, feeling safe enough to surrender to the movement of limbs and shaking of hips, of heads flung back and skirts flashing bare legs. The crowd lining the floor began to clap and sing along, and Sierra hung on to her sister as they spun and lip-synced full force.

She caught Kane's eye and her heart leapt. His gaze was focused on her, a wide grin curving his lips, obviously enjoying the show.

That's when Sierra made her final decision.

Tonight, Kane Masterson would finally be in her bed.

Kane watched her dance and felt transformed.

There was something about seeing her so free and expressive, not giving a shit who was looking, not giving a crap who she impressed, that made her the sexiest woman he'd ever seen.

"You got it bad, man."

He turned to see Marco watching him with his usual grin. The young man sported his usual shaggy brown hair that screamed surfer dude, but his golden-brown eyes were clear, and not foggy with his tendency to smoke weed on Hump Day or weekends. "I do," Kane admitted. "Has there ever been a woman you couldn't forget?"

"Yeah." His gaze held a tumble of memory. "I was in love bad once but I lost her. Couldn't get my shit together."

"You were too young. I'm past thirty, and I'm just getting my shit together."

Marco laughed. "Doubt it. Look at you. All Bond-like and smooth. You're also a good guy. Helped Brick out when he needed it. Helped Judy out with the sea turtle watches. Helped me with that finance program I would've never figured out. Maleficent said Mrs. Simone told her you drive her around so she doesn't have to pay for Ubers and discovered you were secretly paying for half of her groceries because she's on social security. Sierra would be nuts to reject you."

Kane scratched his head and considered his words. "But does that make me a good person for a relationship? I keep things to myself. In fact, I have something big to tell her and I'm afraid it may break us."

"Communication in a relationship is key to it all. You gotta tell her. They always find out the truth anyway. If you lie, you lose her. Better to confess and beg for forgiveness."

He pondered the words. "Smart advice."

Marco gave a long sigh as he stared longingly to the dance floor. Kane caught Maleficent laughing with Aspen and Sierra, spinning on her heel, her fuchsia strands of hair whipping in the air. "Maybe you can do me a solid and help me with Mal. I'm crazy about her, but she won't give me the time of day."

"She's older than you, Marco."

"By eight years, man. I've been living on my own terms since I was seventeen. Had to take care of myself since no one else would. I know how I feel and what I can handle. I just want a shot to show her I think we can be great together."

Surprise hit. It was easy for everyone to dismiss Marco. But Kane also knew there had been a lot of changes in him the past year. He got serious about his business and began making a profit. He stopped taking off lunches and closing up at all hours. He began studying marketing. He was also well-read and could dive deep into various conversations.

Kane wondered if he was being too quick to judge like so many others. Mal had gone after a man who was a few decades older when she was with Brick's grandfather, Ziggy. Why not be open to someone younger if he was the right fit?

"Before you decide to change yourself, you gotta be serious about that woman. She's not out for play, Marco. She wants a real relationship."

"So do I."

Kane looked him in the eye and only saw resolve and a new maturity that had been brewing for a while. "Okay. I can help you. But you have to play the long game. Women need time to see a man in a new light. The first steps are easy because it's surface. The deeper levels will need to be revealed slowly. Are you sure you want to do this?"

"Yeah. Am I getting a makeover? 'Cause that's fire, man. Just like in all those romance novels where the heroine is transformed except, I'm the hero."

Kane blinked. "Sure." He gave Marco's casual cargo pants and black t-shirt a shudder. He was actually wearing leather sandals. "You're not Jesus.

You are a serious businessman like she is. Take your clothes seriously, and it's the beginning."

"Got it."

"And you gotta get rid of the hair."

Marco paused, then sighed. "I'd do it for her."

"We'll talk more about this later." Kane glanced toward Sierra with a slow smile. "I have something important to do."

He thumped Marco on the shoulder and headed to the dance floor.

It was time to tell the woman he loved the truth.

Chapter Nineteen

"A good shoe is not one that dresses you but undresses you."
— Christian Louboutin

When Kane claimed her on the dance floor, she was ready to go.

One long look was all it took. The party was beginning to wind down. She was giddy, happy, and a little bit tipsy. The only thing she wanted was for Kane to take her home, take her in his arms, and take her to bed.

They said their goodbyes, making their way to Aspen and Brick.

Aspen squealed and gave her a hug. "Sierra, these sea turtle soaps are my favorite thing ever. I cannot believe you thought of something so unique!"

Sierra laughed. "To be honest, that was all Kane's idea. He found them on Etsy and suggested we use them as favors."

Brick shook his head, a smirk edging his lips. "Etsy, huh? Had no idea you could be so…creative."

Kane's brow shot up. "You making fun of me, bruh?"

Aspen gasped. "I hope not! I'd rather have a sensitive, caring man rather than someone who's afraid to stand up to his bullying friends." The warning glare was caught and received. Brick gave his friend a look for getting him in trouble.

"Just a joke. I love them."

Kane snorted, but his half hug to Brick was genuine. "Glad you had a good time."

"It was perfect," Aspen gushed. "And now I'm ready to go home and collapse."

Brick growled. "I'm ready to go home and do other things, baby."

Aspen blushed.

Kane threw up his hands. "And that's our cue to leave."

"Talk to you in the morning," Sierra called, holding Kane's hand as they walked out. The air was sticky. By the time they had the air conditioner on in the car, her hair was clinging to her neck. She scooped the strands up in a fist and lifted them from her nape. She chattered on about the party, pointing out the highlights. Kane nodded and smiled but was oddly quiet. As if he was thinking hard about something.

"You okay?" she asked.

"Yeah. I had a great time. Haven't seen Brick so happy."

"Same with Aspen. I'm so glad they found each other. It was meant to be."

He gave a slow nod, but his jaw tightened. Tension swirled from his figure. "I'd like to talk tonight if you're up for it?"

Arousal gathered between her legs. She sensed there was one reason he wanted to talk, and it had to do with taking their relationship to the next level. Sierra knew she'd demanded to know more about his past before they slept together. And he'd insisted Montgomery would accept him, which hadn't happened yet. But after sharing their intimate FaceTime moments, and the way her heart was beginning to unfold every time she saw him, Sierra was ready to jump.

"Sure. We can…talk."

"Good."

Relief threaded through his voice. She hid a smile as they pulled up to her house and went inside together.

"Mommy's home," she called out, waiting for the familiar light footsteps of her new best friend. She turned to Kane. "You may want to step back from me so he's not threatened. I'd hate to see you get clawed again."

"I'm not worried."

His casual tone made her roll her eyes. Always macho.

Montgomery prowled in, whiskers twitching, giving a loud meow in greeting. She sank to her knees and opened her arms, and he pushed against her, mushing his face to the inside of her thigh. "Such a good boy," she crooned, petting him with pure love. "Did you have a nice evening? Do you want a treat?"

She took her time, then slowly rose to her feet. "Kane's visiting tonight. Remember he took care of you when Mommy was away? Maybe you can try to be nice?"

"I'll get the treat," Kane said, retreating to the kitchen.

When he returned, he approached the cat with a confident ease that was brand-new. She frowned. "Kane, just leave it there, don't try to give it to him yourself or—"

In one smooth motion, Kane offered up the morsel and Montgomery slowly took it from his fingers like an aristocratic gentleman allowing someone to feed him.

Her jaw dropped.

"Good job, Mo. It's nice to see you buddy." He didn't try to stroke him but smiled, standing back up. "We've reached an agreement. I won't stand in his way, and he'll allow me in his house. I think—"

Sierra interrupted him by jumping into his arms, grabbing his face, and kissing him hungrily.

He stumbled back, obviously caught off guard, but she didn't retreat, knowing he'd catch her weight. In seconds, he was kissing her back, holding her head while his lips moved over hers and his tongue plunged deep, claiming her in the way that made her toes curl.

"I want you," she whispered against his lips, already tugging off his sleek jacket and working on the buttons of his shirt. "I've wanted you all night."

"Me, too, but wait, sweetheart. Are you too drunk? Maybe we should talk first like I suggested?"

If he wasn't so obviously hard, she may have taken it as a rejection, but Sierra knew he wanted her just as much. "No. I'm not drunk." Her fingers tripped over a button, then glided through the rest without a hitch. "You made friends with Montgomery." She ripped off the shirt, her hands splayed wide to touch all those amazing hard muscles, sliding down his six pack abs to curl beneath his pants.

He spit out a curse, pupils dilated. "Wait—maybe we can—"

She plunged both hands underneath his briefs and cupped his hard cock. Squeezing lightly, mouth salivating for his taste, she dropped to her knees.

"Fuck, oh, fuck."

She was too far gone to slow down. A biting hunger pushed her to lower his zipper, yank his pants and underwear down, and open her mouth.

His animal groan raked past her ears as she took him fully in, her tongue swirling around his thick length, then sucking hard as her name was chanted in a mantra. His hands gripped the back of her head not to guide her, but to helplessly clench his fingers in her hair while he surrendered.

Power flowed through her even though she was the one on her knees. She let his taste fill her, his pleas sweet music, as she pushed him brutally to the edge. His knees shook. His breath came in ragged pants. She drank in every one of his responses only to offer more and more and more.

Hard hands yanked her up from the ground and with one quick movement, he scooped her into his arms. "I am not going to lose control five minutes into my first night with you," he declared. A fine trembling still gripped his muscles and Sierra couldn't help but give him a satisfied purr.

"Afraid you can't handle me off-screen?"

His quick grin promised sweet retribution. "Do I hear a challenge, flirt?"

She laughed as he placed her down, stripped off her clothes, and lay her out on the bed. Deliberately, she spread her arms and legs, a willing sacrifice. Already, she was throbbing for him. The slightest pressure would push her over so this wasn't a fight she was going to win.

Lucky for her losing was the goal.

He joined her on the bed, taking advantage of her vulnerable position. Slowly, he settled himself between her legs, stroking her thighs, pushing up her knees so he was poised before her dripping entrance.

Their gazes locked. The playful banter faded away under the demanding sting of his stare. Sierra shuddered.

"Don't tease me," she said.

His green eyes darkened. "I can't. I need to be inside you. Every part of me aches with wanting."

"I'm on birth control."

He blinked. His hand shook as he stroked her, his erection brushing her swollen folds. "I haven't slept with anyone in a long time and I was tested."

Sierra lifted her arms with invitation. He interlaced his fingers with hers, locked on her face. Slowly, he pushed himself inside inch by inch until he was completely buried to the hilt. The pressure of being filled up caused her to tremble beneath him, gripping his hand harder. Her breath rushed out. "Oh, God," she whimpered.

He stilled. A fine sheen of sweat gleamed on his brow. "You okay?"

"Yes. Don't stop. Never stop."

His body tightened. Kane pulled out completely, hips jerking as he pushed back in and set a steady rhythm. Each time he dragged his dick over her pulsing clit, giving her a perfect friction, taking her up until every inch of her body was on fire, poised with a fine-tuned tension that gripped every muscle.

"Say it," he demanded, jaw tight, eyes fierce with demand. "Say what I want to hear."

"Kane!"

Something broke inside him. He pushed her hands over her head and growled, setting a blistering pace until she poised on the edge, desperate for the orgasm shimmering before her. Shaking with pure need, she arched up, digging her heels into his back.

Kane reached between them and rubbed her aching clit. At the same time, he slammed so deep inside her, there was nowhere to hide, he owned every piece of her body.

The orgasm washed over her, seizing each part in a tsunami of sensation. Her nails dug into his hands and his name ripped from her lips, over and over and over…

"Yes. Just like that. God, I can feel you come all over me. Give me more."

He didn't stop, and she fell into a second orgasm, steeped in pleasure so sharp it was almost pain.

Only then did he let himself go, chasing his own release. She gripped him with her thighs and savored the expression on his face, knowing it was all for her.

They collapsed in the tangled sheets. Their breath came in uneven pants. He groaned and lay beside her, heads together, his heavy arm laying over her stomach, chaining her to him.

"Well, that talk went well," he muttered.

She laughed. "So. Well. I can't wait to have the conversation again."

Kane pressed a kiss to her temple. "Give me five. We had a few dialogue points to go over."

Sierra snuggled against him, sated and stupidly happy. The first time they were together, it was like a roller coaster, falling down the hill and surrendering a piece of herself to a stranger. But he was no longer unfamiliar. He was a part of her life and community and even family. There were no longer any excuses. Now, lying next to him, she could admit it was as if all the years apart were just a blank space where they could make themselves back to one another.

She was no longer afraid of not being chosen. And yes, he had a past they needed to discuss. But in the past month, they'd built trust and a solid foundation.

"I do want to talk," she said softly. "There are things to share that are important."

He was quiet for a while. "I love you, Sierra."

Her heart stopped. She lifted her head from the pillow and stared at him in shock. "What did you say?"

His smile held a touch of sadness she wanted to erase. "I've always loved you. There's never been anyone but you in my heart. I know I made some hard choices. Choices you won't understand until I give you another part of me—a part I always hid. But I can't lose you again."

Her insides lit up with so much emotion, she felt as if she could float away. "You just said it. Right now. In bed. Aren't you supposed to doubt men who say I love you in bed?"

Humor flickered over his face. "Only you would question the location and circumstances. And no, that's when you're having sex. Sex is over and we're cuddling. Most men clam up at the cuddling part."

"Yeah, I think you're right."

He gently touched her cheek. In his gaze, she found everything she'd ever dreamed of having from a man, yet the words bubbled up from her throat and got caught. The small spark of fear poked out and stirred to life. What was wrong with her? He'd given her what she asked for and more. What was the truth really keeping her from letting go of her final defenses?

"Sierra?"

Her voice came out choked. "Yeah?"

"I'm not looking for a response. I don't need the words back now. But you deserved to know my feelings are never going to change and that I'm in this for the long-term." His fingers traced the outline of her swollen lips. "I'm in this forever. If that scares the living hell out of you, I get it. And I don't care. I'll wait for as long as it takes."

It was too much. Raw emotions churned with the insecurities of knowing how easy it was to lose the things and people you loved. It was easier to hold back and be safe from shattering apart with grief and disappointment. But she could give him one thing he deserved to hear. "I'm scared."

"I know."

"Not of you. Of me. Of—"

"I know."

His soft words of assurance almost broke her. In that moment, it was as if Kane stared right into the monster's gaze and didn't flinch. "How?"

"Because when bad things happen, it's easy to believe it will happen again. You lost your parents and your husband. Anything can be taken. What if you allow yourself to love me and I leave?"

The shock of his calm declaration paralyzed her. He'd dragged out the secrets from the dark and shook them out in the light. The part Sierra hated—the weakness she'd been hiding from everyone, even her sister. How she'd wished she could be the strong, fierce woman who put herself out there again and again, taking heartbreak and loss in stride to fight another day. It was the type of characters Aspen wrote about.

"Will you leave?"

"No."

"But what if you—"

"Die?"

She shuddered, and he held her tighter. "Yes."

"I'll still be with you, every moment, whispering in your ear that you can do it because I believe in you."

Tears stung her eyes. She buried her face in the crook of his neck, breathing in his smell, surrendering to the grip of his arms. He continued speaking, the darkness soothing all the rough edges of naked insight. "When we first met, I was on my way to everything I ever dreamed of. You see, I'd gotten lucky. Property development is a ruthless business, but a mentor took me in, and decided to teach me everything he knew. Said I reminded him of his younger self, and I had a magic ingredient the others didn't. I remember being so damn proud when he said it, like I was finally special." She waited, eased by him sharing his own demons. "Hunger. He said I was hungry for every opportunity. I had a thirst to win at all costs, which couldn't be taught."

"What was his name?" she asked.

"John. His name was John."

Sierra sensed the story taking shape was bigger than a simple memory. "I'm listening," she said softly. This time, it was her who held him, urging him forward.

He drew a breath. "John worked closely with me until I knew everything and began making a big name for myself. I decided to get my brother involved, and he began working for the company, too. John pushed both of us hard, but my brother wasn't like me. He didn't thrive on high pressure deals and big stakes, so he didn't do as well. I was hard on him, thinking he just needed to believe in himself and push past his boundaries. Unfortunately, I was wrong. On all counts."

"What happened?"

"Derek always had a problem with alcohol, like my father. I ignored the signs of the rising pressure. I refused to see how the job was breaking my brother apart, and he began drinking again, then using drugs. He had a complete meltdown and went off the grid. Lived on the street for a while. It was a hard time."

"God, I'm so sorry, Kane. What did you do?"

"Worked harder. Told myself it was for both of us. In the meantime, there were some inquiries in the firm that money was missing and rumors of embezzlement began to skirt around. I ignored it, focused on my own shit, listening to whatever John told me to do."

Sierra's heart beat madly in her chest as he paused. She waited, fingers interlaced with his, knowing what was coming next.

"There was an inquisition. They found my deals led straight to the wonky accounting and dove deeper. Seems I was siphoning off money into other investments under John's guidance, and the trail led clearly to me. They arrested me and threw me in jail for fraud."

She closed her eyes in agony, trying to picture Kane in shock, betrayed by the one person he'd believed in. "It was John, wasn't it?"

A humorless laugh shook him. "Yep. He'd been using me as a shield and when the shit hit the fan, he made sure the crime led to me. I was held for forty-eight hours, but in that time period, I realized my whole life could be over. At first, I didn't want to believe it. I thought John was innocent and someone was framing both of us. Until I got a visit from a lawyer who laid out the terms quite clearly. They'd let me go quietly, because they didn't want a scandal. I had to sign a nondisclosure not to share any details, and the company would drop the charges. It would be a blip on my record but I couldn't say a word about anything. Then the lawyer said John was the one who made the deal on my behalf, in order to save me."

She sucked in a breath at the horror of the situation. "You had no choice. You had to take the deal."

Kane nodded. "I did. At first, when I found out the truth, I wanted to fight. I had these illusions of being some whistleblower who ripped the truth out. Going to the newspapers or exposing John. But then I was reminded that my brother had just gotten into rehab. An expensive one. A yearlong program that cost a crapload of money. John said it would be taken care of. That all I had to do was stay quiet, disappear, and move on. So, I did. I made the best decision I could."

"That's when you came to the Outer Banks."

"Yeah. Brick took me in, even though I never gave him any details.

You're the first one I told the story to."

The facts fell into place to create a fuller picture of the man lying beside her. The consistent betrayals he dealt with in the fight to be more than where he came from. The love and loyalty to his brother. The fierce devotion he showed Sierra from the moment they met, no matter how she'd pushed him away. Then why had he lied when she asked him about jail?

"But you said you hurt people?"

He gave a short nod. "I did. I made a promise to my brother and broke it. I sacrificed his mental health for my own wants. You were right about the man I was when we first met, Sierra. I was too focused on my goals and didn't care what got in the way. So, yeah. I hurt a lot of people. Mostly myself."

Everything became clear, and the rest of her walls crumbled. She rolled over him, breasts crushed against his hair-roughened chest, legs splayed open, his growing erection notched in the damp center between her thighs. Pressing her forehead to his, palms cupping his cheeks, she spoke fiercely against his mouth.

"You are an extraordinary man, Kane Masterson. You are a gift to everyone who meets you, and fuck every single person who ever told you differently. Do you understand me?"

She didn't wait for an answer. Instead, she took his mouth in a deep, passionate kiss at the same exact time she sank herself onto his throbbing cock.

Kane jerked, groaning, as she surrendered her entire self to this shattering moment.

Arching her hips, her tongue plunged inside, gathering his musky taste, hands gripping his head still, while she began working herself against him, hips grinding in a demanding rhythm that left them both no choice but to ride out the electrifying pleasure.

His hands cupped her ass, squeezing, teeth sinking into her lower lip as he shuddered beneath her.

"Fuck me like I'm yours," he muttered against her, eyes lit with lust and a fierce love he allowed her to see. "Fuck me so I forget."

The memory of her plea their first night together hit her full force. Unleashing the last of her barriers, Sierra reared up, throwing her head back, and rode him hard. Like she was possessing him. Like she was claiming him.

His dick scraped across her sensitive clit. With a blistering curse, he shoved her up, then slammed her down, hitting that magical spot that shimmered deep inside.

"Kane!"

"Come now, beautiful. Give it to me."

With a scream, she let herself go and the climax gripped her in a brutal wave. He came seconds later, her name on his lips, and then she collapsed on top, still shaking from the intensity of her release.

Their choppy breathing filled the air. The scent of sex rose to her nostrils. Sweat dampened her skin.

Sierra said the words.

"I love you. I think I loved you the moment I saw you at the bar and you talked about our fake kids having lice. I think I couldn't stand to date another man for years because I was always searching for you."

She blinked, no longer afraid. Those beautiful green eyes grew damp with tears. He pressed a gentle kiss to her lips, a kiss of such humble tenderness, her heart finally felt whole.

"Why say it now?" His lips twitched in self-derision. "It wasn't because I gave you a sob story, I hope. Or orgasms."

Her smile was trembly but joyful. "Because if you can be brave, so can I."

Kane didn't respond. Just held her close while they both settled into the silence, knowing everything had just changed forever.

Chapter Twenty

Kane sat in the sunroom, cradling a mug of coffee. Sunrise had just exploded over the skyline, and the beginning of the day was either giving the world a shred of hope or dread.

Right now, he was experiencing both.

His thoughts triggered to last night. There had been no more games or holding back. No more fear or lies. Kane finally knew exactly what it was like to offer the entirety of his soul to another, and wait for judgment.

Sierra had not only listened, but understood.

She loved him.

His eyes closed as raw emotion surged within. He was a stranger to love. Had not believed it existed until she walked in that bar and changed his life. It'd been a long road to find each other again, but after all this time, Kane claimed the woman he loved.

He couldn't lose her now.

The light patter of paws rose to his ears. Mo sat on his haunches, regarding him through lazy slitted eyes. "Sorry, buddy. Am I in your spot?"

Whiskers twitched.

"Your breakfast is out and I cleaned your litter box. That has to count for something."

His giant head cocked. He lifted his paw and began licking it, as if telling Kane he didn't give a shit.

"Fine. You'll have to get used to me staying overnight, though. I don't care if you want to come in the bed later to sleep, but you need to respect our privacy when things are—heated."

Mo licked the other paw.

Kane sighed. "I cannot believe I'm talking to a cat like Dr. Doolittle."

Mo finished his grooming and leapt through the air. Kane braced, still training himself not to show fear from those sharp claws, and waited as Mo landed on his lap. He kneaded his legs, circling. Then settled in his crotch, where it was most warm.

And dangerous.

Kane breathed quietly. One wrong move and his balls would be in big trouble. It took a few moments but Kane finally relaxed, enjoying the cat's solid warmth in a strange type of comfort. Maybe he was getting to be an animal lover after all. Mo was…kinda cool.

Kane drank his coffee and tried to come up with the perfect way to tell Sierra that she was losing her business. He should've told her last night, but no way was his brain working after she jumped into his arms.

It was the last piece of truth he needed to share. Once they worked through the problem together, nothing would ever keep them apart again.

He settled into the quiet of the morning and waited for her to wake up.

Sierra climbed out of bed, donned a short, silky robe, and walked to the kitchen. It was ridiculously early, especially after all the hours of love-making, but something had roused her. The house was quiet and not even Mo circled her feet, looking for breakfast.

She made herself a cup of coffee from the Keurig and went to look for her two favorite men.

Her footsteps led to the sunroom, and she paused before the French doors, taking in the scene before her.

Mo sat on Kane's lap, sleeping soundly. Kane held his own coffee, his gaze trained on the view outside, obviously lost in thought. Her heart leapt as she stared at him, and a deep-seated knowing lodged within her chest.

She loved him. She was no longer afraid of the future, as long as they were together. The future was bright and shiny before her, because last night had exorcised the demons. They'd spent hours talking and sharing, until only their bodies could show how much they felt, reaching for each other over and over.

Last night was even more beautiful than their first. Because this time, neither of them held back any secrets.

This time, they'd called out each other's names in the dark and the light.

Kane's head swiveled around and caught her gaze. "I didn't hear you come in."

She smiled and walked close, leaning down to kiss his rough cheek. "I was enjoying the view."

His fingers curled against Mo's orange fur. "Yeah, we were having a moment. Of course, one screw up and I'll be celibate."

Sierra laughed and touched his broad shoulder. "You were deep in thought. Where did you go?"

He blinked, giving her that lopsided smile. But his eyes were filled with shadows. "I was thinking about your store and how we're similar in how we see the world. Your shoes aren't just sexy—they tell me about a piece of you. I love seeing how beautiful things can become a way to not only express yourself, but dream."

Sierra stared at him. His pain made him poetic in a way that touched her deeply. It was rare a man viewed fashion with such respect. Curiosity urged her to question him further. He seemed slightly melancholic. "Was there anything specific that made you appreciate good clothes?"

"When I was in the city, I was fascinated by the men that went to work every morning. The power suits and silk ties. The smart leather shoes. They held briefcases and spoke commands into their earbuds while they rushed through the crowded streets. God, I was so impressed. They looked important and…worthy. Like they belonged in every way I couldn't."

He released a hard breath. "Somehow, I got it in my head if I dressed a certain way, I'd fool them all. I became obsessed with how I presented myself. I studied male fashion, and with each new crisp dress shirt or Italian loafers, I got closer to believing I was worthy. Cologne hid the memory of garbage. The swish of silk or fine cotton masked the scars. A bold watch told people you were someone to pay attention to. My college was the street and studying every man that intrigued me."

"I never asked how you started in such an industry?" She leaned over and wrapped her arms around him, squeezing in comfort.

"I lied. My résumé was impressive and showed a degree I didn't have. I learned how to bullshit and give them what they wanted to see. I grabbed an intern spot at a property firm, which was pure torture. Endless hours, little pay, and I was treated like shit. But damn, I loved it and I took that opportunity and made sure it was a stepping stone. Soon, I was offered a real position. I got a place—postage stamp but good enough—and got Derek out of my dad's."

The sheer grit and determination to transform his circumstances stunned her. No one would ever know what this man carried with him on a daily basis. How the love for his brother and need to be better drove him forward.

"I stayed there and soaked up all they could give. Then I got an offer from Global—specifically John, who told me the job was a ticket to my dreams." A humorless laugh escaped his lips. "I forgot about the one lesson in life."

"What?"

"There's always a price to pay for what you want."

A shiver bumped through her. Sierra held him tight as if to ward off the negative statement. "These are pretty deep thoughts before two cups of coffee."

He arched his neck back to meet her gaze. "Sorry, I have no idea why I turned maudlin after the most beautiful night of my life."

"Maybe you need a full stomach. I'll cook breakfast."

She tried to pull away but he tugged her hand, easing her beside him. Montgomery finally woke up enough to treat her to a few purrs and rubs before jumping down and disappearing. Sierra took her cat's place and snuggled on Kane's lap.

"I need to talk to you. I meant to tell you this last night but I got distracted."

"Gonna blame it on me?" she teased.

Sierra expected him to laugh, but his expression stayed serious. A frown creased her brow. "What is it, Kane? Are you having regrets?"

The shock in his eyes eased her worry. "Fuck, no. I've never been happier. Having you in my life is everything, and I love you."

She settled back. "Then anything else can be handled."

"It's about Flirt. I have some bad news."

It took her a few moments to process. "Wait—you have news about my store? Is this about Benny and the rumors the others were talking about at the party?"

Kane nodded. His hands rubbed her back, keeping her close. "Yeah. My boss came to me about an opportunity at Stealth. It's a bigger property company—similar to New York. They're looking for property to build one of those fancy resorts, and found out Benny was in trouble with the bank. Seems he has a gambling problem."

Sierra cursed and shook her head. "Damn him. That's where all our repair money went. I suspected something was up when he wouldn't renew."

"Benny got himself in trouble, and Stealth took the opportunity to close in." He paused, holding her hand. "Sierra, they're going to buy the property. Which means they'll force you to close down Flirt."

Shock kept her quiet until her brain clicked on. Then a stream of curse words exploded from her mouth. "I'm getting sick of all these cookie cutter hotels taking over our town. But this makes no sense? Flirt is on a small piece of real estate. There's not enough land to build anything else."

Sympathy flickered over his carved features. "Benny also owned acres of land behind the stores. He's selling it for a huge price, and Stealth will clear all of that out to build."

"Those bastards." She jumped up and began to furiously pace. "I won't let them. I'll get a lawyer and fight. Join in with Carlos and Deanna and see if there's anything we can use to slow down the process. Maybe wildlife restrictions?"

"Already cleared by the town—they kept it real quiet until ready to move. These bigger companies know how to avoid talk or ways to fight until it's too late."

"I can't believe this. If only I'd known sooner! No wonder that damn coward has been ghosting us. How much time until this happens?"

Sierra knew it was bad when her gaze met his. "The contracts are getting signed next week. Within the month it will be over. I'm sure they'll give you some grace period to find another place. Look, I've been scouring all the available lots, and I'm thinking you can temporarily go next to Marco and Brick. There's a small end store there that may fit your needs."

She shook her head. "No, it's too out of the way. I need a place with foot traffic or I'm dead before I even open. I think—wait. What do you mean you've been looking? How long have you known about Stealth?"

A trickle of ice slipped down her spine. Her gaze narrowed at the guilty expression that settled on his face. "A few weeks," he said carefully.

She blinked. "You have to be kidding. That's impossible."

"Sierra, I'm sorry. You have no idea how torn I am about this whole fucked-up thing. When I went to Stealth, they asked me to present them with a list of available properties for this resort, which I did. Then I was told they settled on Sunrise—Benny's real estate—and I couldn't talk them out of it. I tried, I really did. I've spent the past few weeks looking at other opportunities or loopholes but the deal is tight. There's no way to get out of it. Believe me, I tried."

Sierra's brain seemed to short-circuit. The facts he was sharing were off. The past month had shown no indication Flirt was being considered. He hadn't warned her. Hell, he was telling her this news like reporting a funeral instead of outrage. "Kane. Why didn't you tell me about this when you first found out?"

He winced. Scratched his head and rose from the chair, as if he didn't want to get caught in a vulnerable position. "I couldn't. I was bound by the Stealth contract not to say anything. I shouldn't even be telling you any of this right now, but you need to know the truth. I'm so sorry, sweetheart. But I honestly believe we can find something better. I'll help you with everything—I swear."

The words stuck in her throat but she forced them out. "Who's in charge of the deal, Kane?"

Silence.

He shifted his weight. Those green eyes flickered with regret. "Me."

Her friend Inez had once done a cold plunge at a spa. She explained how it was like immediately numbing every inch of skin and cell; a full-body brain-freezing experience. A shock so traumatic, she thought she'd die if she had to stay in the water one extra second.

Sierra finally knew what it felt like.

The warmth and beauty of last night faded into nothing. Sierra thought over their time together. The building of trust. The slow climb toward intimacy. The sharing of souls that was a true game changer.

All that time, he'd been hired to demolish her store.

And he hadn't even warned her.

Kane threw up his hands and spoke slow, as if he was trying to tame a wild animal. "Sierra, I know this is a shock. I know you're pissed and don't blame you. I wanted to tell you immediately, but I spent the time trying to find a way to save Flirt. I made a spreadsheet of every other property in the area that has potential and we'll go through them one by one. You can yell and scream at me, I deserve it. I'm sick that I even got this job but there was nothing I could do. I just need you to try and understand."

Her eyes widened. Was he serious? Was this a joke? Did the man she love actually believe he had no other choice but to take the juicy deal to destroy Flirt?

And hadn't even second-guessed she should be warned?

She'd dropped right into one of her sister's fictional worlds, but this was a hostile, sci-fi revenge story. Not a romance.

Her voice sounded far away. "I need to get some things straight. You're employed right now with Duncan. But you were given an opportunity to—prove yourself with Stealth?"

"Exactly. Duncan, was the one who came to me after realizing I was being held back. If I close this deal, I move to a full-time position at Stealth. The pay is outstanding and so are the opportunities."

"I see. But in order to get this, you need to close down three beloved stores in Duck. And this will occur within the month, no matter how we try to fight."

"Yes." He moved forward but she jumped back. Frustration radiated from his figure, but he kept their distance. "God, what do you want me to say? I know you'll need some time to process. I know this sucks and sounds horrible—but Sierra, it doesn't matter if I walked away from the deal. I already tried to stop it, and they clearly said if it's not me, someone else will take over. The end will still be the same."

"Except you wouldn't have been the one to do it."

Confusion shimmered in his green eyes. "I was going to walk away, I swear. But I thought maybe if I stayed, I'd be able to push hard for some concessions. Ways to help you that someone else wouldn't. Does that make sense?"

She looked at him while her heart crumbled slowly in her chest. What was left was numbness and grief twisted together.

She'd been so wrong. There was no trust between them. And he would always choose his career first.

Kane always chose the money. God, in a sick way, how could she blame him? He'd been trained his whole life to look after himself and his brother. Everything else had to be sacrificed.

Including her.

He just couldn't see it. Kane was a master at rationalizing all of his actions in order to get everything he wanted.

Thankfully, her body and mind shut down for safety. "I think you need to go."

"Sierra, we need to talk—"

"No, Kane. I mean it. I need to be alone right now. It's too…much."

He muttered a curse. His hair was ruffled and mussed from the hours her fingers ran through the strands. Her inner thighs still burned from the sting of razor burn. Kane's mouth firmed in a thin line as he regarded her. "Okay. I'll leave you alone to process. But then we need to talk this through and figure it out."

Sierra turned from him, desperate for distance. "Sure."

His words came out with implacable command. "We will talk later."

She heard him get dressed, sensing his hot stare behind her, but he finally left.

Dear God, what was she going to do?

Tears stung her eyes. Her emotions were raw from last night and the terrible truth he'd just shared. Maybe more sleep? She'd wake up a bit clearer and decide from there?

Sierra climbed back under the covers but the scent of clove and spice haunted her. Her head spun with endless questions and scenarios but everything led to one conclusion.

Kane had not chosen her.

Oh, he gave solid reasons of why he decided to remain on the deal. But the bottom line?

Work would always be more important than her.

And that was something that she may not be able to forgive. The one thing she needed more than anything.

The one thing Kane Masterson may never be able to give.

Sierra buried her face in the pillow and let herself cry.

Chapter Twenty-One

"The stiletto is a feminine weapon that men just don't have."
— Christian Louboutin

"I'm going to kill him."

Sierra watched her sister pace back and forth in the kitchen. Her body vibrated with fury as she shook her fists and muttered to imaginary voices in her head. Montgomery peeked out but didn't like the stressful vibe, so he ditched them immediately.

Sierra sat on one of the stools at the granite counter and drank wine. After her break-down, she'd decided to call Aspen. Even though she hated bothering her so soon after the engagement party, Sierra knew her sister was the only one who could help.

"What is he trying to pull—some awful third act break-up? This is not okay. This is bigger than a usual black moment in a romance. This man literally stitched your heart back together, vowed his undying love, and told you the next morning he was going to destroy your store? Personally? The store that means everything to you?"

Sierra kept drinking and didn't answer. She knew Aspen wasn't looking for answers to her questions. It was her way of processing the mess.

"I swear, I'm putting him in my next novel and he's going to have a tiny dick!"

She couldn't help the laughter that burst out of her. God, she loved her crazy-ass sister. "Good. Make him ugly, too. With awful shoes."

"The worst. When I get done writing his character, the whole town won't have anything to do with him."

Aspen paused and glanced over. They giggled, breaking the tension. With a sigh, Aspen took the stool opposite and poured more wine. "Okay, I'm calmer now. Tell me what the current situation is."

Sierra shrugged. "I told him I need time. I cried all night, and today I called you. He's reached out twice but I texted him not to bother until I want to talk."

"Good. This is on your terms, not his." She shook her head in wonderment. "What planet is he from where he believed this would all end up okay?"

Sierra snorted. "Not sure. He kept saying I'd lose Flirt anyway, so if he was the one in charge, it'd be—better? Does that sound bizarre to you?"

"Yes. How many relationships has this man been in?"

"None."

Aspen blinked. "Zero? A man as hot as that? Are you sure?"

"Yeah, I am. He told me he's never been in love and has no idea how to navigate a serious relationship. I guess my first lesson should have been communication instead of a thousand orgasms."

Her sister rolled her eyes. "Who could blame you? You were hard up and the man is obviously a God in bed."

Sierra groaned and rubbed her forehead. "What am I going to do, Aspen? I've grown this store and just started doubling profits. How do I start over? Will I need to close permanently? Get a real job in some cubicle?"

"Now, who's dramatic? Listen, you will find another place. Maybe it will be smaller or a less perfect location but look at what Marco did with his souvenir shop. It's about thinking outside the box. Yes, a beach shop is better with walk-in traffic but it's not a deal-breaker. You're just depressed. Your lioness spirit will kick in soon and you'll find a way to move forward."

She looked up and nodded. "Yeah. I guess. Kane kept saying he looked everywhere, like if he solved my problem of a new location, I wouldn't care he's the one closing the deal. How can I ever trust him again?"

Aspen nibbled at her lip. "He fucked up, but hear me out. What if he honestly didn't think this was a deal-breaker? I mean, I'd rather plead for his stupidity than his manipulation. The man is obviously in love with you. Is there any way you can forgive him?"

"You're thinking of the way Brick forgave you, right?"

Her sister sighed. "Yeah. I did something like Kane because I was so focused on my crap. Who I've always been. I forgot to realize how I'd changed and wanted something different. Kane may have the same stuff going on."

"It's a good point. For now, I booked a meeting with Benny under a fake name, saying it was about the sale. It's the only way I can get a face-to-face."

Aspen laughed. "You're such a badass. What about the other tenants?"

"I called and told them both what was going on. Carlos said he'd probably retire because he was tired of selling toys, and Deanna said she could find another place for the café. Neither of them want to fight it now. They weren't happy but took it pretty well. "

"So, there won't be any protests like chaining yourself to the demolition site?"

Sierra threw a napkin at her. "No, this is reality. Kane texted me a spreadsheet of other sites for the store with all these stats."

"Too soon. He should've begged for your forgiveness and kept his mouth shut."

"Men."

They drank and sat and eventually Sierra felt more like herself. Still broken-hearted over Kane's choices. Still angry at him keeping the truth and trying to control the situation. Still scared he'd never be able to be the man she could trust and lean on without fail.

But better.

"I wish Mom was here."

Sierra refilled her glass and gave her sister a sympathetic look. "I know, babe. But I told you, Mom would be really proud of you. And I'm here for anything you need."

"Not for me, silly. For you. I know you're still mad at her."

Startled, she stared at her sister. Sierra tried not to show Aspen how Mom's death affected the way she lived her own life. She'd always disapproved of the way her mother lived bold and carelessly, not caring about her responsibilities. Aspen was more like her, with big dreams and stars in her eyes. The outcome of dying in a plane crash chasing some off-track adventure showed Sierra it was better to keep her feet firmly on the ground. So, she'd married her first serious boyfriend and tried to do the right things. She surrounded herself with safety and lived a full life, but without risk.

When she told Kane she loved him, she'd taken the leap. Finding out about his deceit only confirmed her doubts. Sierra now worried she'd been wrong to believe she could have a happily ever after on Mom's and Aspen's terms.

Sierra tried to wave off the remark. "It's psychology 101. I felt abandoned so I turned to anger. Nothing for you to worry about, Aspen."

"No, it's not that. You're more like Mom than you think. But you never got a chance to explore that part of you." Frustration gleamed in her brown eyes. "I remember when you were younger and how vibrant you were. You lit up a room and everyone wanted to be around you. Boys swarmed for dates, and all the popular girls loved you. Your laugh was the loudest and most joyous. God, I was so jealous of you. To have such a bright light like Mom did."

Her jaw dropped. "I was never like that!"

Aspen smiled sadly. "Yeah, you were. You just forgot. After Mom and Dad died, you changed so much. You became so adult and more serious. I was happy, too, because it meant I didn't have to take care of anything. I was so wrecked and then I met Ryan in college and had that awful affair. And believe me—I know things happen for a reason and we both made the best of ourselves. I love who we are and turned out to be. But I can't help being a little sad I never got to see that part of you blossom."

Her sister paused, allowing the words to sink in.

"I also think being with Kane brought back your spark. You're different with him. Freer. Less careful. So, even though we both hate him a little now, I don't want you to give up if there's a chance you can forgive him. Okay?"

Emotion washed over her. She reached across the counter and grabbed her sister's hand. Tears stung her eyes. God, she was crying all the time now. It was so annoying.

"Thanks, Aspen. I'm so happy you moved to OBX. I hated doing life without you."

Aspen squeezed her hands. "Me, too, babe. Me, too."

"Dude, you fucked up. Like, seriously."

"I know," Kane said glumly. "I seem to be doing that a lot."

They sat in the Jeep together, staring at the empty parking lot. The tours were over for the day, and Kane had sought out his best friend for help. Usually, he'd try to figure crap out alone, but Brick's words kept filtering through his brain. The suggestion he needed to reach out more and share in relationships. Maybe if he'd taken his advice, Kane would have done better with Sierra.

Brick shook his head. "I mean, this is bad. You literally said you love her, shared your past, then a few hours later, announced you'd be the one demolishing her store."

Kane rubbed his palms over his face. "That sounds terrible. I swear, I planned this better. I intended to tell her after your party, but I got distracted."

"Sex is not the way to fix issues, dude."

"Really? Like you didn't spend your whole summer avoiding issues with Aspen by taking her to bed?"

"Totally different. Plus, I learned. I'm kind of evolved now."

Kane groaned. "Spare me the details. I'm here asking for help. This isn't easy for me!"

"Sorry. Take me through the whole thing again."

He did. His friend tapped his lip, obviously deep in thought. "Men and women think differently. You're looking at this with a purely rational perspective, but you need to consider the emotional part. Stealth was going to buy out that property anyway—you were just the means to an end. As an outsider, you were also a plus. People get stirred up around here and that will raise some blowback."

"I expected that. I don't mind playing the role of bad guy. I'm used to it."

Brick gave him a long look. Unease made Kane shift in his seat. Why did he sense some hard truths coming he wouldn't like?

"You may be used to it, but do you still want that role?"

"Huh?"

"Listen, what John did to you? That was a betrayal most of us wouldn't get over easy. It makes so much sense now—I knew you'd never turn dirty."

"Thanks."

"Welcome. You're used to doing this job and looking at black and white. It's what you know. But Sierra only sees the man she loves betraying her. She doesn't give a shit about logic or explanations. You're the one leading the charge to destroy her store."

"I know." Brick was right. Who cared how he tried to make it seem if the result was the same? "I hoped if I gave her time, and found her a new place, she'd see I didn't take this job to hurt her. It was simply bad luck."

"I guess I'm wondering how bad you really want this job with Stealth in the first place?"

Kane didn't stop to think about his answer. "It's what I do. It's my career."

"I had a career in New York, too. Built my whole world around being a top finance executive. Now, I'm running Ziggy's Tours and happier than I've ever been. You've never given yourself a chance to imagine a different type of career."

Kane paused. His friend was right. Once, they'd planned on making a huge mark in the industry, but Brick had pivoted and created a new life. A better life.

But Kane was different. He loved the game and the risk, the big money and deals to be made. Without it, he'd be bored.

Right?

"Hey guys. What's up?"

They both turned as Marco joined them. He opened the back door and climbed in the seat, comfortably settling in. His shaggy hair hung in his eyes. He wore jeans with holes in the knees that were real and not cut for style. His orange t-shirt said Salt Water Cures All Problems.

"Hey," Kane said.

"What'cha talking about?"

Brick hesitated. "Relationship stuff."

"Cool. I'm good at that. Need help? Or I can ditch if it's personal stuff."

Usually, Kane would be polite but change the subject. Other than Brick, Sierra, and Derek, no one knew too much about him or his past. Surprisingly, he wanted to open up more. Something about this place stirred an urge to stretch his comfort zone and invite more people to his inner circle. "I'm in love with Sierra, but I got an opportunity for a big job which forces me to be the main guy who buys out the property Flirt is on and destroys her business."

"Oh, shit. That's a pretty big problem."

"I know. Brick was giving me some advice."

"What's in it for you?" Marco asked.

Kane cocked his head. "You mean the job? Well, a lot. I've been trying to get back to the high stakes deals where I can make a lot of money. This company—Stealth—offered me a big contract if I finish the deal. I can pretty much re-create what I had in the city."

Marco nodded. "Money, power, health benefits, status. Right?"

"Yeah."

"But if you do, Sierra feels betrayed."

"Yep. But I'm thinking I can get her to understand. She's a businesswoman. She knows how these things work, and that it's separate from my feelings for her."

Silence settled over the Jeep. He figured Marco would just offer him some sympathy, some support, and some weed. Kane still felt good about sharing.

"Any advice?" Brick asked Marco.

Marco scratched his head. "Usually I'd cite romance novels but this screams movie. Either of you see *You've Got Mail?*"

Kane looked at Brick. "Is that the one with Tom Hanks?"

"Yeah. And Meg Ryan. It's a female fave."

"I never saw it," Kane said. "Do I have to?"

"No, I'll explain. The plot revolves around a small bookshop owner—Meg Ryan. She inherits her mom's place and seems super happy but then Tom Hanks opens up a big chain bookstore right down the block. It's got more inventory and discounts and coffee. So, Meg is really pissed and tries to fight the store, but she can't compete and ends up being forced to close her mom's shop."

Kane didn't like the way this whole dialogue was going. "So, I'm Tom Hanks?"

"Right. Sierra is Meg. While this is going on, they're falling in love with each other over the Internet but don't know who the other is. And in real life, they're enemies, but there's also this weird chemistry between them and they like each other, too, but the circumstances are really messed up."

Brick snapped his fingers. "Yeah, I remember now! Hanks finds out who she is first, right? And sets up some meeting?"

"That's right. They finally meet toward the end of the movie—oh, he takes care of her when she's sick which is a big turning point—and he reveals he's the one she's been talking to."

Hope stirred. "Wait—they end up together?"

Marco nodded. "Romcoms always have a happy ending."

"This is great news. You're saying Meg realizes Tom had no other choice and it wasn't personal, and forgives him? And accepts she had to close down her bookstore and it wasn't his fault because he was just the man behind the company?"

"Yes."

Kane grinned, his spirit lighter. "Marco, this is great news! So, you think Sierra will accept this eventually? She'll find a new location for her store, forgive me, and we all win?"

Marco let out a long sigh. "No. Sorry. That's just how the movie ends. But almost every woman I ever spoke with hates the end of that movie."

His heart sank. "What are you talking about!"

"They all told me Tom Hanks should never have been forgiven because each time Meg thinks about her mom's bookstore, she'll think of Tom destroying her legacy. Basically, Meg should've told Tom Hanks he was an asshole and just left him behind and started a new life."

Kane dropped his head. "This is the worst pep talk I've ever had in my life."

Brick patted him on the shoulder. "I know. But it's truth."

Marco shrugged. "Sorry. I'd say you shouldn't take the new job and fight for your woman. Love is more important than business. Right?"

With one swift movement, Kane got out of the Jeep and shut the door behind him. "Marco, don't go into counseling. I've never felt crappier. I'm out of here."

"I can go with you," Brick offered. "We can watch basketball and eat Duck Donuts and drink beer with Dug?"

"No, thanks. I need to be by myself and get my head together. Then go see if Sierra is ready to listen."

Marco waved goodbye. "Maybe we can get together this weekend?"

"Maybe not," Kane muttered, walking to his own car.

He heard Brick's voice in the background. "Give him some time, Marco. I kind of agree with you on that movie. Tom was an asshole."

Yeah. Maybe Kane was better not to share next time.

Chapter Twenty-Two

"The average woman falls in love seven times a year. Only six are with shoes."
– Kenneth Cole

Sierra rang the bell and waited.

The shock on Kane's face confirmed he hadn't expected her to seek him out. She was the one always running. From him. From herself. From the past. From risk and messy emotions and uncertainty.

But it was time she faced her demons head-on and stopped being so damn afraid.

"Sierra." Her name fell from his lips like a song, a prayer, and a plea all at once. A shudder coursed through her. "Come in."

She stepped past him into the living room. God, he was beautiful. Russet hair mussed. Emerald green eyes filled with fierce hope as he stared back at her. Worn jeans hitched low on his hips. A simple cotton t-shirt molding his chest. Feet bare.

He was obviously a mess and she loved him like this. Vulnerable. Open. He was a man unafraid of his emotions yet he hid behind other walls. It was time they were real with each other.

"Thanks. I've been thinking a lot. And I'm ready to talk."

"I'm glad. I missed you." He stepped forward, then stopped. Cursed. "I just want to touch you. I'm sick about this whole thing and how we ended our conversation."

"Me, too." After time with her sister, Sierra was finally able to pull back and glimpse the whole picture. "I saw Benny."

His body stiffened. "How did it go?"

She gave a half shrug and moved further into the room. "Not well. He tried to duck out on me. I pushed for answers. He finally told me the deal was confirmed and it wasn't his fault." Her lips curled without humor. "The legal notices will go out soon. He said he'd write me a referral as a landlord when I found a new place."

Kane nodded. "Sounds about right. I'm sure after Benny sells, he'll be out of here. Said he had a brother in Colorado and he's tired of the beach."

"Won't be a loss."

"Nope."

"I got a lawyer."

Sympathy shone in his green eyes. "It won't help," he said softly. "Stealth has deep pockets and there's nothing to challenge about the deal."

Sierra shrugged. "I know. I needed to do it for me."

A proud smile curved his lips. "Good for you."

"Is that something you'd also handle?"

He rubbed his chin, unease flickering over his face. "A prospective lawsuit? No, that'll go to their lawyers. Once we sign the contracts, I'll be the lead on the project until everyone's assigned their role and things run smoothly."

"What did Stealth offer?"

His voice was flat. "Everything. A full-time job with all the perks. Managing a small team where I get to do my own deals. Opportunities for growth and global development. A shitload of money and benefits."

A ghost of a smile touched her lips. Was it wrong that she could be proud of him at the same time she resented his choice? He was a brilliant man, who loved so hard. Sierra wanted his success, but not at this cost. Not at the expense of Flirt. "I guess that'd be really hard to pass up. You're very good at your job."

"I am. It's one of the only things in my life I always held confidence in," he said, sounding thoughtful. "After the Global debacle, I knew it'd be difficult to find another opportunity like this."

"You don't like working for Duncan?"

Kane cocked his head. "Actually, I do. Not at first. Too much of a slow lane than what I was used to. But now? I respect the hell out of him and what he built. He wanted nothing to do with Stealth but figured I did."

"Too bad medical office buildings weren't as exciting as pricey hotels."

The joke fell flat. They stared at one another in silence.

"It's just business, right?" she said softly.

Kane closed the distance and cupped her cheeks, pressing his forehead to hers. "No. Just business doesn't break your heart like this. Or make you question someone you love. I'm so sorry, sweetheart. Tell me what you want me to do and I'll do it."

Sierra ached to beg him to step away from the deal. To fight. To tell Stealth to fuck off and that Flirt was more important than their stupid luxury resort. But of course, she knew she was reacting with her heart—not her head. If she ordered Kane to do her bidding, she'd always wonder if there'd be regrets.

She'd always wonder if she'd been second choice.

"I can't. I think you need to do what you feel, Kane. If you say no, you're closing yourself off from bigger opportunities. You may not get another chance like this." Her chest tightened but she pushed on. "This is important to you. You've built your entire life around being successful in this field. It's how you define yourself."

"Like Flirt is to you."

She hesitated, then tried to explain. "No. Flirt is what I built when I figured out who I really was. Separate from my marriage, or family, or what I believed I could be good at. And though I intend to fight, if I lose the store, I'll still know who I am."

Kane let out a long breath. His hands stroked back her hair with such gentleness, she ached to give in. Tell him she didn't care—as long as she had him.

"Are you saying I don't know who I am?"

"No. I'm simply asking you to make your own decision."

"If I'm going to lose you, I'll walk away from the deal."

Those damn tears threatened again. She wrapped her fingers around his wrists and gripped him hard. Met his gaze head-on. "No, Kane. Because if you do, it's the same thing as you taking Flirt away. I'll be destroying a career you love. Which means we both need to make our own choices to move forward."

The words came from gritted teeth. "This is a lose-lose situation. Is that what you're telling me?"

"No. I simply can't tell you what will happen this time. Will I forgive you? Will I understand? Can we move forward in time, accepting both of our decisions the way we need in a relationship? It's a test—but it's for both of us. Can you see that now?"

The realization seemed to hit him like a sucker punch. His arms dropped to his sides as he stared at her; confusion and pain and want morphing together at the same time. "I love you, Sierra. This isn't a game to me. You're everything."

Her heart broke. And she knew if it was the truth, his decision would have been simple. This man owned demons that had made him who he was. He may not be ready to make such a sacrifice.

Could they survive together if he couldn't? Did she love him enough to accept his limits and live with doubt? Wondering if there would always be another goal around the corner more important?

Sierra didn't have the answers yet. "When will this all be official?"

Frustration simmered from his aura. "We sign the final contracts Friday."

"Then I need to start making preparations. Tell Brooklyn and Prim. Contact my suppliers. I owe them the truth."

"Let me help you, Sierra." His plea was heartfelt. "I can help relocate Flirt and do anything you need. I can make this so much easier by using my resources for a smooth transition."

"Do you really think that will make it all better?"

His jaw tightened. "Of course not. But you don't have to handle this all by yourself."

"I have no issues handling the business side of things. That's not the type of need I have, Kane. I never did." She turned away. "Let's take some time and focus on our priorities. We can touch base later."

"Why do you sound like you're scheduling me into your calendar?"

Her voice turned cold. "Because I am. I can't have you sleeping in my bed and be on opposite sides when I wake up. My brain will explode. Kudos to you for being an expert at this stuff."

His rigidity broke and once again, Kane reached for her. "I'm sorry. I don't think I've ever been this scared. Not in jail. Not when I had to protect Derek from my father. Not even when I showed up at Brick's with nothing. Because if I lose you, I lose my very soul."

She wanted to step away but her body automatically softened, welcoming his hands on her. Sierra half closed her eyes, allowing herself a few precious moments to forget. His warmth and strength seeped into her skin. She buried her face in his neck, savoring his spicy scent, wishing things were different.

"Sierra?"

"Yeah?"

"Did you ever see that movie *You've Got Mail?*"

Confused, she tilted her chin up and gave him a questioning look.

"With Meg Ryan? Yeah. Why?"

His gaze dove deep, searching. "What did you think of the ending?"

She blinked. Studied his face to figure out why the dialogue turned so strange. "Umm, it was a regular romcom. Happy ever after. Wasn't that deep."

"Did you agree with what Tom Hanks did to her?"

Sierra frowned. "Not really. But he had no choice, I guess."

He didn't answer. Seemed to pick through her statement as if looking for clues. "You were satisfied with their happily ever after ending?"

She stepped out of his embrace and stared at him. The mystery of the question suddenly became crystal clear. "It was exactly what the audience expected Hollywood to deliver. But honestly? No. Tom Hanks took her mother's store away, and he didn't even look gutted. He was too focused on his win."

She turned on her heel and headed to the door. "Tom Hanks sucks."

Sierra left without another word and wondered what their own ending would be.

It was almost over.

Kane finished packing up his laptop and the papers he'd need for the meeting. Sierra had kept her distance, focused on gathering her resources to block the sale. His pain mixed with the soaring pride he felt for not only her business savvy but also her fuck-you attitude. If there'd been any way to sabotage the deal, Kane would've grabbed the opportunity. But between Benny's willingness and Stealth's wealth and power, this was going to go down quickly and relatively painlessly.

The board was already poised to agree to Stealth's plans for the resort. Contacts had been well-oiled and greased. Kane had done his job well, staying within legal lines, and Jack was pleased.

There was nothing left to do but deliver everyone to the boardroom and make things official.

Kane left his office. On the way down the hall, he noticed his boss at his desk, the door open. "Kane? Come on in."

He peeked his head in. "Duncan. I'm on my way to Stealth."

"Closing the deal, huh?"

"Yeah." He shifted his weight. Worry steeped his shoulders, but

Kane forced a smile. "We're ready to finalize."

"Congratulations. Sit down for a minute. If I know you, you'll be there an hour early anyway."

He laughed, obeying the request. His leg jiggled up and down with tension. "How are things going? Did you finish up the Jefferson contract?"

"We did, thanks to you. You've got a gift, but I'm sure you know it. Are you looking forward to working at Stealth?"

"Sure."

One white brow shot up. "Figured your dream job would evoke a more passionate response."

"Sorry. I've had a lot on my mind lately."

"Like being forced to close Flirt?"

He jerked back, speechless. Duncan's face was calm, those blue eyes staring back with a clear focus. "Wh-what did you say?"

"I heard that it's Sunrise you're closing on today. That's where Sierra's store is, correct?"

Pure hot anger rushed through him. "Did you set this up, Duncan? How did you know I was seeing Sierra or that was her store?"

His boss didn't seem intimidated. Kane was thrown off by the obvious kindness in the man's response. "Kane, this is a small town. My wife heard something from Deanna, who runs the café, and as a regular of Flirt, she also heard you're dating her. I was asked if I knew anything, and told her no. This is all confidential. But I was concerned about the choice you're being forced to make."

Kane groaned and shook his head. "I keep forgetting I'm not in the city anymore."

"I can't imagine how difficult this was for you and I didn't want to interfere. But I also wanted you to know I'm here if you needed anything. To talk. Advice. Support. I pride myself on running my firm with care, and forcing you to take this on was never my intention."

Relief loosened his muscles. There seemed to be no manipulation or hidden purpose with Duncan. Kane had been studying him and his employees for a while, and all actions kept confirming he was different from John. Honest. Direct. Fair.

With values other than making money.

"Let's just say I had no idea this deal with Stealth would turn out this way," Kane finally said, picking his way through his thoughts. "And yes, I've been looking for another option for Flirt, but there's not much out there that will work."

"The beach towns are difficult to find affordable rent. Deals like this make it harder."

"Is that why you didn't want to take it on?"

Duncan gave him a shrewd look. "Exactly. Once, I was in your position. I ended up closing down a good friend's restaurant. Things got messy."

"Were you both able to work it out?"

"No." The answer was simple in its brutality. "She never forgave me."

"Even though it would've happened anyway?"

"Yes, it didn't matter to her. Would I have made a different choice?" Duncan cocked his head, considering. "Probably not. I was young and hungry to grow the company. It was only later on I began losing my taste for doing whatever was needed. I downsized and stepped back from some of the bigger sharks, like Stealth. But they respect me and try to throw other business my way. It's another reason they have their eye on you."

"Because you hired me and they trust you."

Duncan's nod gave him a whole new perspective. All this time, Kane figured his reputation had stirred their interest but it was really Duncan. His respect for the man bumped up several notches.

Duncan was telling him something no one had ever offered before.

He had a choice.

Oh, sure, Kane knew he always had a choice to walk away, but his entire life had been about closing deals and moving forward. The faster the better, because it meant more money and less time to fail. It was also another reason his brother fell apart. Emotion needed to be tucked away. Derek had always been soft-hearted but Kane had been able to do all the hard things to keep them both afloat.

Except...

The thought trickled through his brain like slow-moving sludge. Except, what if there was no more reason to race to the top?

What if he was happy without Stealth and a shiny new job that may take him from the life he was carving out here?

What if he could just say...no?

"It's too late," Kane muttered, more to himself than his boss. "The deal's done. I can't stop it."

"No, you can't. But if you decide to walk away, I'll back you up."

Shock barreled through him. "What? You'd have to fire me. Stealth would need a sacrifice or they'd stop playing nice with you."

Duncan shrugged one tweed covered shoulder. "Who cares? I don't need their support. I've made plenty of money, my company is secure, and I never take orders from others. Not anymore. That's exactly why I built this place."

"You'd let me stay?"

His boss laughed. "Kane, are you kidding? You can stay here as long as you want. You're one of the best employees I have. You closed more medical offices these past six months than I have in two years. I know we're pretty boring here, so I figured it was only a matter of time before you needed more. But if you honestly don't want to go with Stealth and walk away from this deal, nothing will happen to you."

Kane realized he didn't even have to make the hard choice.

Yeah, he'd walk away from the shiny trappings of a big-time deal. But he'd never have to see the betrayal on Sierra's face when he inked the final contract. He could stay working for Duncan, or find something else that interested him.

Had he ever even tried to envision new possibilities?

Kane thought of John and his betrayal. He thought of the years building armor to keep pushing for more, hungry for opportunity and safety. He thought of Brick telling him about happiness on the other side of this career they'd once both believed in. He thought of how he'd changed since coming to the Outer Banks, and how he liked the man he was finally becoming.

And knew right then he was going to walk away from all of it.

Duncan grinned. "I can tell you made your decision."

His throat tightened. "Thank you, Duncan. I told myself I had no choice but it was a lie. It was simply easier to do the same crap I always did without question."

"Want me to make a phone call for you?"

Kane shook his head. "No, this is on me and I'll handle it face-to-face. And then I'll need to figure out a way to get Sierra to forgive me."

Duncan winced. "Yeah, women are harder than any business deal. In my experience, the best thing to do is tell her the truth. Then beg."

"Good plan." He rose from the chair and shook his boss's hand. "It's an honor to work for you."

Kane walked out of the office with a new purpose.

He was about to blow it all up, and he'd never been so damn happy.

Chapter Twenty-Three

"Never underestimate the power of a shoe."
– Giuseppe Zanotti

Sierra sat on the velvet sofa, staring into the dark. She'd flipped the sign to Closed at Flirt, and sent Brooklyn and Prim home for an early evening. Traffic was slow, a thunderstorm brewed, and they were all depressed.

The meeting had been brutal. Her employees were a small, tight-knit group that would now be out of work. Though she'd laid out her plan to fight the property sale, they all knew it was simply a delay. She didn't own the property, or the land. Her lease was technically up. Her lawyer had been clear it would cost her a bundle to file paperwork that would have no effect.

Today, it would be official. Within the month, Flirt would close its doors.

And Kane Masterson had led the charge.

Nausea curled her belly. Would she be able to forgive or get past this awful resentment? Maybe time would heal all wounds.

Maybe not.

A low purr interrupted her thoughts and she sighed, cuddling Montgomery. He pushed his massive head against her, whiskers tickling, and she held him in the dark, in the store that she loved more than anything.

The rain pelted the windows. The scent of lavender candles hung in the air. When she first opened, Sierra would sit here after closing, smiling with pride at what she'd been able to create from nothing. The store had been her true North, guiding her creativity and passion, teaching her hard lessons about business and life, day to day to day.

Eventually, she'd reconnect with her strength. Every closing meant a new beginning. Maybe she would find another location. Maybe she would look outside of Duck and Corolla and these smaller beach towns and go further from the area. She'd have a commute but it may be more cost effective.

Or maybe she'd try to do something online. Pop-up shops were an option. Or gathering her designer contacts and putting together a special Flirt exclusive online.

A tiny spark flared, reminding her she'd weathered too many storms to drown now.

But tonight, Sierra would allow herself to steep in emotion.

Her phone buzzed.

Kane.

She declined the call. Not now. Not when he was fresh from signing the contracts and wanted to rationalize further on all the ways he had no other choice.

Fuck that.

A text flashed. *Where r u?*

Sierra ignored that, too. She pet Montgomery and allowed the silence and beauty around her to soothe her sick heart. She had no idea how much time had passed when there was a sudden bang from the front door. Oh, God, had she forgot to lock it?

She gently slid Montgomery off her lap and jumped up, squinting in the dark. "We're closed! You can come back—"

"Tom Hanks was an asshole. And so am I."

She watched in shock as Kane strode forward with forceful determination. He was soaked, dripping water on the floor as his Armani leather shoes squelched with each step. With his hair plastered to his scalp, three-piece suit hanging loose on his body, and green eyes ablaze, Sierra blinked in astonishment as he finally reached her. "What are you doing?"

"Begging your forgiveness for hurting you."

Despair overtook her. "I can't do this tonight, Kane. You did what you had to, but don't expect me to have this talk right now because it's over and you're suddenly filled with guilt."

Pain etched his features. "You don't have to say a word. Please just listen."

She wrapped her arms around herself to ward off the urge to go to him, even after he betrayed her. "Fine. Talk."

"I backed out of the deal. I was on my way to Stealth, and ended up speaking with Duncan in his office. We talked and he shared some stuff with me, about his past. Things that made me realize I never stopped to ask myself what I really wanted *now*. I just kept going after the same goals because it was what I knew. I'd structured my life to achieve in order to prove myself. Closing this deal was just another task, even at the expense of you."

Sierra kept still and listened. He blew out a breath, shoved his wet hair back from his face, and continued. "I can't stand here and lie to you. Up until that moment, I planned on closing the deal. I was stuck in a mindset that no longer served me, but I couldn't see it until I spoke with Duncan."

"What did he say that made a difference?" she asked.

"He said he'd once been like me. Focused on achievement and success. He'd betrayed a friend and still pushed on. But he began to change and see things differently. He realized he no longer wanted power and money—he wanted a life he loved. He walked away from it all and started his own company on his terms."

She nodded. "Makes sense. So, you were able to connect with his story?"

"Yes. For the first time, I realized I got to choose. I wasn't the same kid who was desperate to prove himself, to save Derek and myself. Money and power no longer made me feel full. Since I arrived here and met you again, everything's changed, but I kept trying to go back to where I was, thinking that was my true self. Brick tried to warn me but I couldn't see it. God, I was so wrong. So fucking stupid. And it almost lost me the love of my life."

His words struck full-force. Her chest loosened as hope bloomed. This wasn't a practiced speech to try and win her over. It was as if a wall had broken within him and this raw confession poured from his very soul. "What did you do after your talk?"

"Duncan said he'd back me up no matter what my choice was. I never had that type of support before. I was trained to win at all costs and suddenly, there was no doubt what I wanted." His gaze burned with regret and promise. "You. I don't need anything else except you, Sierra. How I could possibly think a job or money would ever be more important than loving you? I don't think I'll ever forgive myself. I'm not sure you can either, but damned if I won't do everything in my power to try and show you I'll never make you doubt me again."

Her lower lip trembled. "What about Stealth?"

"Oh, they were pissed. I attended the meeting and blew it all up. Let's just say my name won't be synonymous with trust in this field now. And the deal will still go through. I just managed to delay it but Jack will make sure it's smoothed out."

Sierra dragged in a breath. "So, you'll stay working for Duncan. Do you really think you'll be happy flipping medical offices the rest of your life?"

"No."

"I didn't think so." She squared her shoulders, refusing to cower from the truth. "What are you going to do? Start your own business?"

The flash of white teeth threw her off. "Nope. I want to do something different. I may work for Duncan for a while. Maybe I'll get Brick to rehire me as a tour guide. I liked that. The possibilities are endless. And I want to explore them all with you by my side."

Her eyes widened. "You're okay not knowing?"

His gaze turned serious. "I think it's the best thing for me. I never gave myself the opportunity before. It's overdue." He reached out slowly and cupped her cheek. "Would you be okay helping me figure it out?"

"Yes." Sierra nibbled on her lower lip. "I need to be sure you have no regrets."

"Oh, baby, I have too many to list. That I made you question how much I love you. That I blew up our trust. I don't give a shit about Stealth or a fancy job or my old demons. I want a new start with you. I can prove I'm worthy if you give me a chance."

"I think I can do that," she whispered, leaning forward. Her heart beat madly in her chest. "Except we both may be unemployed for a while. Until I figure out what's next for me."

"Then we'll figure it out together. I love you, Sierra. Life makes no sense unless I'm with you. I'm sorry it took me this long. If you want to find a new place for Flirt, we will. If you want to do something different, you'll succeed. I believe in you. I forgot you don't need me to take care of you or fix shit. You just need a partner by your side."

She wrapped her arms around his neck. "Have you been reading Aspen's books? That's a swoon-worthy line to close this chapter out."

His lips stopped inches from hers. "Actually, Marco gave me that one."

"He's still managing to surprise me." She smiled slowly. "Now, kiss me Kane Masterson."

He did.

Chapter Twenty-Four

"Maybe the reason Cinderella was so happy wasn't because of the Prince…but because of the shoes."
— Carrie Bradshaw

"Put your hands together and let's welcome our couple for the first time as Mr. and Mrs. Babel!"

The crowd at Sunfish roared and clapped as her beautiful sister stepped through the doorway, hand in hand with her new husband. Tears blurred Sierra's eyes as they walked into the center of the room for their first dance. Brick gathered Aspen in his arms, gaze locked on her with such intense love, the guests seemed to all sigh at once. Head tilted up to look at him, veil floating behind her, Aspen whispered something in his ear. He laughed. And the music started.

"I can't believe he's a closet Swiftie," Kane murmured. The song, *This Love*, played in all its glory as the couple moved together, lost in their own world. "When we get married, I want something cool and old school. Maybe *Love Song* by the Cure."

Sierra laughed and bumped his shoulder. "Stop making fun of Brick. And no, we will not be dancing to the Cure."

"I like Imagine Dragons, too."

She rolled her eyes. "Stop teasing. I need to take photos."

Sierra heard him chuckle as she snapped nonstop to capture the moment. The dance ended, and everyone cheered as the crowd surged and swallowed them up. She sighed with satisfaction at the joy filling up the room just by being close to such a beautiful love.

Maybe she had a bit more of Mom than she thought. Since Kane reentered her life, her thoughts had become quite poetic.

"What thought put that smile on your lips?"

She looked at the man she loved. He was almost too beautiful to look at, in his sleek white tux, hair neatly tamed, beard trimmed to accent his full lips, emerald eyes sparking with mischief. "Always you."

His face softened but arousal spiked the air. "Good. I can't wait to ruin your lipstick later. You're so damn beautiful."

His promise made her immediately wet between her thighs. His chuckle told her he knew. Not one to easily lose, she leaned close. "And I can't wait to stand in front of you in nothing but these heels."

His pupils dilated and he looked suddenly uncomfortable, shifting his weight.

Sierra laughed wickedly and dove into the crowd. Her sister's veil was askew and as maid of honor, she had to go fix it. She also needed to calm her nerves. His mention of marriage had gotten her a bit dreamy and she couldn't lose her focus on Aspen. This was going to be a perfect day and she was honored to be the one be by her side.

Mom and Dad would be so proud.

Of both of them.

The past few months had been a whirlwind of change. Kane had been right. The deal with Benny and Stealth had gone down a few weeks later, and Flirt was officially closed. Turning the lights off and saying goodbye to the empty space had broken a piece of her heart, but Sierra knew it was the beginning of a new chapter. Kane took some major heat from trying to blow up the deal, but Duncan stuck to his word and backed him up. Watching Kane learn to trust another male mentor figure was special. In the midst of saying goodbye to her store, there were other gifts received.

Gossip spread about Kane's actions, and he became a bit of a hero. When he got approached by a local luxury real estate firm to see if he'd be interested in selling homes, Sierra noticed him light up. He'd been diving deep into the industry these past few months while working for Duncan.

It took her a while to stop worrying he'd regret his decision. Kane simply showed up and proved himself daily. Slowly, Sierra realized the final barrier of trust between them crumbled to ruins.

He'd chosen her.

Sierra was in her own growth period. She opened a web store to test the waters, but realized quickly she liked the one-on-one interaction with clients. A few of her pop-up stores were a big hit, but the locations were only temporary. For now, she was experimenting with various venues, but making enough money to take her time.

She sensed she was waiting for something meant for her.

Until then, she threw herself into this new life that offered no guarantees except one.

Kane loved her more than anything.

Her thoughts were interrupted when she ran into a distinguished southern gentleman with white hair, white mustache, and kind blue eyes. "Sierra, it's nice to meet you. I'm Duncan Allen."

Her eyes widened with recognition. "How lovely to meet you! Kane has spoken so highly of you. I cannot believe we haven't met before this."

His laugh was robust. "I could say the same. He comes to the office with a spring in his step, which I know is all you. And my wife, Jessica, was a regular shopper at Flirt. I'm truly sorry about the loss of your shop."

Duncan's obvious empathy was soothing. "Thank you. I'm grateful you offered Kane the support he needed. We owe you a lot."

"Nonsense. Us locals have to stick together." His bushy brows lowered in a thoughtful frown. "I didn't intend to talk business at your sister's wedding, but wondered if you had a few minutes to chat? We can bring Kane over."

"Of course, I'd love to chat. Let's go outside where it's quieter."

They grabbed Kane and headed outside to one of the empty tables. Duncan lit up a cigar and they exchanged casual chit-chat for a bit. "I had an opportunity that came up I'd love to discuss with you. Unfortunately, it's something I'd need a decision on rather quickly. I think I have a place that would fit well for Flirt."

Her heart stopped. She shared a glance with Kane, but it was obvious he knew nothing about it. "I'd love to hear about it," she said.

"My sister owns a building she's been leasing for a while, decided to sell it to me. Her children live in Maryland, and she's looking to move and be with her grandchildren. One of her tenants unfortunately passed, and there is one space open to rental. I'd like to offer it to you, Sierra."

She blinked. Excitement simmered. "Where is it located?"

"On the Duck waterfront—northeast corner. The current shop is Jane's Candy Shop."

Reality crashed in. She knew the spot well, and it was prime. She forced a smile. "That's so generous, Duncan, but I'm afraid the rent isn't something I can afford." Oh, sure, she could probably take a big reach and get a loan but Sierra also didn't want that type of pressure to sell a certain level in order to pay her mortgage. No thanks. She wanted her store to be her safe haven, not a place of fear.

"Normally, I'd agree, but my sister had struck a unique deal with Jane. They were friends for a while, so the rent was fixed. It's been that way for a decade. Probably more affordable than the Sunset location Flirt was in previously."

Sierra frowned. "That's lovely, but it's now an opportunity for you to make a lot more money. I'm very sorry about Jane's passing. That must be hard on your sister to lose a good friend."

"Thank you." He tilted his head, staring at her with a twinkle in his eyes. "Sierra, I'd like to offer you the same deal. I'm not looking to make more profit. I'm looking for a place that's solid, with a tenant I can trust. Flirt is a mainstay in Duck and many of us miss it. Including my wife. She's been grouchier since you closed without getting her shopping gene workout."

They all laughed.

Duncan continued. "Think about it. Let me know if you're interested. The sharks will be circling the moment they realize there's an empty storefront, and you're my first choice. There's no hard feelings if it's not what you want. And of course, it has nothing to do with Kane working for me or any favors. It's simply the right thing for everyone."

He gave another smile, finished his cigar, and rose. "Now, I better get going. I heard it was an open event and wanted to take the time to meet you. Enjoy the wedding."

They said their goodbyes. Sierra turned to Kane, trembling with excitement. "Did that just happen?" she asked, partially in shock. "Did he just offer me prime real estate at a fixed rent I can afford?"

Kane grinned. "Hell yes, he did. Your store made a mark, sweetheart. Because you put your heart and soul in it, and people responded. For Duncan, that's just good business, not a giveaway."

"I want it."

The words shot out of her mouth without hesitation. Her insides settled. This was her sign.

Flirt was about to have a new home. A better one. She'd just needed to trust and let go.

Kane picked her up and swung her around, "Should I chase Duncan down and tell him?"

"No—let's wait until after the wedding. I want to keep the news for just us." She glanced down the street where Duncan had disappeared. "I had no idea your boss was so striking. From your descriptions of him, I imagined someone more low-key and plain."

"As Armani quoted, 'Elegance doesn't mean being noticed. It means being remembered.'"

Her head spun in shock. She blinked. "You—you know designer shoe quotes?"

"Of course. I'm not uncivilized."

She stared at him with all the raw emotions swirling inside, no longer afraid to let herself surrender to it all. "I'm so in love with you, Kane Masterson."

And then she kissed him, lipstick be damned, giving herself up to the sensations flooding her body, embracing the feeling of safety and home she always experienced around Kane.

Aspen poked her head out. "Will you stop making out and get your ass in here? I have to pee and you forced me to wear this giant dress so you better hold it up for me."

They both burst into laughter and rejoined the wedding.

Much later, Sierra stood in front of the man she loved in nothing but her Louboutin's and claimed her own happily ever after ending.

The End

Want more of Kane and Sierra? Go to
https://dl.bookfunnel.com/zb71f4m5ey to claim your
BONUS EPILOGUE!

Discover the Outer Banks Series

Book of the Month

She's desperate for another bestseller… and she'll go to any length to get it. Even if it means sacrificing her pride to chase the hottest bachelor in town and get him to break her heart…

Once the literary world's golden girl, Aspen Lourde can't seem to produce another successful book, and the pressure's on to prove she's not just a one-hit-wonder. But there's a catch: her bestseller was a heartbreak hit, straight from her own love life disaster. Without any fresh romantic turmoil to fuel her pen, Aspen needs inspiration quick enough to create a book her agent can sell to her publisher. So she escapes for the summer to the Outer Banks with a plan to live a story worth writing.

Brick Babel is a romance novelist's dream: a local heartthrob with a reputation as wild as the horses running free in the town. He's everything Aspen needs for a muse kickstart—gorgeous, moody, and notoriously unattainable. His affairs are legendary in the small town, and every woman warns her off, including her sister.

Too bad a good heartbreak is exactly what she needs to meet her deadline.

But Brick refuses to play the game, rejecting all of her advances. When Aspen hears his tour company is on the verge of bankruptcy, she offers him a deal: fake a whirlwind summer romance, then ditch her, drama guaranteed.

Desperate to save his grandfather's business, Brick agrees to the ridiculous deal. What starts as a contractual fling spirals out of control as lines blur and real feelings emerge. Brick's falling hard, and Aspen's rethinking her plot twist. The novel might be her ticket back to the top, but at what cost?

Because Aspen's finally found her muse, but some stories may be too true to share.

Book of the Month isn't just about finding love where you least expect it.

It's about finding yourself in the pages of life's unexpected chapters.

Book Club Questions

1. *The Reluctant Flirt* opens with a backstory from both Sierra and Kane. Each of these events change the characters' trajectory. Discuss how both of them changed afterward. What were the challenges they faced due to these events?

2. Montgomery (Mo) becomes an important part of the story. Do you like to read about animals in your books? What did he bring to the story that you enjoyed?

3. Sierra and Aspen lost their parents at a young age. Discuss Sierra and Aspen's relationship and issues they face being orphans.

4. Kane faces a big decision when his job wants him to close Sierra's store. Did you agree with his decision and actions? Why or why not?

5. Sierra's store, Flirt, is part of her identity and creative outlet. Did you ever have a dream to own a store or start a business? What would it be?

6. Sierra and Kane spend one night together but don't meet again for four years. How have things changed between them? Individually? Do you agree they wouldn't have been able to have a successful relationship if Sierra had stayed that morning?

7. Did the shoe quotes add or detract from your enjoyment in the chapters?

8. Speaking of shoes, Sierra loves them. Do you have a passion for something particular? What is it?

Discover More Jennifer Probst

Christmas in Cape May
A Sunshine Sisters Novella

Devon Pratt loves many things in life. The beauty of flowers. The yin and yang of energy. The power of positivity in people. And everything to do with the Christmas season.

As a floral shop owner in the beach town of Cape May, she looks forward to decorating both the town and running the annual holiday party to benefit the local animal shelter. Too bad the new owner of her favorite venue is more like the Grinch than Santa. Working with him will be a challenge, but she's too full of seasonal cheer to let him annoy her, right?

Jameson Franklin hates many things in life. Crowds. Fake cheer. Ostentatious décor. And especially Christmas. The season is full of things he'd rather avoid, but since taking over the popular restaurant Vintage temporarily for his cousin as a favor, he's trying to play nice with the locals. Too bad the florist is insisting on overrunning his sacred space with blooms, dogs, and an endless positive persistence that pushes all of his buttons. But when too many heated confrontations lead to heated encounters, he begins to wonder what it would be like to love not only Christmas, but Devon Pratt.

Let the festivities begin.

* * * *

Something Just Like This
A Stay Novella

Jonathan Lake is the beloved NYC mayor who's making a run for governor. His widowed status and close relationship with his daughter casts him as the darling of the press, and the candidate to beat, but behind the flash of the cameras, things are spinning out of control. It all has to do with his strait laced, ruthlessly organized assistant. Her skills and reserved demeanor are perfect to run his campaign, but her brilliant brain has become a temptation he's been fighting for too long. Can he convince her to take a chance on a long-term campaign for love or will his efforts end up in scandal?

Alyssa Block has admired the NYC mayor for a long time, but her secret crush is kept ruthlessly buried under a mountain of work. Besides, she's not his type, and office scandals are not in her job description. But when they retreat to an upstate horse farm for a secluded weekend, the spark between them catches flame, and Jonathan sets those stinging blue eyes on winning her. Can she convince him to focus on the upcoming election, or will she succumb to the sweet promise of a different future?

* * * *

The Marriage Arrangement
A Marriage to a Billionaire Novella

She had run from her demons…

Caterina Victoria Windsor fled her family winery after a humiliating broken engagement, and spent the past year in Italy rebuilding her world. But when Ripley Savage shows up with a plan to bring her back home, and an outrageous demand for her to marry him, she has no choice but to return to face her past. But when simple attraction begins to run deeper, Cat has to decide if she's strong enough to trust again…and strong enough to stay…

He vowed to bring her back home to be his wife…

Rip Savage saved Windsor Winery, but the only way to make it truly his is to marry into the family. He's not about to walk away from the only thing he's ever wanted, even if he has to tame the spoiled brat who left her legacy and her father behind without a care. When he convinces her to agree to a marriage arrangement and return home, he never counted on the fierce sexual attraction between them to grow into something more. But when deeper emotions emerge, Rip has to fight for something he wants even more than Windsor Winery: his future wife.

* * * *

Somehow, Some Way
A Billionaire Builders Novella

Bolivar Randy Heart (aka Brady) knows exactly what he wants next in life: the perfect wife. Raised in a strict traditional family household, he seeks a woman who is sweet, conservative, and eager to settle down. With his well-known protective and dominant streak, he needs a woman to offer him balance in a world where he relishes control.

Too bad the newly hired, gorgeous rehab addict is blasting through all his preconceptions and wrecking his ideals…one nail at a time…

Charlotte Grayson knows who she is and refuses to apologize. Growing up poor made her appreciate the simple things in life, and her new job at Pierce Brothers Construction is perfect to help her carve out a career in renovating houses. When an opportunity to transform a dilapidated house in a dangerous neighborhood pops up, she goes in full throttle. Unfortunately, she's forced to work with the firm's sexy architect who's driving her crazy with his archaic views on women.

Too bad he's beginning to tempt her to take a chance on more than just work…one stroke at a time…

Somehow, some way, they need to work together to renovate a house without killing each other…or surrendering to the white-hot chemistry knocking at the front door.

* * * *

Searching for Mine
A Searching For Novella

The Ultimate Anti-Hero Meets His Match…

Connor Dunkle knows what he wants in a woman, and it's the three B's. Beauty. Body. Boobs. Other women need not apply. With his good looks and easygoing charm, he's used to getting what he wants—and who. Until he comes face to face with the one woman who's slowly making his life hell…and enjoying every moment…

Ella Blake is a single mom and a professor at the local Verily College who's climbed up the ranks the hard way. Her ten-year-old son is a constant challenge, and her students are driving her crazy—namely Connor Dunkle, who's failing her class and trying to charm his way into a better grade. Fuming at his chauvinistic tendencies, Ella teaches him the ultimate lesson by giving him a *special* project to help his grade. When sparks fly, neither of them are ready to face their true feelings, but will love teach them the ultimate lesson of all?

* * * *

Begin Again
A Stay Novella

Chloe Lake is finally living her dream. As the daughter of the governor, she's consistently in the spotlight, and after being dubbed the Most Eligible Bachelorette of NYC, both her career and personal life has exploded. Fortunately, her work as an advocate for animal welfare requires constant publicity and funding, so she embraces her role and plays for the camera—anything for the sake of her beloved rescues.

But when a big case is on the line, she's faced with the one obstacle she never counted on: the boy who broke her heart is back, and in order to gain justice, they need to work together.

Chloe swears she can handle it until old feelings resurface, and she's faced with a heartbreaking choice.

Will this time end differently—or are they destined to be only each other's first love—instead of forever?

Owen Salt fell hard for Chloe when he was a screwed-up kid in college, and spent the next years changing himself into the man his grandfather believed he was capable of. But when his career led him across the country, he knew he needed to leave the woman he loved behind. He's never forgotten her, but as the new darling of the press, now she's way out of his league. When work brings him back to fight for justice by her side, he swears he can handle it.

But he's never really gotten over his first love—and he wants one more opportunity to prove he's a man who's worthy.

Can Owen convince the woman who holds his heart to take a second chance on forever—or is it too late for them both?

For fans of Jennifer Probst's Stay series, *Begin Again* is book five in that series.

About Jennifer Probst

Jennifer Probst wrote her first book at twelve years old. She bound it in a folder, read it to her classmates, and hasn't stopped writing since. She holds a masters in English Literature and lives in the beautiful Hudson Valley in upstate New York. Her family keeps her active, stressed, joyous, and sad her house will never be truly clean. Her passions include horse racing, Scrabble, rescue dogs, Italian food, and wine—not necessarily in that order.

She is the New York Times, USA Today, and Wall Street Journal bestselling author of over 50 books in contemporary romance fiction. She was thrilled her book, The Marriage Bargain, spent 26 weeks on the New York Times. Her work has been translated in over a dozen countries, sold over a million copies, and was dubbed a "romance phenom" by Kirkus Reviews.

She loves hearing from readers. Visit her website for updates on new releases, and get a free book at www.jenniferprobst.com.

On Behalf of Blue Box Press,

Liz Berry and Jillian Stein would like to thank ~

Steve Berry
Benjamin Stein
Kim Guidroz
Chelle Olson
Tanaka Kangara
Stacey Tardif
Suzy Baldwin
Chris Graham
Jessica Saunders
Grace Wenk
Ann-Marie Nieves
Dylan Stockton
Kate Boggs
Richard Blake
and Simon Lipskar

Made in United States
North Haven, CT
22 July 2025

70923454R00143